and more from Papatia, *insha'Allah*." — *Brooke Benoit, A Clichéd Life*

"...I must say after a long time I came across a book that had kept me intrigued since the first page." — *Aisha Idris, The Bookish Nomad*

ALSO BY PAPATIA
FEAUXZAR

Fixed Up!

The Nanny

Respect the Letters

What Am I? (Book 1 & Book 2)

The Dreams

The Fortieth Name

Praise for Papatia Feauxzar's

The Ducktrinors

"...The Ducktrinors is a bit of a mix; sci-fi, romance, crime. I have read many sci-fi books over the years and always found them very imaginative. Papatia has brought in many believable but imaginative futuristic elements to the novel..." — *Fozia Shah, Muslim Mummy*

"...Though at times I felt that things moved ahead too fast and that the author should have warranted us with some more details, it was nevertheless a page turner till the end. It was an enthralling read and I would definitely recommend it to all the *Harry Potter* and *Hunger Games* fans out there! ..." — *Aleeza Shoaib, Munna, Baba & Me*

"... The novel is fast-paced and simply yet well written which are plus points for gripping attention of young adult readers. Enjoyed the characters of Dawood and Ali... hope she won't leave us hanging for so long to read the next volume of The Ducktrinors. Recommending the book for teenagers and readers who never grow old ..." — *Zeneefa Zaneer, Thinkalolic Mom*

"This book is one of the most original works of Muslim fiction I have come across. Veering away from the usual, it's set in a time that is almost the end of the world. It reads very much like a sci-fi novel, with futuristic gadgets and gizmos and incredible technological advances, however there is still a heavy dose of Islamic references. It's a first book in what promises to be an interesting series. It dares to imagine what Islam might be in the far-off future..." — *Ayesha Desai, Raising Young Believers*

"...THE DUCKTRINORS combines two powerful genres: the school story and the scientific fantasy. And to a great extent, the author depicts reality by demonstrating an advanced version of the occurrences of this present time. I must confess that I really enjoyed reading this book as I impatiently await the next part. This is definitely a keep for the pleasure of my future adventure-thirsty children. I highly recommend this 'must read' for every teenager, young adult and adult alike. I must say that this is the very first attempt at producing an intriguing Islamic science fiction as the book spells utter creativity and ingenuity. I won't be surprised to see a motion picture of it in the future." — *Wardah Abbas, The Rose's Pen*

"...The imagination of the writer is good and has done quite well in describing the scene for your mind to imagine well. Reading some chapters will remind you of a *Harry Potter* book. I feel the novel is for teenagers and younger audience but I still loved reading it to the child inside my heart..." — *Sana Khan, A Day Dreamer's Diary*

"...The Ducktrinors is the first of its kind in the realm of Muslim fiction, and it is a powerful, poignant, and compelling one. Feauxzar has given us a wonderful, insightful, and interesting work of fiction to enjoy and give to our young ones ..." — *Tohib Adejumo,* Author of *Love in Ramadan*

"...Actually, I'd recommend *The Ducktrinors*, simply because of the feeling I had when I finished the novel: I felt good... The aspects that give me pause, however, are the very aspects I find endearing. Hanifa's character handles quite a lot..."— *Sarabi, Muslimah Media Watch*

"...I believe that stories like these are what we need in present day societies to rattle our consciences and jolt us out of our comfort zones—to gratingly remind us that it is our moral right to take the reigns and make a difference to our lives and to the lives of those around us. Hanifa is the woman in all of us; she can be presumptuous, bossy and at times conceited. She is human and experiences emotions of love and attraction—emotions which are real but are often condemned in Islam. However, and of more significance is her facility to rise above her mortal being, to reveal resilience to the struggle and steadfastness to her Islamic beliefs. A must read — recommended for both males and females over 18." *Dr. Zaheera Jina* — **Riding the Samosa Express:** *Personal Narratives of Marriage and Beyond*

"Hats off sissy. What can I say? Truly RESPECT your imagination. Please bring on Malik fast!" — *Fawziyyah Emiabata, Muslim Teen Reads*

"Finally! Papatia Feauxzar has tapped her distinct noveling style into a fast-paced, futuristic novel with a decidedly Muslim flavor. ... I think that I've read almost all of her stories, and Ducktrinors is definitely my favorite, so far. Although it's written mostly for a younger audience, Papatia has crafted another fun, slightly-awkward, but smart female protagonist in Hanifa Ducktrinor, and I enjoyed watching her problem-solve to save the world (and her own behind!). Or begin to, since this is a bit of a cliffhanger. I'm also excited that this is a series, as we just don't get enough of them! Looking forward to more

THE
DUCKTRINORS

Book 1 & Book 2 of the Jihad Series

PAPATIA FEAUXZAR

Dallas, Texas

THE DUCKTRINORS (Book 1 & Book 2)

Copyright © 2015 - 2018 by Papatia Feauxzar.

All rights reserved. Printed in the United States of America. No part of this book may be used or reproduced in any manner whatsoever without written permission except in the case of brief quotations embodied in critical articles or reviews.

This book is a work of fiction. Names, characters, businesses, organizations, places, events and incidents either are the product of the author's imagination or are used fictitiously. Any resemblance to actual persons, living or dead, events, or locales is entirely coincidental.

For information contact:

Djarabi Kitabs Publishing

PO BOX 703733

Dallas, TX 75370

https://www.djarabikitabs.com

Cover and jacket design by Adelina Ferizi

Illustrations by Kaltrina Ferizi

Library of Congress Control Number: 2018935705

Hardback ISBN: 978-1-947148-80-2

EBook ISBN: 978-1-947148-83-3

Paperback ISBN: 978-1-947148-10-9

First Edition: March 2018

10 9 8 7 6 5 4 3 2 1

To Her and my Muhajaba Yankee niece because I love you both and because you are our legacies

To my little Mujahid Cowboy and Them because you're the coolness of my eyes

We will all meet one day insha'Allah.

AUTHOR'S NOTE

"I seek refuge in Allah from Satan, the accursed one, in the name of Allah, the Most Merciful, the Most Compassionate."

My wish is that you find **The Ducktrinors Book I & Book II** an exciting page turner. It's a story that should have only been told by either Hanifa or Malik's point of views. However, I couldn't bring myself to do it and mute the voices of the other crucial characters in the process. Like every author out there, I have a special bond with these characters I don't want to give up. And as a reader, at least one of these fictional characters will resonate with you.

So, this story had to be told mostly. Another reason it had to be told is because of the historical events profoundly weaved throughout the plot. Many writers try to show and tell. And there is no official ruling that we have to. It's a personal choice a writer makes and the debate on the matter continues. What I know is that I like to tell and show. This helps me hint at the plot and avoid tedious scene descriptions. Keep that mind as you read dear reader. Throughout the years, I have realized that this style of storytelling fits me best. I pray this sci-fi dystopian Muslim young adult story suits your fancy.

Enjoy and please leave a review!

Papatia Feauxzar

Jumada Al-Thani 1, 1439

(February 16th, 2018)

"The people will see a time of patience in which someone adhering to his religion will be as if he were grasping a hot coal."

(At-Tirmidhi 2260)

THE

DUCKTRINORS

(Book 1 & Book 2)

INSPIRATIONS

The Quran *Sherif* has been a major inspiration in writing this book. *Alhamdullilah.* So check out some of the verses that have inspired me.

"*O you who have believed, do not take My enemies and your enemies as allies, extending to them affection while they have disbelieved in what came to you of the truth, having driven out the Prophet and yourselves [only] because you believe in Allah, your Lord. If you have come out for jihad in My cause and seeking means to My approval, [take them not as friends]. You confide to them affection, but I am most knowing of what you have concealed and what you have declared. And whoever does it among you has certainly strayed from the soundness of the way.*" (Quran 60:1)

"*Allah does not forbid you from those who do not fight you because of religion and do not expel you from your homes - from being righteous toward them and acting justly toward them. Indeed, Allah loves those who act justly.*" (Quran 60:8)

"*And [recall] when you said, 'O Moses, we can never endure one [kind of] food. So call upon your Lord to bring forth for us from the earth its green herbs and its cucumbers and its garlic and its lentils and its onions.' [Moses] said, 'Would you exchange what is better for what is less? Go into [any] settlement and indeed, you will have what you have asked.' And they were covered with humiliation and poverty and returned with anger from*

Allah [upon them]. That was because they [repeatedly] disbelieved in the signs of Allah and killed the prophets without right. That was because they disobeyed and were [habitually] transgressing." (Quran 2:61)

"Indeed, those who believed and those who were Jews or Christians or Sabeans [before Prophet Muhammad] - those [among them] who believed in Allah and the Last Day and did righteousness - will have their reward with their Lord, and no fear will there be concerning them, nor will they grieve." (Quran 2:62)

"And [recall] when We took your covenant, [O Children of Israel, to abide by the Torah] and We raised over you the mount, [saying], 'Take what We have given you with determination and remember what is in it that perhaps you may become righteous.'" (Quran 2:63)

CONTENTS

A FEW THINGS ABOUT THE MADHAHIB IN THIS SERIES

**Sunnis: Largest branch of Islam
Tabi'een (Sunni generation after the Sahabas, who were the companions of the Prophet *sallallahu aleihi wassalam*):
Imam Abu Hanifa

Tabi al Tabi'een (Sunni generation after the Tabi'een):
Imam Malik ibn Anas
Imam Shafi'i

Salaf-I-Salhin (Early righteous servants):
Imam Ahmad ibn Hanbal

*The Sahabas, the Tabi'een, and the Tabi al Tabi'een are also early righteous servants.

**Shiites: Second largest denomination of Islam
Jafari Madhab after Imam Jafar Ibn Muhammad al-Sadiq

CHARACTER LIST

THE GOOD GUYS:

Hanifa Ducktrinor: protagonist, a seventeen-year-old girl of Ethiopian origin

Buraqa: Hanifa's personal horses

Dawud: an eleven-year-old orphan boy who is Hanifa's friend, protégé and a computer savvy hacker

Ali: a man in his early twenties working for the rebellion

Mustapha Kreedor: Hanifa's paternal grandfather

Malik Ducktrinor: second protagonist, an eighteen-year-old boy of African origin

Aadil: Malik's friend and a soccer enthusiast

Khalid ibn al-Walid: Sobriquet for an online friend of Malik who's a sword enthusiast

Nusaybah bint Ka'ab: Sobriquet for an online friend of Malik who's a sword enthusiast

Umm Manee: Sobriquet for an online friend of Malik who's a sword enthusiast

Salah Ad-Din: Sobriquet for an online friend of Malik who's a sword enthusiast

THE BAD GUYS

Sylas: the antagonist, leader of the Seculars at Hanifa's school; Castle 5

Judas: Sylas's sidekick

Hamani: Sylas's scientist

Sir Landry Big: The worldwide leader of the Seculars

Corayto: Sir Landry Big's right hand man and newest press secretary

Ata: an ambitious Secular officer

Marcel: Sir Landry Big's son

The Fundamentalists: an extremist Muslim group

The Zulmists: an extremist Muslim group

Almourabitoun: an extremist Muslim group
Bonita Miller a.k.a. Bonnie Mills: Malik's teacher
The Crew Sad: an extremist Christian group
The Radical Zionists: an extremist Jewish group
Bloody Mongols: a nationalist movement claiming lineage to
Ghenghis Khan

OTHER CHARACTERS:

Muallim: Malik's ascetic teacher
Sayf Ibn Zulfiqar (SIZ): Malik's sword. The acronym is
pronounced *seez*
Adama Mustapha Junior Ducktrinor: Hanifa's father
Eva Ducktrinor: Hanifa's mother
Shafiya: Malik's younger sister
Pristine: Malik's youngest sister
Ana Undeapsidud: Hanifa's friend from the first day of school
Hamza: a Brazilian Secular officer, crypto Muslim
Ridwan: an African American Secular officer, crypto Muslim
Hind: a British Secular officer, crypto Muslim
Coraline Hanifin: a French Secular officer, crypto Jew
Yakuta: a Japanese Secular officer, crypto Muslim
Makhnani: Secular officer, crypto Muslim
Bashir: a Saudi Secular officer, crypto Muslim
Nadhir: a Lebanese Secular officer, crypto Muslim
Nadirah Beauregard: an African Secular officer, crypto Muslim
Nasreen: an Iranian Secular officer, crypto Christian
Najma Perales: a Mexican Secular officer, crypto Muslim
Ya-Sin L'Heureux (a.k.a. Cindy/Sin-D): a Brazilian Secular
officer, crypto Muslim
Binnur: a Turkish Secular officer, crypto Muslim
Tim Undeapsidud: Ana's older brother, a genius architect and a
hacker
Sarah: a Caucasian American Secular officer, non-
denominational
Hazera: a Bosnian Secular officer and a former Secular (laid
back) Muslim

Romeehna Torales: a Brazilian Secular officer, crypto Muslim
Tahany: an Egyptian Secular officer, crypto Muslim
The Mujahideen: a Muslim resistance group from Texas
The Four Caliphs (The 4Cs): A Muslim SWAT team
The Hui-Han Descendants: a group of Chinese Muslims
supporting the Ducktrinors
The Righteous Murabitun: a group of Moroccan Muslims
supporting the Ducktrinors
The Futuristic Muwahhidun: a group of Moroccan Muslims
supporting the Ducktrinors
The Brave Moriscos: a group of Spanish Muslims supporting
the Ducktrinors
The Last Mamlucks: a group of Egyptian Muslim supporting
the Ducktrinors
The Deli Sultans (a.k.a. The Crazy Sultans): a group of Muslim
Indians and exiled Turkish supporting the Ducktrinors
Team Muhammad: a Muslim African American group who
named themselves after three inspiring Muslims aside from
their Prophet (saw); Bilali Muhammad, Ibtihaj Muhammad,
Dalila Muhammad. They support the Ducktrinors as well
The Bold Malê: a group of Brazilian Muslims supporting the
Ducktrinors
Hindus For Peace: an interfaith Hindu group
Peaceful Christians United: an interfaith Christian group
Shalom Keepers: an interfaith Jewish group
Agnostic and Atheist United: a humanitarian non-theist and
civil right group

MAGAZINES

The Muezzin: the Muslim electronic magazine (e-zine) that
relays the successes and failures of the oppressed
Al Bayanne: a Muslim e-zine and radio located in Africa
The Irreligious: the Secular daily tablet that spreads lies around
the globe and promotes rewards for joining the Secular cause.
The daily tablet is also known as *The Profane*.

SECRET MEANS OF COMMUNICATION

Aljamiados: Latinized Arabic by the Moriscoes due to the ban on using Arabic as the main language. Mustapha Kemal Ataturk had done something similar in the Ottoman Empire.

CHAPTER ONE : SCHOOL

Hanifa

Timeline: The first day of school in Brazil

AFTER RELOCATING SO MANY times from America, Asia, Europe, and South Africa, Hanifa knew what kind of speech her parents would inflict upon her on the first day of school. She braced herself while also hoping that, today, either they would make an exception, or she could make a quick escape before The Speech. After all, her extra-good behavior over the past year had to count for something.

"I leave you in the hands of Allah," she said, hugging her dad and mom and kissing their hands quickly to follow her brother and two sisters to school. She had picked up this mixture of etiquettes from living in so many places around the globe.

"Not so fast, Hanifa," her mom said.

"Hanifa," her father started, raising one eyebrow, "you're not to talk about religion, the world coming to an end, or calendars. They are forbidden topics. Are we crystal clear?"

Aww man! I was that close to exiting the room, she thought. "Yes," she mumbled, her cheeks burning.

"We want you to promise that this time, in this new town, you will be more careful." Her mother shook her index finger in Hanifa's face.

Hanifa nodded, put her hands in her pockets, walked to the front door, and grumbled over her shoulder, "Okay...I promise not to activate code *fitnah*."

"That's right!" her dad said. "Otherwise kiss Brazil goodbye and you will go back to being homeschooled."

Hanifa nodded, wincing at the idea of being grounded, and closed the door behind her.

"They gave you The Speech again?" her brother Malik asked as soon as she caught up to him and the girls. His serious hazel eyes examined her.

"Yeah, they don't trust me, and I can understand that. But how many times do I have to apologize or show them I can keep my mouth shut? What happened last year was an honest mistake, okay?" Tears filled her eyes.

"I know, but they have a point. We barely escaped from South Africa the last time you made an honest mistake. So, they'll keep reminding you that danger is surrounding us and that you have to be extra careful—not only for your own safety, but for ours too. Just remember that it will be homeschool for *all* of us this time. I don't think you enjoyed your wings being cut off. I wouldn't. It sucks."

Hanifa kept quiet. Her parents must be tired of changing jobs so often. It had been easy for her father to land handy jobs to hide his overqualified skills and his real identity. Her mom on the other hand, had to revamp herself from home every time they changed cities. She had been a cake caterer, a flower artist, a healing and herb specialist, and most recently, a seamstress. The only stable things in all her jobs were her accounting skills she used to run her small home business. *I guess I need to be a little more careful since everyone is affected by my actions.* On a heel of that thought, she continued walking, staring at the white sneakers peeking out from under her long, pleated skirt. Once they reached the shuttle stop, she just focused on spotting the right silver-gray SUPER-SPEED SHUTTLE (SSS), allowing the world around her to draw into her peripheral vision, to lighten her mood.

Paraty, Brazil was beautiful. The seasons were opposite to places located to the north of the equator, but of course these days, fake plastic trees lined the city and had even replaced the rain forest. Having lived in the US, where it was currently summer, it felt like Paraty was coming out of a winter with temperatures varying from 66°F to 79°F as proclaimed by the signs banks and pharmacies helpfully displayed in front of their establishments. It was definitely a pleasant temperature, ideal for tourism. The mountains tops were still coated with snow and they reflected their white peaks in the clear sea around the island. The island's tall green trees were also visible in the sea as the sun shined bright on the horizon.

SSSs of different colors flew off over Hanifa's head, and they stirred pleasant breezes that caressed her face. *We have fake tress but at least the air is clean.* At that thought, she glanced at her siblings to see if they were enjoying the moment like she was, but she couldn't read their expressions; they looked lost in their own thoughts.

Hanifa continued to take in her surroundings, and soon a silver-gray SSS lowered itself and stopped by the students. They hopped in and an automated voice said, "WATCH YOUR STEPS AND TAKE A SEAT, CHILDREN OF THE FUTURE."

What future? The world is ending soon. Crap! I need to stop thinking about the end of our times. Too late. Thoughts about religious predictions had taken over Hanifa's mind.

The hexagon SSS was auto-piloted and could

accommodate six students. They had two angular couches facing each other. She took a seat by one of the four floor-to-ceiling windows. Malik sat next to Hanifa, her school bag between them. He fixed his hat, an old man's cloth cap he got in Eastern Europe, straightened his long, caramel-toned neck, and put two cordless earplugs in his ears to listen to the news.

Shafiya and Pristine sat facing them. As they settled in, the hexagon car took off; its orange laser fired behind it. Hanifa was seventeen autumns old. There was only a three-season gap between her and her older brother Malik.

Shafiya was fourteen springs old. She sat perfectly still except for her backpack rocking back and forth on her toes. She wore a red trapeze Zulu hat, an elbow-length white shirt, and an old pair of loose blue jeans. Her brown kiwi-skin complexion made her look like a real Zulu native. Her round face and button nose sealed the deal. Shafiya knew how cute she was.

Pristine, who was twelve summers old, mimicked Shafiya's behavior by rocking her bag too. Her feet were barely visible under her brown maxi skirt and bag. Facing down, her frizzy curly hair hugged her beige long-sleeve blouse as she hummed a melodious religious acappella.

Through the windows, the coastal mountains seemed so small. Hanifa leaned back on her couch to contemplate the view. Her slouched hat touched the back of her seat as she absentmindedly blew the uncontained strands of pressed hair off her face.

From the corner of her eye, she saw Malik glancing at her. "Hey, are you going to need any help? I mean, being your first time at school and all."

"No, I'll be fine," Hanifa replied, popping a chocolate protein bar into her mouth. Ramadan had ended a little over thirty nights ago, and her stomach was still used to small meals. Though Calendars were forbidden, Hanifa's parents knew exactly what year it was and had told Hanifa and her siblings that they would share the date with them when the time was right. For the Seculars— Immortal wannabes— marking time was only a reminder that the end was near. When it was a religious or otherwise auspicious day that they needed to observe by fasting or with extra prayers, their parents would let them know.

"OK, holler at us if you need to," Shafiya said, chiming in.

Hanifa nodded and looked through the window, a pang of fear seeping into her heart.

***

At school, as soon as the foursome jumped off of the SSS they somewhat blended into the colorful crowd. Muslims like them were created to stand out anyway, not blend in. The students' clothes barely covered their bodies. The majority of them wore bright, transparent clothes. While the female students had patches of fabric to hide their breasts and genital areas, everything else was hanging out. If you didn't dress like that, you weren't a cool kid. Hanifa averted her gaze to avoid looking at their *awrat* parts. She decided to explore the school setting instead.

On each side of the primary lane leading to the school

buildings, there was an impeccable artificial green lawn that seemed to continue infinitely. As her siblings walked ahead toward the school, Hanifa stood still, mesmerized by the architecture. She looked up, trying to fathom the height of the buildings. The glass windows shined intensely. The robotic janitors certainly did a good job. The light blue glass reflecting the rising sun made her look forward to other pleasant surprises.

"You can't even see the top of any of the five towers because they're so buried in the darn sky," a young female voice said.

Hanifa twirled around to see a tall blonde rocking a bowl haircut, dressed in a transparent blouse as well. Before Hanifa had time to answer, the girl added, "Hi, you're new?" in perfect Portuguese.

Hanifa nodded, her mouth still hanging open. *The end of times are definitely here,* she noted, taking in skyscrapers that seemed to go on forever. She checked the impulse to speak her mind aloud and kept that comment to herself. She promised her parents she would not talk of religion or use any forbidden words.

The blonde extended her hand to Hanifa. "I'm Ana Undeapsidud."

"I'm Hanifa Ducktrinor. And yes, it's my first day. What gave it away?" Hanifa also replied in Portuguese with a slight accent.

"You looked up. Only new students do that. Regular students forget that they go on forever." Ana shook Hanifa's right hand. "Anyway Hanifa, nice to meet you."

It now made sense to Hanifa why they called the school "The Five Skyscrapers Castle School" or just

"Castle 5." She hadn't even bothered to look up the school before physically attending. She was just too happy to be outside the house for a change.

"Come on, let me show you around," Ana said. "You look so lost but you speak the language so well." Ana dragged Hanifa away from the curbside to one of the school towers.

"Yeah? Thanks! We travel a lot, so my parents made sure we knew the major languages: English, French, Spanish, Portuguese, Cantonese, German... You get the gist." Hanifa shrugged like it was no big deal.

"I see. Impressive. Anyway, the first building on the left is for kindergarten. The next one is for elementary school. Then, the next two toward the right are for middle and high school, and the last tower on the right is for university students."

"That's really cool. At my last school, it wasn't all

together like that," Hanifa remarked.

"Really? So how was it?"

"Each school was in a different area of the city, but we still carpooled to stay together, for safety," Hanifa said as they walked toward the school buildings.

"And where did you come from?"

"South Africa," Hanifa said.

"Are you South African? Why did you leave?"

"No, we're originally from East Africa—Ethiopia to be precise." Hanifa twisted the corner of her mouth.

"Why the face? Bad memories from Africa?" Ana paused, pulling up her leggings with one hooked finger.

"Well, I talked about religion and the end of—"

CHAPTER TWO : SCHOOL TROUBLES

Hanifa

ANA IMMEDIATELY JUMPED AND covered Hanifa's mouth. She looked left and right. "Shhh…there are spies everywhere! Even the walls spy. *Seriously.* They could report you to Sylas Yumaneter." Then, she removed her hands from Hanifa's mouth.

"Who is Sylas Yumaneter?" Hanifa whispered back.

"He's the Secular Deputy of the school. Any funny business about what you were about to mention is reported to him. He's twenty-one, and he either takes care of insurgents personally, or blows the whistle to the authorities when he doesn't feel like dealing with the issue."

"Authorities…you mean the Seculars?"

"Correct. Oh, and Sylas controls the headmaster, the president, and the dean of the school. They all fear him despite the fact that they're much older than he is. Sir Landry Big holds the reigns to the education system if you ask me."

"Sylas must have some dirt on them then," said Hanifa. "I still wonder how the Seculars came to power so fast, though I have an idea based on my Mom's tales. Anyway, there's no more freedom."

"That, my new friend, we agree on. Come on," Ana said as they entered the high school tower, "let me show you the connecting elevators to the other towers. I'll show you the pictures of the headmaster, president, and dean, too. Their pictures are pretty much for show—they rarely come to school since they don't have any power here. And since school isn't required, no one will get on your case if you don't show up for class. But if you decide to study, they monitor you very closely. You can obtain one of the best degrees in the world attending this school, like my older brother Tim, because the school is renowned and resourceful."

"No kidding?" Hanifa was surprised by the "no mandatory school" part. "My siblings never mentioned that, probably for fear of being homeschooled like me." *But nothing escapes Mom and Dad. I'm sure they know. They have to know and perhaps that's a way for them to stay low key.* Hanifa quickly thought, and Ana continued to talk.

"Ah! Sneaky. Yeah, the teacher is a computer chalkboard. Anyway, I assume you're about my age. I'm eighteen."

"That's a bum that school isn't required. And yeah, I'm seventeen autumns old. I take it the high school and university towers will be where you and I will mostly hang out. I can't wait to take university courses."

Ana led them to the elevators, taking Hanifa to each floor of the high school and higher-education towers. As they toured the school, Hanifa wondered if she would run into Malik in those two towers since he was only a few seasons older than her. But because the school was so enormous, that possibility was very slim.

"This is sick!" Hanifa exclaimed. "It's like a hotel! So many rooms!"

"Ha! I tell you. And you know what? If you know the right people and are adventurous enough, you can find anybody on campus at any time."

"How is that possible? This school's huge!" Hanifa said.

"The student IDs are tracked. There's this application only available in a secret place in or around the library called Shadow Hunter. You just search the name of the person you have in mind, and it finds them."

"Is that legal?" Hanifa asked skeptically.

Ana grinned. "Probably not, but who cares? It must be fun! I think it's in the library because no one goes there to study."

"It must be fun indeed. I have an idea: how about we try to find it and pinpoint Sylas?" Hanifa proposed.

"Do you have a death wish? Trust me, you don't want to be noticed by this guy. Besides, I heard the program has a tough time finding him, according to Tim. He's always at multiple places at the same time. There are a lot of rumors about him. Some say that he's a vampire and possesses clones of himself. Others say that he kidnaps children to perform evil rituals," Ana said spookily. Her eyes grew one size bigger.

The Muezzin was probably right! Hanifa thought, reflecting on an article she'd read from the rebellion's e-zine. "Creepy. Okay, so maybe it wouldn't be a good idea to try to find him," Hanifa added, wincing. "But there is no fire without fumes…"

"Good! Let's forget him. The library is over here." Ana led the way once again, dismissing Hanifa's last insinuation.

The library was lined with neatly shelved books and had long rows of pristine tabletop computers with no legs. The tabletop computers were some sort of newly developed, ultrathin material with individual tablets seamlessly built right into them that, without any support, gravitated above the ground. All of this was possible by a new invisible magnetic field technology between the tabletop and the floor.

"Wow, look at all these old books. I'm going to have a field day in here," Hanifa said as she jumped in glee.

"Who's your friend, Ana?" a deep monotone voice asked from behind them.

Ana froze. "We were just leaving," she managed to say, pulling at the arm of Hanifa's long-sleeved green blouse.

"No we aren't. We just got here," Hanifa said. She stared at the fit, silver-haired young white man who held her gaze with *amazing* red eyes if she said so herself. *But who has silver hair these days? Only robots and clones do from what I've seen in the past. Maybe the rumor is right,* Hanifa considered.

"Maybe you should listen to Ana. My name is Sylas Yumaneter, Secular Deputy. And this is Judas," he said, pointing his thin chin to the redheaded young man next to him.

Judas grinned widely, his huge belly emphasized by his hands in his pant pockets.

Oh snap! Hanifa thought.

"You girls should be in class by now. We're administering a Secular recruitment test right now," he said, moving his head toward his right shoulder to reveal the few test takers behind him.

"Sorry to disturb. Ana was just helping me with orientation on my first day."

"I see. Come back when we're done, unless you want to sit for it."

"No thank you. We're sorry for disturbing your exam—we didn't see a sign."

"Afraid you won't do well?" Sylas asked.

"No, joining the Seculars' army isn't my thing." Hanifa shrugged.

"Every year students line up to become part of the army. You mean to tell me we don't interest you?"

"Correct," Hanifa said, looking him straight in his eyes.

"Maybe you're just lying and not bright enough to pass the test."

"With all due respect, Sylas, I'm afraid I could ace this exam if I wanted to," said Hanifa. "It was nice to put a face to the name, though. Ana, let's go."

"You guys can leave when I say you can. I didn't catch your name," Sylas continued.

"My name is Hanifa, like…" *Telling him that I was named after a Muslim Imam will not help my case here.* She ate her remaining words.

"Like whom?"

"Nobody. I don't know why I said that," Hanifa said, scratching her head.

"Hmm, Hanifa is not a common name, but it rings a bell." Sylas put his right hand to his heart and closed his eyes, as if trying to recall some long-forgotten detail. He toyed with the white fabric of his deputy attire until he gave up.

"Anyway, Judas, pass me a tablet so that Hanifa over here can show me what she's made of." Judas gave him the tablet and Sylas pushed Hanifa into a seat, putting the tablet in front of her.

Snap! How did I get myself in this situation? I was supposed to avoid his kind like the plague.

"Ana, take a seat. No need for you to take the test since we already tested you."

Ana sat down, pouting.

"How long is the test?" Hanifa asked. Taking a forced test on the first day of school wasn't how she had planned her return to normal school.

"Shh," a test taker shushed her. The icy gray in the raven-haired girl's eyes made Hanifa shiver. She swiftly turned her head back around to focus on the task she had to perform.

"Sorry," whispered Hanifa. Her eyes nearly bulged out of their sockets, her lips pursed.

"Just a couple hours," Sylas said, grinning. Then he walked back over to resume his seat at the table.

Hanifa stared at the white tablet screen for a minute. It read "Secular Army Admission Test." She glanced at the apprehensive Ana sitting in the corner of the library, then swiped her finger left to right.

The next screen that popped up gave the different sections of the test. The test's table of contents showed major ancient religions as the first part, then secular politics, mathematics, biology, chemistry, accounting, ancient civilizations, and pop culture.

Ancient religions? That should be a piece a cake, she thought. The Quran talks about all the religions. That and all the history books she read would come in handy here. There were a few questions on each major religion. She selected the answers she thought were correct and moved on quickly. Hanifa still wanted to finish the school tour she had started with Ana.

When she answered all the required questions from the first section, the next part popped up on the screen: secular politics. *Thank you, Uncle Abe, for making me take interest in this subject.* She was sure she would do well on this part as well. Moving fast, she selected the answers with her finger.

Mathematics, biology, chemistry, and accounting were subjects that were easy to Hanifa; her whole family was science- and numbers-oriented. Her father was an engineer.

Her grandfather too. Her mother, on the other hand, had been an accountant before marrying her father. With all the knowledge they'd instilled in her, she was naturally inclined to pass this section as well. *Sylas, I'll prove to you that Allah gave me brains!* She snickered.

Then a thought occurred to her: *What if he thinks you cheated? Or worse. What if he thinks you're religious? Nah. Why give a test to people if you're going to be suspicious of their results? Besides, it's not like I had time to prepare for this stupid exam.*

She pushed her thoughts aside and focused on the last part of the exam: ancient civilizations and pop culture. The last part wasn't so bad, but she was sure she missed a few questions because she was starting to get mentally tired. *Yup, trying to recall old, remote things will do it. I need some water.* She pinched her forehead in concentration.

Hanifa exhaled and looked around her. Sylas was whispering to Ana. He smiled as she quietly giggled and listened. Then she flirtatiously tucked strands of her blonde hair behind her ears.

Hanifa was taken aback by the sight of their closeness. *Surely, she would have told me if they were a thing. But then again, she barely knows me.*

Hanifa continued looking around the vast library. There were still a few test takers left. Thankfully, the raven-haired girl was gone.

When she was done, Hanifa gave Sylas the tablet back and said, "Now I know why you're the leader of the Seculars in this school. You can be imposing. No offense, Sir."

"None taken. Judas always says the same. Isn't that right, Judas?" From the corner of his eye, he eyed his sidekick, who nodded to approve. "I'll let you know about the results."

"If I pass the test, my answer is still no. I only took the test because you didn't give me a choice, and because I wanted to prove that I wasn't dumb." Hanifa crossed her arms over her chest.

"Dumb? I never thought so. Just consider the possibility of joining us under my lead. There are benefits to the position." He winked and added, "You girls can go now.

Ciao!"

"Finally!" Ana threw her arms up in the air. "How was the test?" she asked, pulling Hanifa out of the library.

"Not bad," Hanifa replied, though she was worn out. She dragged her feet along as Ana pulled her strongly. They continued the day touring and eating delicious Brazilian food from the cafeteria such as mashed sweet plantains and spicy soup with hints of coriander and paprika followed by ripe baked plantain banana with ice cream as dessert. It was a change for Ana who told Hanifa that she ate a lot of prepackaged meals.

They also indulged on many different cakes, puddings, and other high-calorie sweets. High on sugar, they ran throughout the school like reconnected childhood friends.

***

"How was your first day of school?" Mrs. Eva Ducktrinor asked her children at the dinner table. Malik, Shafiya, and Pristine recounted their stories in turn while Hanifa stayed quiet.

"Mom, all my classmates loved my Zulu hat I got from South Africa!" Shafiya said, barely containing her joy.

"They *did?*" She sounded happy for her daughter. "I knew you didn't have anything to worry about."

Shafiya smiled and continued eating her roasted chicken and seasoned brown rice.

"They thought my skirt was too long and wiping the floor," Pristine said with her face tilted down. She was playing with the steamed vegetables on her plate, hardly eating anything.

"They don't know anything. People barely dress today. Your skirt was beautiful and very classy," her mother comforted her. "What about you Hanifa? How was your day?"

"It was okay. I met a new friend—Ana."

"Good. I'm glad you're socializing," her father said, cutting his meat with a knife.

"Did you tell her you want to be a courageous Coreishy woman when you grow up?" Mrs. Ducktrinor asked, putting a piece of okra in her mouth.

"No! Of course I held my tongue." *Well, kinda.* She recalled keeping her thoughts about the height of the school to herself, but she also remembered Ana covering her mouth when she mentioned "religion" and was about to say the word "times." She also stopped herself from telling Sylas the origin of her name if that counted for self-control.

"I trust you, otherwise I wouldn't have sent you to school," her father said, clearing his throat.

Hanifa looked down at her lap with squinted eyes. Just then, the electronic doorbell announced a loud message from visitors. "GOOD EVENING, FELLOW CITIZENS, THIS IS THE SECULARS' PATROL. OPEN UP."

The Ducktrinors exchanged looks around the table before their eyes zeroed on the dumbfounded Hanifa.

CHAPTER THREE : BEDTIME STORY

Hanifa

Timeline: Hanifa's childhood

"I'M A COREISHY WOMAN!" ten-year-old Hanifa said, her head held up high, both of her hands at her hips. Then she mounted her wooden horse while her yellow cape, secured around her neck, gracefully draped the horse as she sat back, covering its tail. A fan blew air on her, making her cape billow behind her back. Hanifa's ten-year-old mind didn't know the implications of such a desire to be a fierce woman, but it certainly marveled at the valor it entailed.

Her parents exchanged loving looks and smiled. Looking back, they must have known the chances Hanifa would become a well-educated woman and a community servant— like Fatima Muhammad Al-Fihri Al Quraysh or the courageous Nusaybah bint Ka'ab—were close to nil in their times of *fitna*.

"When I grow up," Hanifa said, "I will bring people together, and I will always continue to seek knowledge! *Rabbi Zidni Ilma*—Oh Allah increase me in knowledge. *Ameen*."

"*Ameen* and good luck! But you know education and charity are considered a source of a likely communism and revolt," Malik piped in. "How are you going to keep a low profile when Seculars see higher education and giving charity as pillars on which all organized religions are built on?"

"There is always a way to stay on the straight path, like Dad says," Hanifa said, winking and pseudo-galloping. "I'll just have to be smarter and beat them at their game." She finished with a nod and an approving *hmm!* "Isn't that right Dad and

Mom?"

"Who knows?" her mother said with a wide smile. "Everything and anything is possible. Hanifa, we will do our part in your upbringing, continue to encourage you to be the best version of yourself and support your dreams *insha'Allah*."

"*Insha'Allah*," Hanifa added and continued playing on her horse.

Malik, a plastic sword pulled at the ready, stood by the fan that blew air on her, making her yellow cape billow on her back. She had sloppily stitched $(CO)_2$ short for *COurageous COreishy*, on the yellow cape and bedazzled it.

"Hurry up so we can have a duel!" he grumbled at his sister, and started fending off the invisible air in front of him. "Besides, I thought the best of Coreishy women rode camels—you're on a wooden horse. Whatever, I don't care."

"Heh, they rode any kind of animals," Hanifa said as she continued to play on her horse.

Later that day, after the *magrib* prayer, they sat in *halaqa* formation on the beautiful rugs laid on the floor of the prayer room. During *halaqa*, they would sit in a semi-circle around their father or mother, or both, to learn and talk about Islam and the different *madhabs* or *madhahib* they were named after.

"Hanifa, what would a follower of Imam Hanifa's school of thought do if he was bleeding and had to make ablutions?" her father asked.

"I know the answer," Malik said, raising his hand excitedly.

"Wait your turn, son," their father said firmly, yet gently.

Hanifa mirrored her father's smile. "In the Hanafi Madhab, my *wudu* would be void. So, I would have to make ablutions with the *niyat* of the Maliki Madhab."

"Correct, Hanifa. You need to make ablutions with the

intention of Imam Malik's Madhab because, according to his teachers, one's *wudu* isn't void."

Hanifa nodded and then her father continued the education session, questioning her a few more times on other differences between the *madhabs* before turning his attention to Malik. "Malik, Shafiya is only seven years old. Let's say I'm a follower of the Shafi Madhab and that I kiss her hand while being a *mahram* or non-*maharam*. Is my *wudu* void?"

"No, it's not void," Malik replied firmly. *He seems so mature and sure of himself,* Hanifa thought.

"Why not?" his father asked.

"Because Shafiya isn't of marriageable age, my *wudu* isn't void if I merely touched her," Malik added with a proud grin.

"Excellent. Okay, good job answering questions today. Pristine, my *hanbal* princess, come here," he said to his youngest daughter, who had five birthday candles to her name. She got up gracefully, yet sassy-like, to go sit on her father's lap, her pink *abaya* swirling around her sock-covered ankles. "One day when you're all grown up, I'll ask you questions on the Hanbali Madhab," he told her, nudging her button nose.

"Deal!" she said as she high-fived his offered palm with a peck and giggled.

Then the family made a few laps of *dhikr* on their rosaries before they started a round of *duas*, beginning with the youngest person in the room to the oldest. Pristine went first and recited an easy and powerful *dua* in Arabic from memory: "*Rabbana la tuzikh qulubana ba'ada iz hadaythana wa hablana min-ladunka rahmatan innaka antal wahhab.*" (*Our Lord, let not our hearts deviate after You have guided us and grant us from Yourself mercy. Indeed, You are the Bestower.*) (Quran 3:8)

The rest of the family uttered, "*Ameen.*"

It was Shafiya's turn. The family continued to utter "*Ameen*" until she finished her recital. Then Hanifa's turn came, followed by Malik and finally their father's. He closed the *halaqa* session with his *dua* and they closed with the *isha* prayer right after. Dinner normally followed the last obligatory prayer of the day where they thanked their parents for the food upon finishing eating. Afterwards, they brushed their teeth and went to their rooms to study before bedtime—Hanifa's favorite part of the day. Her father always went to her room to say goodnight after her mom had stopped by.

"Baba?"

"Yes, dear."

"Can you please tell me the story of The Companions of the Cave?" Hanifa asked her father as he tucked her in.

"I tell you that story every night, Hanee," he said to her.

"I know," she replied, pouting. "But I'll give you more hugs and kisses if you tell it to me again tonight." Her hazel eyes gleamed with excitement.

"Okay…" Somewhat dramatically, her father went into character while dimming the lights in her room, then he began narrating the story of the *As-hab al Kahf* with renewed vigor and energetic gestures.

"A long, loooooong time ago, there were a group of Christian men who believed in Allah. The ruler of their town was a TYRANT!" The way her father emphasized "tyrant" made Hanifa jump but it didn't stop her from tuning in. She tightened her grip on the hems of her comforter and drank her father in, eyes wide open.

"He forced his people to worship idols and false deities. The group of young men refused and decided to flee to escape persecution. They prayed and implored Allah to protect them." Hanifa's father yawned. "Do you want me to read the rest of the story from the Quran?"

Hanifa nodded, bouncing her head up and down excitedly. She wanted to hear his melodious, poetic voice as he recited *surah* 18 of the holy book from his memory. Her father finished, taking in a deep breath. He sat down next to her and kissed her on the forehead. "And you know the rest, my dear."

"Yes, I know! When Issa, *aleihi salam*, or Jesus—son of Mary—returns, the cave currently located in Tarsus, Turkey will open and the companions of the cave will come out. Together with Mahdi, *aleihi salam*, his vouching cloud, they will help him defeat *Yajuj* and *Majuj*."

"That's right!" her father said and continued, "Now, enough about bedtime stories. You need to sleep. We have a *halaqa* session as usual tomorrow after the *fajr* prayer and I don't want you opposing to waking up because you had little sleep."

"Okay Dad…But before you go, I have another question." She paused and sat up. "When I grow up, do you think I can fight with them too?"

"You've never asked me such a serious question before, Hanee." He stayed quiet for a moment while she examined his cryptic facial features. "I don't know, little one. The end of times is near but it might not be in our lifetime for us to take a part in it. But it would be an honor and a miracle if it happens in our lifetime."

"That'll be so cool!" She beamed.

"Alright, say your prayers and may Allah protect you during the night," he said, getting up with a heave.

Snap... My escape tactics to avoid sleeping didn't work. "*Ameen,*" she mumbled as she slumped back into bed while he closed the door behind him and turned off the light.

One day, I'll lead an expedition to Tarsus, find the cave, and fight alongside the companions—Mahdi, and Issa, aleihi salam-insha'Allah, Hanifa thought before drifting peacefully off to sleep.

CHAPTER FOUR : BEDTIME STORY

Malik

Timeline: Malik's childhood

"HURRY UP SO WE can have a duel!" Malik had grumbled to Hanifa for the umpteenth time before she got off her wooden horse.

"Fine! Let's do it. I'll win and you will do the visual effects. You better be creative," Hanifa sassed.

"Safi!" Malik called and his second sister showed up.

"We need a referee as usual. Mom and Dad always side with Hanifa because she's younger," Malik said, eyeing his parents suspiciously.

"Yes, you do and I understand. I need to share the spotlight but sometimes I feel like it's unfair," he added before they had the chance to place a word.

The parents gasped and Malik didn't linger long on their reactions. He knew she was their favorite and sometimes he felt like he didn't *completely* belong in the Ducktrinors' home.

"Sure," the young Safi replied and took her position. It was serious business.

"Thanks sis," Malik said, turning his attention to Safi and then faced Hanifa. "Don't worry, you will have time to be creative since I'll win anyways," Malik said sure of himself. With widening grins, the siblings pulled their wooden swords at the ready. Within seconds, they were fending off each other's attacks making hollow sounds that resonated in the air.

Malik won points by touching Hanifa's shoulders, knees, and head covered *hijab*. Hanifa on the other hand won the fight by making impact on his chest, shoulders, both knees, and hip.

"Well Malik, Hanifa wins…Sorry, it was clear as day," Safi said, delivering the verdict.

"You guys are all against me! Next time, I'll ask my friend to arbitrate! Sayf Ibn Zulfiqar is not supposed to lose because it's the best sword there is!" Malik said, irritated. Yes, he named his play sword Sayf Ibn Zulfiqar even though it wasn't split at the tip.

"Alright," Hanifa replied, shrugging. "It's time to be creative brother."

"You're a good sword fighter Malik but you can't win all the duels if we're being honest. See, Safi thought her sister deserved it so maybe we aren't playing favorites like you think," one of the parents said after Malik had seen them deliberate for a moment before they agreed to the verdict.

Hmph! Malik let out exasperated. "What's the scenario?" he asked, ignoring their comments to question Hanifa.

"We're being attacked and you are the savior. What do you do?"

"Thank God!" Malik's response was due to the fact that other times, he had been asked to be a pirate defending his ship or the prince that saves the princess of Persia from armed guards and a tyrant king. He had to do a monologue sketch on his own and play all the parts while his family enjoyed the display of him running about in all directions like a chicken with its head cut off. As they laughed endlessly because he tried to entertain them by including funny moments like when he pretended to pull down the pants of the guards or pretended to give them water when it was a laxative drink.

When the *Eid* approached, Malik was also known to make corny jokes. "It's not a proper moon war without a saber fight!" He often told Hanifa as she laughed holding her belly.

In all, Malik was a funny person when he didn't wear his taciturn hat. So Malik cupped his chin for something that seemed like less than a minute and then his face lit up! "I got it!"

"No rush, you have time to prepare the props and you can entertain us tonight after dinner *insha'Allah*," Hanifa said with the wisdom of a grown up girl.

"Bossy girl," Malik teased and recognized the ghost of a wicked grin flash in her face.

***

Later that night, after Malik had performed the best play of his life with all the craft materials the family possessed in their homeschooling supplies, he got ready for bed. He couldn't wait to ask his father for a new and inspiring story. When the knob of his door turned, he could barely contain his excitement. His cheeks were burning with anticipation. As soon as his father entered the room, Malik let out, "Baba, can you please tell me another story about a miracle performed by a Muslim scholar?"

"I pretty much told you everything I know," Adama replied, twisting the corner of his lips as he played with his chin. The only thing Malik thought they shared in common: playing with their chin. He always thought that his family wasn't completely his family but his parents had always reassured him and told him that his doubts were silly. "Just because the resemblance isn't striking like with the girls and us it doesn't mean you aren't our son," his mom had said to him once. Malik had accepted the response but still had doubts and he didn't know why.

"Let me see," his father said still thinking, pulling the young man from his distracting thoughts.

Malik sighed anyway, grumbled, and then pulled the cover on his slender body. "*Naam,* may Allah protect you during the night Baba. Night."

"That's it?"

"Well, there is no reason to stay up since that would have been your next move." He turned his head to face his father and at that moment he noticed a spark in the old man's eyes.

"A story just hit me! Have you ever heard of Somuncu Baba?"

"I don't remember you telling me his story Baba," Malik replied suddenly feeling awake.

"His real name was Sheikh Hamid-i Vali. According to

my sources, he was a grandchild of our beloved Prophet Muhammad *sallallahu aleihi wassalam*," Adama added as he sat down by the side of the bed.

"This is so cool *masha'Allah*! What did he do? Please tell me! I hope a great *keeramat*!" Malik said, sitting up. His hazel brown eyes glistened with excitement.

"Oh he was great... *Masha'Allah*," his father replied matter-of-factly, meeting his son's eyes. He tilted his head to one side as his eyes made a 180 degree in their orbits to vouch for that fact. A sly smile covered his face as he started his narration of this *awliya* he had mentioned earlier.

"*Subhanallah* Baba! So after the opening of the mosque where he conducted the *tafsir* of *surah Al Fatiha* seven ways, he was able to be at all the doors of the mosque and greet every attendee on their way out?" Malik asked as his eyes bulged in amazement.

"Yup! That is what my sources say. And that my son is an Islamic miracle performed by a scholar or a *keeramat* in Arabic," Adama recognized, shaking his head in disbelief.

"One day, I'll be a great teacher and scholar *insha'Allah* and I'll perform a *keeramat* as well for the sake of Islam."

"Well son, that is a dream to live up to. Your father will be jealous of you when that happens, and it will come from a good place *insha'Allah*." Adama winked as he tousled Malik's curly dark locks and added, "May Allah help you realize your dreams and goals and may they be *mubarak* for you, *ameen*. Alright boy, good night. Sleep tight and may He protect you during the night. *Ameen*."

"*Ameen* Baba, thank you and same to you."

Adama got up from the side of the bed and Malik slumped back to bed, pulling the soft covers to his chest before peacefully drifting off to sleep. He hoped he could travel to a beautiful place that night so as he closed his eyes shut, he had whispered, "Ya Allah, let me visit a beautiful and enchanting place tonight." Then he recited the *hawqala* and ended with *ameen* as he did every night before he passed out. That night he met **Tawfiq aka Fiqh Tsion As-Staree** [1] as his soul travelled about in known and unknown dimensions. They became great friends.

---

[1] Tawfiq is a fictional character of Papatia Feauxzar who is lightly mentioned in a short story titled 'Fiqh Tsion's Tells of Faith'.

CHAPTER FIVE : THE SECULARS

Hanifa

Timeline: The first day of school in Brazil

HANIFA'S FATHER OPENED the door, a tense smile plastered across his face. Hanifa immediately noticed several patrol cars in the neighborhood, all without their emergency lights on.

"Good evening officers. How can I help you?" Mr. Ducktrinor continued to smile at the two black officers standing in front of him. His eyes went from their strong, fit bodies to his neighbors' front doors; the Bordinis, the Berholzs, and the Silvas also had officers at their doors.

Whew, so we weren't the only ones, Hanifa thought as she followed her father's head movements.

"Good evening, Sir. What is your last name?" asked the officer wearing square, opaque shades. He had a deep voice.

"Duck-Ducktrinor," Hanifa's father stammered while the other officer noted his response on a tablet.

"Got him. He's listed," the officer with the tablet declared.

Hanifa saw her father swallow the knot in his throat. From a few feet away, she could see his left fist forming a ball in his pants pocket.

"This is officer Nozier and I'm Officer Sozpitius from the Secular police patrol. Did you shelter anybody in the last hour or so?" His thumb and index fingers pinched the tar belt of his black uniform.

"No," Mr. Ducktrinor said, glancing back at Hanifa and the rest of his family to confirm his words. They all nodded and grouped up behind him. "Is everything okay?"

Officer Nozier buried the tablet in his back pocket and

took a few careful steps back, his head craning like a cat who had heard a noise.

"What's up?" Officer Sozpitius asked, turning his head to his colleague.

"I'm going to re-scan the perimeter. I heard something," Officer Nozier said, looking left and right before starting to sweep the house, the front and backyard with a sophisticated-looking scanner gun.

Officer Sozpitius turned his attention to the family. He glanced at all of their faces as they stood behind Mr. Ducktrinor and said, "We're looking for a fugitive with the last name Kreedor. He's over fifty, at least. He's also extremely dangerous. We believe he's involved with the rebellion. How many people live in this house?"

"Kreedor?" Mr. Ducktrinor repeated and looked at his wife, who Hanifa saw instantly blanch.

"Yes, Kreedor. Do you know anybody by that name?" Officer Sozpitius took a step back, tightly enclosing his hand on his firearm.

"No, I don't. We're six. Me, my wife, and our four children," Mr. Ducktrinor replied, his back pressed to the front door for Officer Sozpitius to count the rest of the family.

The officer relaxed his grip on the gun.

"That's what I got with my scanner gun. No one else is inside," Officer Nozier said, coming up from the grassy front yard. "Please report anything strange and suspicious to us at 966." He still tried to peek through the windows, which were covered with thin, white curtains.

When officer Nozier finally rejoined his partner on the Ducktrinors' doorsteps, Officer Sozpitius said, "We apologize for the intrusion. Good night, Ducktrinors." They tipped their shaved heads and the duo left.

Mr. Ducktrinor closed the door behind them and let out a deep sigh. "Whew, that was nerve-wracking. Who could they be looking for with our previous last name?" He looked at the ceiling, taking another deep breath.

"I don't want to know," his wife replied. "I hope for the fugitive's sake, they don't find him. This is crazy. What are the odds that from all the last names, it's Kreedor?" She shook her head and started making her way back to the dinner table.

"If you ask me, that felt way too close," said Hanifa. "And when the bell announced the patrol, all of you looked at me like I was the one who did something to warrant their visit here. I told you, I didn't get into anything compromising at school. I deserve an apology." She eyed her whole family with a sullen look.

The room quieted, and she crossed her arms around her chest, waiting. But even as she awaited the magical words she was unlikely to receive from her family, she thought, *Why do I expect an apology? They had fair grounds to believe I might have put their lives in danger again. Past mistake or not.*

One by one, the family members sat back in their seats to continue their meal without saying anything to Hanifa. Instead, the conversation turned to the judicial system. Any crime was punishable by law in their times, much like old societies, but a specific type of murder had not been sanctioned.

"At least they try to do their job by trying to arrest a wanted criminal," Mr. Ducktrinor said.

"True," Hanifa's mom commented. "But I'm afraid they've also legalized another type of murder under the pretense of religious cleansing. We can't practice our faith openly or we're likely to be sentenced to death." She drank her glass of water in three sips and continued her small conversation with her husband.

Hanifa's heart sank in her chest. She took a bite of food that she no longer wanted. Truthfully, her appetite had gone the minute her father started grilling her on her first day at school. She knew her father meant well and just wanted safety for his family. Hanifa silently ate her food so that her mother didn't think her dish wasn't tasty.

An older, crispy voice interrupted the family's awkward silence. "*Assalamu aleikum*, family," said a round old man in a high-tech wheelchair, moving towards the dinner table.

Mouths and eyes opened wide as they all turned to look in his direction.

"*Wa aleikum salam*, Grandpa! What are you doing here?" Hanifa asked, jumping out of her seat. She rushed to him, throwing herself onto his lap and clasping her hands behind his neck. She almost smothered him with her hug.

"Your grandpa is weak these days," he said, laughing while tapping her back. A quick minute passed, and she looked back at her father as she sat on her grandfather's lap.

The lightbulb turned on, on her father's face. "Of course, it makes sense! Mustapha Kreedor—the only R.E.D Rebel left to challenge the Seculars." He leered at his father without adding a peace or welcome greeting.

"I see sarcasm is still lurking behind the surface when it comes to you, son. Whatever happened to respecting elders? If you must know, I'm no longer Retired and Exceedingly Dangerous. I'm just a retired engineer who used to be a rebel. The rebellion has dissolved and my health isn't the best these days. I need to lay low going forward."

Hanifa finally loosened her grip on his neck and the rest of her siblings took turns kissing his right hand.

"Why are they looking for you? You almost put our lives in danger, Baba," accused Mr. Ducktrinor as his breath deepened and his brows furrowed.

"We attempted a coup. Since it wasn't successful, the whole rebellion is divided. Some are trying to regroup while others, like me, took the opportunity to make their exit."

Hanifa's parents murmured, exchanging worried looks.

"I must have missed that in the news today," Malik said, brooding. He acted like old people, always listening to the news and wanting to be a real human teacher to replace the robot teacher ubiquitous in schools since recent years. Ubiquitous, a word she had picked up from her Grandpa and loved how saying it twisted her tongue.

"You could have undone everything your son Abu did to keep us safe," Mrs. Ducktrinor said, squeezing her eyes shut and stroking her forehead. She *clearly* wanted to say more but was afraid to come off as disrespectful to her father-in-law.

"And Abu would do it again if he has to, children. Aren't you thankful you can still use the last name Ducktrinor after he created so many dummy Ducktrinor surnames for the Seculars to be able track?" Mustapha asked, wheeling his chair closer to Adama with a finger pressed on a random bottom by the side of the wheel.

"Where does it stop, Baba? As a mole in the Secular system, Abu can get killed for hacking into the system to change our names and lead the Secular intelligence to a dead end every time the Seculars seem too close to knowing we're Muslims."

"I know," Mustapha said. "Hopefully, he won't have to vouch for any of us or die trying to protect us. On a more pressing issue, I thought the Secular patrol was just here. Are you going to help hide me in the basement?"

"Right!" Dad agreed. "How did you pass the scanner gun test? The officer heard you arrive for sure because I heard something, too."

"Oh, I used this new teleporter I designed to keep myself in limbo in the portal until they left the house. This technology is only available amongst the best scientists and engineers of this era," Mustapha gloated. "I arrived before them and had to go back when I heard them questioning you."

"That's very cool, Grandpa. Will you show it to me later?" Hanifa asked.

Her grandfather smiled and agreed as the rest of the family hustled to set up the guest room in the basement and hide him. Adama and Malik hauled Mustapha down the stairs to the basement.

"It would have been nice, if your wheelchair flew in the air." Adama had quipped.

"I'm working on it," Adama replied, sighing clearly exasperated by his son's incessant taunting.

After the flurry of hiding Grandpa died down, Hanifa brought him dinner and ate with him while the rest of the family stayed upstairs.

After dinner, her parents took a walk around the neighborhood to facilitate their digestion and Hanifa and her siblings sat around their grandfather, prodding him for stories. They loved his outlandish, rebellious tales in which he was always a savior and the center of attention with handy gadgets that he had designed.

Mustapha told the children that once he had rendered a whole rebellion safe house invisible with a program he had designed, saving the neck of everyone in the building minutes before the Seculars had arrived on their doorsteps to make arrest.

"So you guys just vanished right in front of their eyes?!" Hanifa asked.

"You bet we did!" he replied.

"So cool!" the children let out in a cacophony of fascinated sounds.

After telling them stories, Mustapha gave them a crash course on engineering even though they had had many of these talks with their father in the past. Hanifa paid more attention since she wanted to know more about his wheelchair.

"What is an engineer?" Mustapha asked the children.

"It's a curious person that designs and constructs things to solve an issue or a problem. It's a person that always thinks about how things work, why things work or don't; the mechanism behind it is what piques their interest. Dad's words, haha!" Hanifa said with a smile and her siblings laughed because they knew she was on point.

"Great answer. To continue, there are many types of engineers; aerospatial, civil, electrical, software, mechanical, you name it. And they all go through the same process. First, they define the problem to be solved, then they research the problem. Next, they develop a possible solution and prepare to design the solution to the problem that needs to be solved. After, they build a prototype, they test the prototype, and finally they evaluate their results. They often face many failures, so they refine their invention and make it better for future users. A good engineer welcomes failure because there is always a lesson to be learned in the process that will help make the end product a revolution!" Mustapha said with passion in his voice and his hands moving in the air with assertion.

"To end and recap here, an engineer's job is to identify the problem, who has the problem that needs solving, and finally why is solving that problem crucial? *Alhamdullilah*, I can safely and proudly say that every member of this family has the curiosity and problem-solving genes. *Masha'Allah*. Now, let me show you how I designed this wheelchair with everything you just learned about the engineering process."

Right on cue, the children gathered closer around him as he made a small digital projector screen with azure blue light appear in the air just above his lap to show them his most coveted trade patented and copyrighted secrets.

***

The next day, standing at the course registration teller machine, Hanifa tried to hide her face under her hoodie from the guards patrolling the school in their white uniforms. The "S" on their chest meant something far away from hope, unlike Superman's Kryptonian crest. Something more like "submit," though of course it meant "Secular." *What are they doing at school? Are they looking for us?* she asked herself.

They had barely escaped from South Africa and had laid low in Brazil until the beginning of the new school year.

The Secular government had dispatched troops all around the globe searching for them until Uncle Abu ("Abe" to the Seculars he had infiltrated) led the Seculars to a dead end, away from Brazil. Now, with Grandpa Mustapha in the picture, things were even more dangerous for the whole family.

With sweaty palms and panic taking over her senses, Hanifa pressed the screen facing her repeatedly until the computer spat out her coursework registration receipt. She slid the flat-screen tablet with the summary of her classes into her backpack and quickly ducked into an alley without even closing her bag or looking.

"Ouch!" she said as she bumped into another person. The contents of her bag emptied onto the ground.

"Watch where you're going!" Ana spat.

"Ana! I'm sorry. I was trying to hide from the officers." The words flew out of Hanifa; this was exactly why her parents didn't trust her. She was a loose mouth.

"Oh, it's you," Ana said, relaxing her facial expression. "I've been looking for you everywhere." She dropped to her knees to help Hanifa pick up the contents of her backpack from the grey marble floor. Her white tutu sprang outward, almost revealing her panties. Ana grabbed an apple, a purple pen, and the tablet. "You carry strange things, Hanifa. No one eats real apples these days. The new paste available in stores does the same thing. And a tablet receipt?" Ana peeked at the courses and shook her head in disbelief.

"Call me old school. I eat healthy, not the latest engineered food that the Secular government endorses. And yes, I came to this school to learn. Deal with it."

"Old school? That you are," Ana mocked, looking at Hanifa's clothes up and down. Then she narrowed her eyes. "*Kôrôkô*s are believed to be extinct, but are you a *Kôrôkô*? You kinda dress like them. I know that because I'm really into fashion."

"Of course not! Nonsense." Hanifa puffed in laughter, shaking her head to get that idea out of Ana's head.

"Hmm, okay...So what are you going to do with a leadership and public speaking class? Or military techniques, for that matter?"

"If you paid attention to school, you would know that military techniques *is* a Secular requirement. But don't tell me, school isn't required here, right?" Hanifa sassed Ana. "As for the other class, I don't admit it to everyone, but I'm afraid of crowds and it would be nice to know how to address a crowd fearlessly." Hanifa looked down. She had stopped grabbing her things from the floor for a quick second. Then bouncing back, she continued, "So what did you want to warn me about?"

"I just wanted to tell you to be careful because they don't play here."

"Why? They don't play anywhere." Hanifa stood up and came face to face with Ana.

"Because you strike me as the daring kind." Ana shrugged.

Hanifa chuckled, and her reaction was only half-lived.

"ATTENTION, YOUR PRESENCE IS NEEDED IN THE GATHERING ROOM," an android voice announced through the speakers. The message repeated several times.

"What now?" Ana sighed while Hanifa stared at the voice enhancers with a skeptical look. With knitted eyebrows, Hanifa and her friend followed the other students to the designated room.

Moments later, students were still making their way to the gathering room. The auditorium filled up quickly. The Secular officers stood on the podium, in the hallway, and in front of the room to monitor the traffic and the seating of the students. When everyone was seated, the flat screen on the podium turned on. A video detailing the "glorious" biography and ascension to power of Sir Landry Big played for some minutes. *Whitewashing*, Hanifa thought.

WE WILL NOW DISPLAY A MESSAGE FROM THE HEAD OF THE SECULAR GOVERNMENT—SIR LANDRY BIG, showed on the screen until an old black man with black shades came on.

"Children of the future, welcome to another school year. This live video is being displayed simultaneously in the schools of all five continents: Eurasia, Australia, Africa, Antarctica, and last but not least, the Americas. You must be wondering why I am addressing you this year instead of my press secretary. Rest assured, you have done no wrong. But, there were some resistances detected recently. It led to a failed coup d'état and the death of my right-hand man and press secretary Trex Klinton. Sincere condolences to his family. To avenge his untimely death and bring things back to normalcy, many arrests have been made and many more will follow.

"The mutineers are hiding in plain sight. If you know anyone who is a rebel, tell us who they are and you will be generously rewarded. Think of the money and social status you can receive."

Hanifa and Ana looked at each other and then turned their faces back to the screen.

"I repeat, if you know anybody who is plotting against the Seculars, turn them in. As always, visit our temples in your facilities and salute our statues with your curtsies on a daily basis. If you're not a Secular, we respect your call. Just don't mention the forbidden words, challenge us, or think you can take us down. And remember, it pays to be one of us."

What a crock of shit. You don't respect our call. You persecute us openly when you know who we are. Hanifa snarled silently.

"Pay your respects to our deputies on the fields. My ministers and I thank you for your devotion and cooperation."

The screen went off and Sylas, followed by Judas and a few others, took the stand.

"I have my eyes on a few of you," he said.

At that moment, Hanifa felt like he was specifically talking to her. Sylas briefly met her gaze. *He could have been looking at anybody in the crowd*, she appeased herself.

"Again, make sure no one you know is being stupid enough to think they can challenge us," he warned.

A few murmurs spread through the gathering room before Sylas spoke one more time.

"You're dismissed." His deep and young voice roared through the auditorium.

Ana eyed the pensive Hanifa. "Well, that was

something."

"It was." Hanifa admitted. *I can't mess up anymore. Darn! It's hard not to speak one's mind.*

"Anyway, now that's over, what do we do for the rest of the day? A yesterday do-over?" Ana asked, winking.

"I don't know about you, Ana, but I have an ancient world civilizations II class to attend," Hanifa replied as she headed to the exit.

"Not again! You don't need to go to school. That's torture," Ana said, throwing her hands in the air in exasperation.

"But I want to. I'm only putting myself through it. You didn't sign up for it. I did," Hanifa retorted.

"All I'm saying is that there's no pressure for you to study or learn, but you still do. I was hoping to hang out with you today, H. Yesterday was so much fun!" Ana pouted.

Hanifa curiously tilted her head to one side to look at Ana. "You don't have any other friends?"

"I do, but none of them are like you. With you I don't

have to compete to be the center of attention or show off my latest clothes. You're different. You're not caught in the material things like me and my *friends*." Ana looked down, slouching her thin, square shoulders.

"I'm sorry to hear that. You can come with me to class. It's not like the android teacher is going to stop you—it's just a flat-screen digital chalkboard. Plus, it's designed not to worry about skippers or students, based on what Sylas said yesterday."

"Yeah, these things just lecture and turn off by themselves when class is over. Come on, where is this class anyway?"

"It says Room ACW1," Hanifa said and they went to find the class.

On their way, they found Sylas standing in the middle of the hallway leading to their classroom. Dressed in his usual white suit, he was gently tapping his left palm with a roll of paper; something that only a few people could afford in Hanifa's times since real trees were scarce. Sylas had a smirk on his face.

Hanifa's eyes grew wide. If there was one person she needed to avoid right now, it was Sylas.

She immediately turned to Ana and said, "Maybe you were right. Let's skip class today."

"Now, you're talking! Wait…it doesn't have anything to do with him, does it?" Ana pointed her chin in Sylas's direction.

"Maybe," Hanifa let out. They turned around, quickly retracing their previous steps. As the girls' clothes flapped noisily, they also heard footsteps chasing after them. They picked up the pace.

"Hanifa! A word please," Sylas called to Hanifa, stopping their attempt to elude him.

This guy really doesn't pick up on cues. "Yes…?" she said, spinning around stiffly.

Ana also stopped, slowly glanced over her shoulder, and, robot-like, turned around.

"Hanifa, I need to discuss your test scores and my

proposition to you about joining my army."

CHAPTER SIX : THE FIRST ARMY

Hanifa

Timeline: A couple years before The Ducktrinors moved to South Africa and then Brazil

HANIFA LOOKED UP HOW to start a high school club in America and found what she was looking for with a couple of keystrokes on her computer. *I don't have to compete with the MSA because my idea is original. Who doesn't want to emulate the best people of our religion who lived before us thousands of centuries ago?* She internally jubilated at the names she had picked for the boys and the girls who would join her club.

"Leadership experience, here I come!" she told her ego. First, she brainstormed ideas about the real focus of her club. "Easy, the main focus of this club should be to lead an expedition to Historic Islamic sites with Tarsus being the first on the list. Step one, check!" She continued to define the club's purpose and goals. She had to think hard because the second step wasn't too different from step one.

"Okay, I want the members to know more about the life of Prophet Muhammad *sallallahu aleihi wassalam*. I want them to know more about the *coreishys* and the *sahabas*," she said, poking her chin with her pencil. After a couple minutes of this, it hit her. She figured that she would ask Muslim Historians in her community to come give speeches about the blessed predecessors of Islam once a month and that club meetings would be held weekly. Finally, she decided the club would hold trips to historical Muslim sites once a month. Mankono, Timbuktu, Bagdad, and Philadelphia were just a few cities she had already listed. Now, the hard part was to register the club at school.

"Miss Ducktrinor, what's the point of the club? The Muslim Student Association does many of the things you want to do with your club," the teacher of Islamic Business Law told her.

"But mine is a little different. And like you said, the MSA *does many*—not all—*of the things* I am planning to do," Hanifa replied.

"No! I can't sign off on your request. You argue too much and we don't need a hot head running loose around here and telling young men and women that they need to go on holy wars. We have a good thing going on here in our safe haven. We don't need you to mess it up or expose us by starting travels around the world with your inflammatory concepts. It will draw too much attention on you and by the same token our safe and low key haven. Remember, believers are hunted in this time, and it's only by the grace of God we are still keeping a low profile. So, young woman, please forget about your crazy ideas of saving the world and leading *hijra* in crazy places not safe for the *ummah* and our children!"

The teacher ousted her from his office and slammed the door in her face.

Crushed? Hanifa wasn't.

"You don't know greatness when you see it," she said under her breath, turning her nose up. She walked away, knowing deep in her heart that she could make her dreams come true even if the teacher didn't approve of her ideas. She spread the word about her club regardless.

"I don't need anybody's permission to do great things," she told anybody who tried to argue with her that her club wasn't approved by the school. Her mindset attracted other free spirits like her and she successfully held her first club meeting at the school *masjid* after the first afternoon prayer of the day on a Saturday. A girl named Asha volunteered to be Vice-President.

"I want to be Secretary," Oumar, a young man in the group said.

"It's yours. Start taking notes!" Hanifa ordered

playfully.

"I have been! It's so awesome!" he replied with obvious excitement.

"Now, we need a finance-inclined person who will help us raise funds since we don't get any support from the school as we aren't approved. This person will also take care of the club budget and expenses," Hanifa pointed out.

One girl had the funds because her parents were rich Muslim merchants, but she wanted to run things, and Hanifa didn't want to give up the President's role. Her first army's fate was doomed from the start.

"Without money, we can't plan events. Without money, there is no point to draft a budget. Without any money raised, we can't keep the club going," Asha tried to tell Hanifa.

"Listen to your girl," Sophia said with a wicked smile on her face.

"I just can't give you the reigns of my 'baby' and coolest invention ever. Sorry, it just can't happen." And this is where her first attempt to build a potential group of followers she could turn into an army had died.

CHAPTER SEVEN : GAGA

Hanifa

Timeline: The second day of school in Brazil

"CAN WE TALK ABOUT it another day? We're late for a class," Hanifa told Sylas, a little out of breath.

"Really? Is that true, Anabelle?" He turned to Ana, crossing his arms over his chest. He stared deeply into her eyes; his scarlet irises sparkled with malice. Ana looked away as if his stare might scorch her.

Anabelle? Hanifa grimaced.

"Y-yes, we got so caught up talking that we didn't realize we were walking in the wrong direction," Ana said, nervously glancing at Hanifa.

"So you two weren't trying to avoid me?" Sylas asked, squeezing his chin between two fingers. He continued humming and creased his eyes at them. The girls pursed their lips and remained calm. "The way I see it, you'll never have time to talk to me. You obviously don't want to be a Secular follower and you were clearly running away from me. So, we'll have to discuss this right here."

"But—"

He ignored Hanifa's pleas and talked over her while he read the tablet in his hands. "You aced major ancient religions, secular politics, mathematics, biology, chemistry, accounting, and ancient civilizations and pop culture." He stopped, looking up at Hanifa. Then he dropped his face again to peek at the tablet.

As his fingers swiped the tablet screen, he said, "Even though you missed a few questions in that last subject, you still aced the rest. This is impressive. You're quite smart. Now, I want you on my team because the knowledge you have will be very valuable to my Secular Army. Many students who take the test don't have half the knowledge you have. How do you know all this stuff?" he asked, slanting his red eyes.

"I-I-I just love to read. That's why I was excited to see a library with so many resources." A knot formed in Hanifa's throat. She clenched her right fist to try to keep her composure. "And, I was partly homeschooled. But thank you for the compliment. But like I already said, I'm not interested in joining the Seculars' army. Can we leave now?"

"Sure. But with time, you'll change your mind; you just need the *right* incentive program. We could do this the easy way or the hard way, your choice." He smiled wolfishly. Then he winked at Ana, who dropped her head. She then put a finger in her collar, tugging at it for some air. She was wearing one of those popular transparent blouses with little patches over her breasts.

Hanifa studied Ana through squinted eyes as they walked away from Sylas. "This guy has a pet name for you? How close are you two?" She tightened her backpack on her shoulders as she waited for an answer.

"Not close at all. We have common friends," she replied, avoiding Hanifa's gaze. Then she said, "By the way, in the ancient pop culture and civilization section of the test, did you know who Lady Gaga was?"

"Don't change the subject. You've been acting awfully strange every time he pops up. Did you bring me to the library knowing all along he would manipulate me into taking the test?" Hanifa eyed Ana suspiciously.

"Of course not," Ana refuted. "Who isn't scared of Sylas? The guy is a lunatic! Besides, if you remember right, I gave you cues that he was bad news! Yesterday, as soon as I saw Sylas in the library, I told him we were leaving, but you said we weren't. Remember that?"

Hanifa pondered on the words for a quick second. "Fine, I believe you. And to answer your question, I have to admit that I didn't know who Lady Gaga was and I actually meant to look her up."

"Really? Well, that's not really a bad thing that you

don't know her," Ana said.

"Why not?" Hanifa asked.

"Lady Gaga was ahead of her time with her clothing fashion. She's a fashion legend and the inspiration behind the way my other friends and I dress. Now, I would rather know things from thousands of centuries ago before her time. It would have made me more valuable to help the ones I love," Ana said, feigning a happy smile.

This girl keeps intriguing me. "The ones you love?" Hanifa asked, stopping to face her.

"I don't want to talk about it," Ana confessed.

Hanifa nodded and didn't press further. "Well, now that he's out of the way, maybe we can go back to class," Hanifa proposed. Ana grunted inaudible words while Hanifa dragged her back towards the classroom.

***

The rest of the day unfurled peacefully as the girls attended several classes together. Between classes, they ate lunch together like they had the day before. Each classroom had long, reclining white chairs and a thin counter without legs as a table. The magnetic field between the floor and the table held the pristine thin counter in place. They were so comfortable that while Hanifa relaxed and enjoyed the lectures, Ana slept during the leadership and public speaking class.

During that class, Hanifa glanced at Ana, shaking her head in disbelief before she continued taking notes. Hanifa learned about self-esteem and self-image in the first portion of the lecture. She paid close attention because she needed to master these qualities if she was to lead and address a crowd to Tarsus. The computerized teacher played some videos and urged the students to take part in the simulated activities. The computerized teacher also gave random topics for the students to pick from.

Hanifa partook in the exercises and practiced delivering speeches staring at a computer showing a crowd of people staring back at her. She had to step in a specific oval space marked on the floor at the front of the class to deliver her prepared speech after five minutes of preparation upon picking the topic she liked. Students were evaluated on their physiological reactions like heart rate, blood pressure, respiration frequency, and sweaty palms. The computer grading system technology was similar to the one used in old lie-detectors. *Old pots still made the best dishes*, Hanifa thought making the connection between the classroom teaching software and past technologies she had read about. *Mom would have said it's generic benchmarking with her fancy finance and accounting terms.*

Altogether, Hanifa enjoyed the public speaking simulations but she couldn't say the same for the rest of her classmates. Like Ana, many students didn't pay attention to the class. Some students actually made fun of her and of the few others who participated in the lecture.

"Look at these nerds!" she heard amongst cackles and other mockeries as she tried to remain focused.

When the monitor stopped lecturing, Hanifa nudged Ana's shoulder to wake her up so that she could attend military techniques.

Ana jumped off the chair like she had been tased. "What happened?"

As the brightly dressed, half-naked students left the room, Hanifa laughed so hard at Ana that tears filled her eyes. Realizing where she was, Ana calmed down and started laughing herself.

Hanifa said, "You weren't kidding about school being not mandatory! Almost no one took notes on their tablets." She pulled the zipper of her backpack and threw it on her back. She held both arms of her bag between her thumbs and index fingers and looked at Ana, who was twisting her face and the corner of her mouth while intently analyzing her colorfully painted nails.

"I told you," Ana said, slipping her royal-blue, five-inch suede heels back on. She then scanned her face with a light copper, shell-shaped hand mirror and her makeup automatically freshened up. Her red lips were even brighter than before and her eyelashes turned voluptuous. She tried to pass the mirror to Hanifa, but Hanifa shook her head. Ana adjusted her blouse and white tutu, patting the skirt back down as they left the room.

During military techniques, Hanifa zoned in and out of her listening trance to smile at Ana, who was staring at her rainbow-like nails again while huffing and puffing to dramatically illustrate her boredom. While Hanifa wanted to tour the school with Ana again, she preferred to learn about armed combat, unarmed combat, and stealth killings. Also her mind kept drifting to the conversation they had at dinner about Sir Landry Big's speech the night before at dinner. It had all started when Malik asked, "What did you guys think of Sir Landry Big's recent speech in the news?"

In all, Sir Landry Big had always had a master mind. He went to school in Europe and then the United States. He even went on student exchange programs in China and Russia. Landry made friends all over the world because of his charisma. He became a diplomat for his country. And as an ambassador, he sought donations from his generous connections to build schools all over the world. These donators saw his efforts as charity. Only Landry knew the real agenda. These schools focused primarily on science majors. While the majority of these schools were not a secret, some of the schools he funded were underground. Officially, these ghost programs didn't exist. This is where most of the orphans and stolen children ended up and became trained killers. These spies and trained assassins became very valuable when, during a meeting of the GX industrialized democracies, he had his assassins poison the drinks of all the attendees before he declared himself the ruler of the world. How he sold this story? He argued that they were plotting the genocide of the human race. And the dumb public believed him!

Then his students and followers flooded each country they were located in and seized the power for their charismatic leader; Sir Landry Big. "He was charming, opposing, authoritarian, and feared all at the same time," Hanifa's Mom, Eva Ducktrinor, adamantly proclaimed. And the way she talked about Sir Landry Big piqued Hanifa's interest. *Mom sounded like she knew him in another life. Does she know this guy?* Not wanting to know the answer to the question, her eyes glanced around the multi-colored classroom once again.

During one of those quick glances Hanifa paid Ana during the class, Ana's ultra thin phone chirped. She looked at the screen and winked at Hanifa. She blew a note to Hanifa. The letters danced and waggled in the air as they made their way to Hanifa, and Ana exited the classroom. Hanifa's mom had once told her about how in the old days, students just passed each other notes on paper instead of the new-era digital letters that disintegrated the minute the recipient had read the message. As the sliding doors closed behind Ana, Hanifa turned her attention back to the lecture and made a mental note to read the message Ana had left.

CHAPTER EIGHT : ANA'S STORY

Ana

Timeline: The second day of school in Brazil

I WISH I HAD as much will as Hanifa with class lectures, Ana thought. She planned to brush her blonde hair and change her clothes before going to meet Sylas.

Meeting Hanifa had stirred her family tragedy to the surface. The Undeapsideds were originally from the beautiful Sydney, Australia; land of the Aboriginals. Irreligion ranked second there after Christianity, and Ana's family had identified with being irreligious—but they weren't harmful. They had moved to Brazil because the family loved the location, the beach, and the food every time they'd gone there for vacation. Plus, Castle 5 was a renowned private school, spawning and spewing out refined students from the few who were interested in studying.

Ana's family had felt pressured from the adherents of all the other religions to convert to theirs. Many of her friends kept telling her, and at first, it was more of a forceful preaching than anything, "All your good actions will be in vain if you don't pick a side in this life before judgement day."

When her family refused to pick sides, they were hunted down. Many died. The religious groups had more political motives than aspiring to better and secure a good afterlife for her kind. The more followers the religious groups had, the easier it was to pass laws and rule the government and the country.

Even after she and her parents had moved to Brazil, a stigma followed them because of the connections her birth country had with Brazil's socialites.

Ana's parents were murdered after being quizzed on

obscure facts dating back centuries about ancient religions and sects, and they provided many wrong answers. Ana couldn't answer either to help the family pass with few wrong answers, so she witnessed them being shot in the backs of their heads like animals. Spared because of her young age and forced to look after herself, she had despised organized religions after that and enlisted in the Secular Army. She had since recruited as many people as she could so they could take down the believers that took her parents' lives from her.

Her older brother Tim, a.k.a. Tariq, had also been spared. They tried to stay together to fend for themselves but Tim found Islam along the way. She'd been incensed by his choice. He was arrested, both because Sylas had wanted something from him, and because his name made him an easy target. Once his arrest dawned on her, Ana felt guilty for ignoring her only living family member and vowed to get him out. She had led so many people astray for the Seculars, and she didn't want to do that anymore.

And Tariq was more peaceful with their parent's death.

He kept telling her, "It was their time to go. Nothing happens only by His will. Of course, the perpetrators will pay for their sins, but Mom and Dad's time on earth was up, Ana. If they didn't die that way, they would have died another way. In their sleep, by car, train, plane, you name it…it was decreed for them to go."

Ana didn't go for Tariq's over-simplistic explanations. It was too easy for her taste, and she held on to her grudge and revenge for a long time before letting go.

***

"Ana, you have to convince her to become a Secular soldier under my lead," Sylas said, looking straight into her eyes. Seated with his feet resting on his office table, he continued, "Stop being a child with the pouted lips and crossed arms."

"Why should I help you? My brother is still your prisoner. We had a deal," Ana said calmly, sitting in the chair in front of him.

"I'm still working on his release. He'll be out soon.

There are a few more hurdles before the Secular government agrees to let him out." Sylas swung his feet down and got up in a heave. "It's not my fault your last name makes you an easy target. Why don't you change it?" he asked, irritably squinting his red eyes at her.

"It's not that simple, you have to know people," Ana said. She knew people, but they were worthless when it came to helping an Undeapsidud. Unfounded discrimination still ran deep in their day and age. "What do you want with her anyway? I like her...she's not like the others." A warm fuzzy feeling overtook her. Butterflies fluttered in her belly every time Hanifa's name came up.

"She has great test scores. She can be a valuable asset to my army. She knows things many people on my team don't. With her on my side, I can spot believers a mile away and get rid of them. With her, I can finally make it far in the Secular government," Sylas said dreamily.

"You're gaga. Aren't you a little too ambitious?" Ana made one eye slightly bigger than the other.

"Don't make that face. Your glamorous eyeliner style looks goofy. And for your information, I'm perfectly rational. You have to dream big and I am," he said confidently. He spread his arms like a bird soaring in the skies.

"Well, I'm not doing *anything* until my brother is released. He's innocent and you know it! Besides, with all the students I have already convinced to join the Secular Army, I shouldn't have to do your biding anymore. You have to honor your promise." Ana jumped out of her seat.

"I promise that she'll be the last one I ask you to convince," he said, walking to her. He gently stroked her face as she continued to pout. "Plus, you don't want Hanifa knowing that you were a very bad girl, do you?" he asked, grinning.

Ana pulled away from him and took a few steps back. Fret quickly took over her face. "You wouldn't dare tell her."

"It's up to you," he said, shrugging. He made a pirouette in front of her and went back to his seat. His spiky grey hair let out silver sparks that made Ana quiver.

A slight gasp escaped her lips. "She doesn't know that I know you that way, and I want to keep it as such. Besides, it was only one time!"

"It doesn't matter. She won't care about the details. I mean, she could infer that we did what we did because you wanted to help your brother. Anyway, make your choice: either your friend joins the army, or she finds out that you put a tracker on her at my request."

Ana felt Sylas' gaze wander to her naked legs. She tugged her thigh-length raffia skirt down. "Fine! I'll talk to her. Just get my brother out! And don't screw with me because I also have 'Eyes' on you!" She stormed out of the room, almost whipping Judas with her trudging arms as he was approaching the doors on her way out. She knew he had no idea what Eyes was.

"Dude! Look where you're going!" Judas said, marching in and waving a fist at her.

Ana continued walking aimlessly until she felt a looming presence directly behind her in the empty school alley.

She gasped. "Oh! It's you. You scared me, guys."

"We should be scary. *I* should scare you." Sylas took a threatening step closer to her.

Ana stepped back. Something about the way he had said those words didn't feel right.

Forcefully, he pounced on her, taking her off guard and leaving her utterly defenseless to stop what came next.

CHAPTER NINE : ANA'S EYES & SYLAS' STORY

Sylas

Timeline: The second day of school in Brazil

A FEW MINUTES BEFORE Ana was assaulted, Judas quickly stepped into Sylas' office before the silver automatic door closed after her. Unbeknownst to Sylas, Ana was recording every move he made between the school, his home, and his other extra-curricular activities for a rainy day.

"What's wrong with her?" Judas asked, his thumb pointing toward where Ana had just made her exit.

"Don't worry about her. Ana is tired of recruiting, but she's easily manageable. We have her brother," Sylas said calmly, staring out the window as though lost in thought.

"Speaking of her brother, he still doesn't want to disclose the location of the original Shadow Hunter." Judas skimmed the tablet in his hands. He sat on the red ottoman facing Sylas as the sun's rays pierced the room.

"Maybe it's time we give him a reason to." Sylas grinned, turning his attention to Judas. Sylas' eyes gleamed. "Follow me."

Sylas left the room, Judas in his stride, and whipped out a pale copy of the Shadow Hunter app from his pocket to *try* to locate Ana. There was still a glitch with the thin tablet version that Judas and his team of programmers had designed for Sylas. Ana's brother's version was believed to be bug-free, except for the limitation of being unable to distinguish between a clone and its original human subject. Many Seculars had cloned themselves for fear of dying. And the war of the believers against clones and their secular owners had become harder. When Sylas captured Tariq to misappropriate the original device from the inventor himself, the real Shadow Hunter was nowhere to be found.

"Sylas is pretty pissed that you won't tell him where it is. So he sent me here to interrogate you. Like I'm going to tell on my brother," Ana had puffed incredulously.

Her brother Tariq seemed pensive about hearing her words and then said, "I hid it in a place of learning and gathering."

"Gee, this whole place is a place of learning," Ana had pointed out. Then Judas entered the room for more questioning but Tariq didn't give out anymore tips even though he was threatened several times.

So Judas had to make do with his own version of the Shadow Hunter which wasn't accurate a hundred percent of the time. It also didn't have the broader range of the original, but it was worth a shot when the person being searched for was nearby.

The app gave Sylas and Judas the estimated direction of

where Ana might be and at a quick pace, they darted in that direction hoping they would hear her actual footsteps.

Once they caught up with her, Sylas and Judas dove on her and drank deeply until Ana turned pale and passed out.

Sylas exclaimed, "She'll be perfect for tonight's party." He wiped the blood off his mouth with the back of his hand and turned his gaze to Judas.

"Yes, she will," Judas added, grinning.

"She's only mine tonight. You know I don't share well."

"You're the boss," Judas replied, throwing up his hands in the air.

***

After every party he hosted drew to a close (usually not until dawn), Sylas would fly himself home in a fancy black flying car. As soon as he got home to his vast, empty mansion, he would go to his study and pour himself a drink like his father used to do with fine wine. Then he would put his feet up on his legless table and pull out the Bible, read some passages, ponder for a moment, and then close it. Then he would grab another book from his vast library. Usually he reached for *A Comprehensive Understanding of Religions*. He would read just a few pages of it and then snap it closed. Next, he would check on the contents of a tall aquarium containing a body that looked just like him. Once he assured himself the contents were perfectly intact, he would call Hamani, his doctor and scientist, and report his body limits and progresses to him like in the following exchange.

"How much more blood do we need to build a body that will be impervious to any threat?"

"A lot more, sir," Hamani replied via speakerphone. "The blood pool is far from being full."

"And this blood sacrifice is taking too long, Mr. Scientist. My patience is running thin. I need this body soon if I want to overthrow Sir Landry Big and take his place."

"Sir, I will do my best so you can meet your deadline. You have my word."

"Great! That's what I want to hear," Sylas said and

hung up.

Then he would go sleep in a rejuvenating box for a few hours before heading back to ruling the school.

Sylas had told Ana during one of their pillow talks that he was born into a believing home. His father, Petr, was a devout Christian man who used to say, "No one can live forever." Sylas loved his grandfather and his Jewish mom, both of whom died way too soon in his opinion. These two deaths in his early life made him lose faith. Soon, he became obsessed with immortality and satanic rituals, even though in his past Bible studies he remembered reading that the devil wasn't to be trusted. He also knew, deep down, that there was a force more powerful, unseen and above all creatures, but he secretly hoped that he could find a loophole in the universe to stay alive forever and eventually outlast Sir Landry Big.

Tired of hearing his father Petr nag at him about life and death, Sylas had killed his wealthy and charitable father, hired a genetic scientist called Hamani, and started cloning himself with the added bonus of his dad's cells. That made him sound sometimes like an old person rather than a young one. He would endure and abuse his real body and push it to the limits. With the cloning, he became even more addicted to pain and hid his real body somewhere safe in his mansion while continuing to experiment on his cloned bodies. When he was actually using his real body, he had green eyes, but when he was using clones, his eyes were red and his hair color was silver. Despite these small differences, his clones were pretty accurate copies of his real body. He had made sure Hamani didn't design them like dumb robots who couldn't think for themselves.

"I want really intuitive clones. You're the scientist! Make it happen!" Ana had heard Sylas yell many times concerning his demonic creations. "Dr. Jekyll" just went along with Sylas's insatiable requests. *The pay must be good*, Ana often thought of the complicated duo relationship when she eavesdropped on them via the Eyes robot.

With all her recordings, Ana had come to the conclusion that Sylas loved women's company and enjoyed to "love-roofie" them by spraying himself with a falling-in-love

pheromone essence that smelled irresistibly delicious.

CHAPTER TEN : IMAM MALIK

Malik

Timeline: Several years before the Ducktrinors moved to Brazil

MALIK KNEW EVERYTHING THERE was to know about the man he was named after. He simply loved acquiring new knowledge. And because Imam Malik was originally from Yemen, Malik Ducktrinor had made sure his family took them there during their travels so he could learn more about Yemen and the Imam to satisfy his curiosity, and by the same token, enrich his educational world.

In Yemen, Malik came to learn many things about that country but two stories remained etched in his mind above others; the historical Yemeni-Saudi conflict which reminded him of many current issues in the *ummah,* and the legendary Yemeni Queen of Sheba also known in some sources as Barakissa. He found her story with King Suleyman fascinating and secretly wished for a similar passionate devotion and love for His Creator first of all and for his future wife, God willing.

Besides his love for learning, Malik enjoyed guiding the *salat*-prayer with his family when he had the chance to.

When the *adhan* for the *magrib* prayer resonated through the small and prosperous city of Greenwuhud calling the believers to the fourth *salat* of the day, Malik smiled blissfully at the melodious voice of the real *muezzin,* warming his mind and soul to the knowledge that it was time for him to perform since his father was often delayed at work so could not pray with the family.

Showtime, Imam Malik, his ego would cheer as he made

his way out of his room to enter the prayer room where his sisters Hanifa, Safi and Pris were already waiting.

Once, Malik heard giggles behind him as he uttered the first *takbir* of the *salat*. His desire to have a brother couldn't have been any stronger in those moments. Malik was outnumbered by girls, and he knew it had to be Pristine because she never took him seriously, but he would ignore the distractions and focus on the prayer. *Shaytan especially Khanzab is using her to get to me so I can doubt myself and riddle this salat of errors so SHOWTIME AGAIN IMAM MALIK.* And like that he tuned out any distractions and led the *salat* as perfectly as he could. Even Walhan couldn't get to Malik with his *waswas* as he was so focused in his act of *ibada*. As he recited the opening chapter *Al Fatiha*, he let the *tafsir* of the *surah* sink into his soul because he had learned to multitask to that level over the years, paying close attention to his surrounding, visible and invisible, like a real *sufi*. The kind of pure *sufism* that once existed in the first years of Islam. Anyway, the feeling was inexplicable and he figured it was the conversation he was having at those brief moments with his Creator. Somuncu Baba had interpreted this *surah* seven different ways that had amazed him. Another *tafsir* he had enjoyed was the one of a prominent scholar in the twenty-first century who had fallen out of favor due to his indiscretions though the scholar was knowledgeable in the *deen*.

In all, Malik had always been aware of the seen and the unseen from an early age because of his *alim* goals of performing Islamically approved miracles. For that reason, he knew early on the difference between a *mujiza*, a *keeramat*, and a *feerasat*. Though he had always been amazed by that last one when performed in really old graphic novels like *Naruto* which he loved to check out from the library or like really old movies like *X-Men*, he had never really wanted to perform them in real life since they were obviously against Islam and so farfetched, yet somewhat believable if you believed in the unseen mentioned in the holy scriptures. For him, it was what you called an oxymoron. That said, he always thought that *taijutsu* was feasible while *ninjutsu* and *genjutsu* were out of the questions because they resembled powers a person associated with the unseen could perform. In fact, a summoning *jutsu* that fell under a *ninjutsu* required blood sacrifice and the summoning of a weird range of animals and elements, whilst *genjutsu* used illusionary techniques to win over the opponent. And that is as far he had let his mind wonder on the ninja techniques while first admitting to himself that if the story his father told him about Somuncu Baba was true, it certainly resembled a real clone teleportation *jutsu,* only that it was done by a believer, changing the way it was called. Then Malik had mused over the possibility of time travel he was very familiar with in the case of the scholar baker, Somuncu Baba.

He was familiar with time travel because he believed that sometimes if one is distracted in a prayer, the small amount of distraction was equaled to 4000 years of worship, give or take a few years. Because 4000 years can't be explained in dunya time, it has to be 4000 years in another dimension; thus that qualified for time travel, and his friend Tawfiq from the future had confirmed his thoughts once.

Tattoos also creeped Malik out because he felt like the

drawings could come to life once real evil encountered you. In his mind, they had a close relationship with hand seals and mystical ninja related techniques. His reservations grew when he learned that angels don't come to a person or a house that has images of living things displayed. Malik had always believed that to remain steadfast in faith and be blessed with bounties and miracles, the closeness of angels was necessary. Some of his friends might argue that good *djinns* achieved that purpose but dealing with *djinns* was forbidden in Islam and he knew better. Unless they offered their protection for free and with no strings attached, he would never get close to them. Even with that, he would still be wary of their generous help.

After the *salams* of the third *rakat* of the *magrib* prayer he was leading, Malik turned around to face the women in the room. They all did some laps around their rosaries. When he thought everyone was done, he started a *dua* and sealed the prayer with *Al Fatiha*. It was *halaqa* time.

The family discussed the *fards* of *wudu* according to the *madhahib* as customary in their daily *halaqa* sessions as repetition is considered pedagogic. When Malik was asked, he answered that they were seven requirements and he enumerated them. At Hanifa's turn, she also enumerated the four requirements. Shafiya ensued and made her mother proud by saying that six things were obligatory to make the ablutions valid. At Pristine's turn, she gave the *fards* of *wudu* according to the Hanbali *madhab*. "We must:

1. Make intention

2. Utter *Bismillah*

3. Wash the face

4. Wash the mouth

5. Wash the nose

6. Wash our two arms

7. Wipe the entire head including the ears

8. Wash our two feet

9. *Tartib* or wash the parts in the designated order

10. *Muwalat* or wash each part right after the other without breaks."

In all, the differences between the creeds were small

and they were more similar than dissimilar.

"Knowing these small details can help you when you are faced with a situation where you need to make *wudu* very quickly in order to pray. These situations can include waking up late for prayer, being in a war or at war. Again, remember these well, as they can come in handy when you least expect it. Understood?" Mrs. Ducktrinor asked.

The children nodded and they closed the *halaqa* session of the day. Malik noticed that his mother always did her *dua* in English when they were in *halaqa*. It said, "Wherever you are and go, may Allah always protect and guide you my children. May He protect your descendants too, *ameen*." Once, the children had asked her why she did that in non-Arabic and her reply was, "Of course I say my *duas* when you aren't around in Arabic because I know the meaning. However, you guys don't know everything about the Arabic language. Besides, Allah always answers the *dua* of a mother and I want you guys to remember that I love you." That is all she would say. And as the children grew and became exposed to more Arabic and learned the language, she still uttered her protection supplications in their native language or in English.

***

The next day, Malik came home running. He quickly sent *salams* greetings his Mom's way without looking and went straight to his room.

"No running in the house Malik," his mother said. He wasn't loud in his sneakers compared to the boots he wore when he rained. He had loved sneakers and he was a sneaker-head for sure.

"Yes Ma'am!"

"Don't be late for *magrib* and don't forget to take a shower," Mrs. Ducktrinor warned from the kitchen.

"I won't," said Malik with a hint of certainty in his voice. His thoughts continued to race. *How am I going to build the best boat in the class? Damn Oceanology! What kind of science project is that? I'm not particularly crafty in building things like Grandpa and Dad. I just want to be a scholar and all these things are just a means to an end.*

As his thoughts raced, he took a shower and went back

downstairs before the prayer time. It was summer in Greenwuhud, USA and the days were longer so he sat at the kitchen table waiting for his mom to finish cooking. Lost in his thoughts, he didn't hear her call his name.

"Malik! Malik! MALIK!"

"Oh sorry Mom, I didn't hear you," replied the eldest son.

"What's bothering you son?"

He sighed first and then said, "I have this science project and I have no idea how I should go about it. The teacher is a talented carpenter and boat builder. I don't know if this time I can wow her. The first prize is a contract with a Marine institute who will patent my invention. I want to win *sooo* bad!"

"Oooo *her.* Somebody has a crush. Teacher's pet, heh?" Eva teased, winking at her son.

"Nah Ma," Malik replied as his brown cheeks flushed.

"Sure. Well, I made spicy fish soup. That would jumpstart the synapses in your brain and speed up your creativity, *insha'Allah*." Eva harrumphed and continued to get dinner ready for her family.

"Mom, I'm serious," Malik added, disappointed at her jokes while she ignored him and hummed a catchy *nasheed* tune as she finished cooking in the kitchen.

Later that evening, Malik was quiet at the table. He ate his food and tuned out the rest of the family. Before sleeping he made a prayer to Allah, "Ya Allah, please inspire me to come up with a brilliant idea to help the believers in the future. *Ameen.*" After that supplication, he wiped his palms on his face and twisted his face in disgust.

"Ew... I soaped my hands several times but I can still smell the fish."

That night Malik dreamed he was on top of a fish sailing as a storm approached. After the rain, the sun shined with such a brightness and there were many fishes in the water and people were sitting on top of them. They were all relieved as they watched the sun rise. The next day Malik woke up intrigued by that dream. Then it hit him! "That's it! I will build a sort of fish-shaped boat! Yes! I will win this competition if it's *mubarak* for me *insha'Allah*."

So Malik built the boat inspired by his dream. He spent days and nights on it. Upon completion, he couldn't wait to show it to his family before the science fair.

When he showed it to his family, they said plenty of *masha'Allah* in addition to words of congratulations, except Pris.

"It's alright," she had said, pouting.

Malik dismissed her and got ready to put his creation away. But he tripped and fell on the study table in his room on which the sort of fish shaped boat was displayed and, to his horror, everything came crashing down.

"I've had enough of her, Mom and Dad! The brat gave me the evil eye! I will give her a serious beating today for all the days she disrespected me and made fun of me!"

"*Subhanallah.* We're so sorry!" his parents uttered, their hands on their mouths in disbelief.

"The science fair is in a few hours and I'm going to land a zero because of this brat," he snarled bitterly.

"Unbelievable! The teacher won't believe me and my classmates will think I tried to pull a fast one because I'm teacher's pet."

"So you are her favorite student after all. Maybe she will give you a makeup assignment."

"No, Mom. This was it. I blew it. Plus, you guys didn't get to the coolest part. It could shape-shift."

"Seriously, like Ms. Frizzle's school bus?" Hanifa asked.

"Exactly…" Malik replied, deflating by the seconds.

"Well, it wasn't meant to be," his mom wagered.

"Who cares about a lame Mobi fish anyway?" Pris sassed and humphed before leaving her brother's room.

***

What Malik didn't know at the time was that his teacher, Bonnie Mills, was a Secular spy. The Seculars were still a small faction recruiting brains for their organization back then.

"Professor, can I speak with you please before the fair?" Malik had asked his teacher the day of the science fair.

"Sure! I can't wait to see what you have done for this fair," said Professor Miller with a wide smile. Real teachers in Malik's time didn't dress any better than students. Professor Miller wore skimpy clothes that were a bit distracting.

"That's exactly what I want to talk to you about. I encountered an issue, Professor Miller."

"Come on Malik, I told you not to be so formal dear. Call me Bonnie Mills," she said almost purring, leaving Malik slightly uncomfortable, letting out a nervous laugh in return.

CHAPTER ELEVEN : OF KINGS, LEADERS, AND PROPHETS

Malik

MALIK SCRATCHED HIS HEAD before looking left and right. The teacher was attractive but distraction and scandal weren't on his to-do list, so he kept his head down while explaining to her that at the last minute his project had fallen apart.

"I'll give you a make-up assignment *again* under one condition," she said with a soft and caressing voice.

Malik raised his head up, bracing himself for the proposition he had feared all along. Something told him that his teacher's next words would be temptation bonified. He studied her flickering green eyes and steadied himself.

"Come over to my place after school today and we will re-create your project. You have interesting ideas. Also, I want you to meet a recruiter for a secret organization. Not a word to anybody. If you say something, I'll know." Bonita Miller wore a serious face before adding, "I know where you live."

The switch between the moods worried Malik. So he just nodded and took her home address. Conflicted, he made his way to the science fair with a less than stellar project to show.

Malik later learned about the small faction—which the Seculars were back then—from his mother. They had a commendable story; an inspiring mission statement. Unfortunately, theory and application are two different things sometimes. The Seculars overthrew the world overnight with their spies spread out across the world: G7, G8, G20, G*Whatever* no longer were. They had taken care of that, plus they killed the political leaders of these powerful countries along with it. People went from the jelly to the jar, from night to morning, under their leadership. The technique used by European politicians to dismantle the Ottoman Empire, Africa, Asia, and India were in turn used by this new brand of Seculars.

They divided the nations knowingly, conquered, and forced-united the world under their lead. At the head was Sir Landry Big from the Ivory Coast who had always despised white supremacists and their agendas to oppress other races and overstay their welcome in Africa. While he was no better because he was also bigoted, he couldn't care less. He was a black man ruling the world and he had been successful at last. As the representative for his country at international meetings, Sir Landry Big had pitted every country of the industrialized democracies against each other. While they killed each other and weakened their economy by financing instigated wars they had no idea about, he just sat back and watched until they had all weakened. This is what brought the Seculars to rule the world, not the lethargy of the *ummah*. Though, this lack of interest on the part of the Muslims also played a role and opened a door for the Seculars to come sit at the power table. No, to rule over the power table.

Later when Malik got home exhausted from a day of dodging inappropriate advances, recruitment offers, and finally getting over his failed science project, Malik looked forward to a refreshing shower before heading to the prayer room. Malik's mother started the daily *halaqa* session by questioning him on the story of Musa *aleihi salam,* also known as Moses.

"In which *surah* of the Quran is Prophet Musa *aleihi salam* mentioned and what is one miracle he performed in the name of Allah?" she had asked, looking at him intently. It was no secret he was the number one lover of faith-related miracles.

"His story is mainly narrated in *surah* 28 of the holy Quran. For miracle, I would have to say that it's the sea he split with his wooden staff," Malik replied with a bright green *kufi* adorning his beautiful hair. With a head high, Malik wore a victorious smile. *She must be thinking that I'm a charmer with that approving nod and smile she's wearing on her face.* Before she could ask another question, Malik added, "One day when we set our plan of *jihad* in motion," he paused and looked at Hanifa, "I'll split the sea too and drown our assailants if it comes to a battle at sea."

"Insha'Allah," said Mrs. Eva Ducktrinor, while Pristine cut in, "Yeah right! In our time, we won't need to do that. That's if we live that long and that's if your fantasies turn into reality! Nobody will be walking then, why can't we just teleport or something like that?"

The rivalry between the oldest and the youngest of the Ducktrinors was back in the air again. Malik just huffed and puffed before saying, "*Insha'Allah*, Mom." He meant to add, *You little brat, I won't argue with your immature comments but I'll prove you wrong one day if God wills it.* All the while, Pristine stared at him defiantly and he could feel her burning stare on his face.

Mrs. Ducktrinor intervened sternly at last after she cleared her throat. "Pristine, it wasn't your turn to talk—and don't be disrespectful to your brother. Otherwise, I won't ask you anymore questions tonight."

"But Mom!"

"No but! I mean it. The next time you cut me off, I'm sending you to your room. I thought your father and I were clear on this. The *halaqa* starts with the oldest child and the *duas* to close the circle of learning starts with the youngest, which is you. It's pointless to want to be the only center of attention. Share the spotlight. You, the Ducktrinors children, are strong as a UNIT, not by yourselves or any other way. Did I make myself PRISTINELY clear Pris?"

"Yes, Ma'am," Pris mumbled under her breath and lowered her head.

"Good! Let's continue. Hanifa tell me what you know of Firaun in this *surah* 28 that your brother mentioned," Eva Ducktrinor demanded.

"Firaun, who is also known as Pharaoh, had two sidekicks working for him aside from his soldiers. His high priest and the first one was called Haman whom Firaun had asked to build a tower so he could climb to the sky in order to meet Allah. A sign of *kufr* for sure. Anyway, the other sidekick was Karoun a.k.a. Coré; a violent arrogant man from Mussa *aleihi salam's* tribe who despised his own people," Hanifa finished.

"Excellent, children!" their mother cheered.

"Shafiya, what is the name of the tribe of Musa *aleihi salam* that Pharaoh and Karoun especially hated?"

"They were called the Bani Isra'il or sons of Israel. The King hated them because of the prophecy while Karoun simply just hated his own tribe and was at the service of Firaun."

"Correct answer, my daughter," Mrs. Ducktrinor said, smiling. "Last question for you; what happened to Karoun?"

"Allah gave the power to Mussa *aleihi salam* to deal with him as he saw fit. He is currently below the ground suffering in oblivion daily as he descends slowly toward the core of the earth, according to some old sources and *tafsir*," Hanifa finished. "Gosh, that must be hell on earth," she remarked, popping her hazel eyes.

"I bet!" her mom agreed and turned her attention to Pristine. "It's written that Shaytan's progeny is nine. Of the nine, which one was likely to have controlled Pharaoh?"

"I believe it was A'wan as he is one controlling rulers," said Pris without blinking. Before her mother could approve of her answer, Pris added, "The one that commands magic is called Laqus." She said these words as she turned her attention to her older brother Malik, a grin spread on her tiny round face. "Be careful Malik as you might fall in his traps in your attempts of pulling off a *keeramat*..."

"That's it, young lady! I warned you. Go to your room!" their mother yelled.

"Mom, don't. It's okay, she has a point. Besides, if you send her away, *Shaytan* would have accomplished his goals and she would miss the learning session and the *isha* prayer as a family. Let's continue," Malik advised.

Tears almost filled his mother's eyes and he didn't know if it was out of pride for raising a calm tempered son unlike herself or because she was losing it. He decided to choose the former because she had a thankful smile on her shiny caramel face.

She continued asking them questions about other prophets (may Allah be pleased with all of them) such as Nuh, and Yunus, Yaqub, and Yusuf. She urged her children to take heed upon finishing the *halaqa* that history repeats itself and they should never let their anger and jealousy get the best of them, otherwise they would regret their actions like in the story of the children of Adam *aleihi salam*; Habil and Qabil. "It's that same jealousy that turned Prophet Yacub's children against their own brother Prophet Yusuf. Understood?"

"Yes, Ma'am," all the children replied on cue.

"Good deal. Alright sassy girl, time to start the *duas*," Mrs. Ducktrinor said, winking at Pristine.

Malik smiled, relieved. Finally, it was her time to shine and Pristine could start acting normal again.

***

Every day of the week was busy for Malik. He went to school five days a week. On Fridays, his parents allowed him to work night shifts at the movie theater. Besides school, it was the only time he had the opportunity to experience young adult life. He didn't date but he couldn't help but notice multitudes of young couples, hand in hand, walking about the vast theater.

His job was pretty easy-going since the movie experience was fully automated these days. A kiosk dispensed tickets, popcorn, drinks, and snacks. The customer just had to input his order on the touch screen and the order was dispensed.

Malik and other ushers had to restock and refill the dispensing machines with corn, oil, salt, different syrup flavors for drinks loaded with high fructose corn syrup, anything needed for the whole movie experience that robots couldn't perform since there weren't as intuitive as humans.

While the job could be boring at times because it was an endless weekly routine, he had to be on his toes.

Why? Because while in old movie theaters, the movie viewers could go in and take a seat in the screen room, in his era, movie goers where given their flying seats at the kiosk. They would hop in, secure the belt, and jet dangerously in the alleys of the movie theaters with no care whatsoever for pedestrians or theater staff.

In the actual screen room where the movie is watched, all the seats hung in the air, hovering above the ground or other viewers as the movie played in the form of a hologram.

Sometimes you would hear, "Hey, can you move a little to this side or down so I can see better?"

It cracked Malik up that in such an advanced age, movie viewers still dealt with other people blocking their view or line of vision. He preferred movie nights with his family members anyway. Plus, his parents were never shy about talking about romantic scenes or intimate matters when it came to those brief moments on screen.

Saturday was family day with more homeschooling lessons like during *halaqa* time, but this time with lots of food and refreshments prepared by the whole family before heading out for a picnic in a park.

Finally, on Sundays, Malik met with his personal mentor *Muallim*, the teacher that his mom always insisted he needed in his life. While his father didn't care much for the teacher, he didn't oppose his wife. "Your mom knows best and that is why she's trying to protect you," Adama Ducktrinor always said when Malik complained that he had a full plate.

"Protect me from what?"

"When the time comes, you will know."

Malik always hated the vagueness in his father's responses and tried not to lose his temper over the secrets he knew they were keeping from him.

"Son, that's enough questions. But for the umpteenth time, I'm not completely qualified in this dimension of Islam your mom is so adamant you master. And think of it as you seeking your PhD in religion and *Muallim* is your major advisor."

"Fine, I'll continue to attend his classes. At least *Muallim* is not boring. Why can't you teach me instead?" And Malik would ask more questions which would stay unanswered.

***

In the USA, things were always sketchy for the youth—especially young black males. For that reason, Malik kept his head down and stayed busy in school. Sure, Greenwuhud was always a safe haven but there were times when they had to leave the comfort of their safety to visit other states. It was outside the safe haven that therein laid the rub. Malik also tried to avoid rough neighborhoods. He kept his calm when randomly frisked by white male officers. In school, he didn't go out of his way to make friends. Only a few stubborn guys insisted on being his friends though he always showed disinterest. Malik, in short, was a very careful person who scrutinized everything. His fear was to be jumped by a mob of haters or pushed or fall down a balcony like history had it with Hamza Warsame. Because his name was conspicuously religious, he faced a lot of unfair treatment. The struggles of being black and Muslim like the ancient hashtag depicted in social media. But he knew that the problem was far older than this. Even in the time of Rassullulah *sallalahu aleihi wassalam*, racial discrimination still existed. So Malik often thought, *I won't play victim. Certain things will never change and I won't let that stop me from achieving greatness.*

When the Ducktrinors moved to Brazil, Malik realized that in Brazil and many other places in the world, things weren't that different. The genocide of black youth was rampant there too and sometimes he wondered why people feared the black race so badly? Was there a memo or a prophecy about Blacks becoming great he hadn't heard about? Because it made no sense to target one race just because of the color of their skin; there is ugly and beautiful in all races. *But hey that's life, every burden is a test*, Malik always inferred. *At least soccer with jinga is a good distraction here.*

His Brazilian friend Aadil was always good company when it came to that. Unlike Malik, who didn't have an alternative non-Muslim first name, Aadil did. He went by Adel. People often assimilated him to the legendary singer Adele from the twenty-first century or even assumed he was a girl before they even met him. "Why don't you go for Adolf instead?" Malik had asked him once.

"Because I'd rather be taken for a woman than be associated with a name that is reminiscent of Adolf Hitler."

"Ah!" Malik said, eureka like, and closed the discussion.

Malik's other friends included a boy and his sister with a sobriquet Khalid ibn al-Walid and Nusaybah bint Ka'ab. Like their nicknames denoted, they were sword lovers.

Another insurgent the group befriended was a girl with the alias Umm Manee. A lone ranger, a nomad, she moved like the wind! Nobody knew much about her but she was very efficient. Some say her name was Esmaralda Perez and that she went by Esma. Malik and his clique started an online movement like the descendants of the twenty-first century Muslims and prayed it worked.

"Dude, people will think we're a hip-hop group because of our name," Aadil had pointed out even though he liked the name as they were all from the East of each of their respective continents.

"So be it. My family is originally from Ethiopia and that's East in Africa. You're From the Middle East Aadil. Khalid and Nusaybah are Indonesians. So it goes without saying. Umm Manee is from Murcia and that's Eastern Spain.

There you have it, we're the Far East Muvmant," Malik finished with a decided tone. This discussion was now tabled indefinitely. So the Far East Muvmant's members time travelled to make sure their organization stayed stellar even after they had passed.

With Malik as their leader, the quartet learned how to meditate and let their minds wander to places and other dimensions. They always sat in a circle in their headquarters: the mosque during times when the five daily prayers weren't in session. Since they weren't all in the same city the majority of time, they always conferenced in. They became very good at paying attention to the clock and the different time zones so they never missed connection time; Umm Manee was the best *al muwaqqit* of the group. She was a diligent time keeper for sure. They always made great friends with the Imams of the mosques they always used because it was a sight to rejoice in the eyes of these community leaders. The Imams always said the same words like they had spoken to each other, "*Masha'Allah!* Children of this age who take the *deen* seriously and are better *sufis* than perhaps most of us. *Subhanallah*, may Allah always guide you on the right path and may you always find what you seek if it's *mubarak* for you, *ameen*."

"*Ameen*," the group usually replied, blushing and flattered beyond repair.

So the youngsters enjoyed visiting historic events in the past or the future and sometimes watched in dismay or amazement the battles Muslim armies had partaken in from afar.

Malik had read "La Mystique de Ghazali" reported and prepared by Abdallah As-Sabr and he had shared with his friends the wisdom and knowledge he had learned to connect with Allah. One *hadith qudsi* in particular in the book struck him, *"Allah says, 'Neither My Heaven or My earth can contain Me, but the heart of My believing servant can contain Me.'"*

"Whoa, that's a lot of power in us we can reach if we truly want it," Malik had said and his teammates had agreed.

As a group, the Far East Muvmant learned about spiritual exercises they needed to partake in to become spiritually powerful and connect with Allah on a deeper level. Some of these included repentance or *at tawbba*, *al mahabba* or love of Allah, gratitude or *as shukkur*, trust in His plan or *at tawakkul*, purity or *ikhlas*, sincerity or *as sidiq*, *at tawwid* or the monotheism of Allah, and patience or *as sabr*.

But with time travel, there are rules and one mistake can undo anything. And they couldn't escape their human erring nature; their organization, like many other Muslim empires before them, also knew an apogee and, as predicted, a decline.

Malik also had online buddies from around the world besides the Far East Muvmant who shared his love for swords. He collected swords and sneaker pictures on his hard drive. He was a minimalist and didn't see the need to collect actual things when this world was temporary and his family was always on the move. His dream: Find the closet of a dead collector or sneaker-head and donate all the shoes to less privileged children around the world.

CHAPTER TWELVE : OF TEACHERS AND STUDENTS

Malik

IN SCHOOL, MALIK PREFERRED science related subjects even though at first, he thought he wasn't intellectually equipped or crafty enough for them. This is how he found out about many inspiring Muslim brains in his private researches. He always found it annoying when he discovered that a Muslim scientist had been extended a Latin name, thus making it impossible to know the guy was Muslim in the first place. Like the controversial and rationalist Maliki scholar Ibn Rushd who had been Latinized as Averroes during the Renaissance. *But you*

Ducktrinors did the same thing with your name to escape persecution, a voice in him often pinned. Malik usually ignored the voice.

In college, he enrolled in Physics, Mathematics, and Oceanology classes like many scholars he had heard about from the tales his father had contributed to. He learned that most of the scholars he looked up to didn't like being the center of attention. "I'm the same but my relationship with the spotlight is a bit complicated," Malik had beamed, even though some teachers favored him. Not a popular kid except when teachers made it difficult to be so, Malik avoided crowds and people knowing too much about him. *The less attention, the less evil eye I will bring to myself,* he had always reckoned. "You're the oldest and the most modest Ducktrinor child," his mother often said with great pride.

"Thanks Mom," was always his response.

He was the kind of student that kept all his syllabi and transcripts very neat. Malik also loved to record the require-ments of other majors. Thus, he became an archivist at a young age because he always wanted to know how and what to teach his future students. *I'll form my own school and become a great scholar insha'Allah,* Malik loved to say to his family during dinner or any other opportunity he got. *Alhamdullilah* he was blessed with knowledge because he sought it and remembered things very easily.

"But what's the point if that's going to blow our cover as believers? You and Hanifa are really something. I want to say, TOO MUCH!" Pris would chime in.

"Shut up!" Malik would reply, loosing his temper. While many thought he was good-tempered, the truth was he was ill-tempered but did his best to control his flaw.

"You shut up, Malik!" Pris would sass more until the parents would intervene.

"Pristine you have a point but please be respectful to your brother once again," Adama would put out and continue, "Malik, we've already been through this. We have no *ummah* these days where your services can be of use. Please try to keep your head down and not attract attention to yourself or us with your plans of opening your own school to teach in a world where people don't want to learn a thing. Besides, it will be a blatant defiance to the system if they catch wind of this. Shoot for library assistant since robots are now the librarians. These robots have the entire database stored in their programs but humans still have to do the heavy lifting at times or the thinking to program them. Such a job would be a great cover for you with all the knowledge you possess."

"No thank you. I won't limit myself. I still don't understand why you accepted a mechanic job for the Seculars when you can be 'Dans la cours des grands' or one of their lead engineers," Malik usually said short of a little sarcasm.

"Well, you still don't understand that all your mother and I do is to try to keep you children safe. The job puts food on the table, pays the utilities plus other necessities, and that's all I care about." And like that, his father always closed the discussion.

It was usually with muddled feelings that Malik stayed quiet during the rest of the meal. But that never stopped him from bringing the tabled subject back in the hopes that his parents would change their minds and support his career goals.

Malik was always energized about acquiring and spreading knowledge. It explained why he was also very athletic. He loved archery and running. But the sport he loved the most was sword fighting and inherently he also took a liking to the derivative of the sport, fencing, because of Hanifa. "I know you take inspiration from the *sahabiyat* like Nusaybah bint Ka'ab but have you ever heard of the African American named Ibtihaj Muhammad?" Malik had asked Hanifa corny like once during one of their playful duels when they were still children.

"No, I've never heard of her."

"Okay, she was amazing *masha'Allah* and brought great pride to her country as well and especially to the Muslims of that era, according to my readings."

Hanifa's eyes glistened with awe as he continued to fill her in on more details of this renowned *Muslimah* fencer.

When their father wasn't around to play with them, Malik would lead his sisters in target practice. He always loved to say, "Never step on the shooting range when others are still shooting just to check your *cible!* It's dangerous." He knew a little French thanks to his mom.

"Chill out, Bro," Hanifa would say and then add, "These arrows are not even real!"

"Right!" Pris would pipe in. As usual she was always about defying her older brother because she wished she had been born first.

Malik would sigh and bow his head in disbelief. "It's about practice and building a habit of safety. What if you get in the habit of jumping in target areas and get used it. One day, when you have real arrows, you will step on the field without a second thought! Be careful sisters," Malik would utter calmly, unlike himself, more disappointed than angry.

"What if there is a high wind and my arrow doesn't go straight but makes a forty-five-degree angle and hits people on my side? What if we're at war? I would be a target no matter what I do. So we wouldn't need to step on the shooting field to be at risk. Wouldn't you agree?" Pristine would often argue with her older brother.

"Hmm hmm! Exactly, if we are at war, it would be pointless. We would be at the mercy of arrows anyways," Hanifa would support Pris.

"Morons! Only a skill-less archer like you two would let his arrow and bow deviate to forty-five degrees and put the life of his comrades in danger. Ugh! I've had enough of you two." Malik would finally loose it and ask his mother the following, "Mom! Do you need any help in the kitchen? Hanifa and Pris are free. I'd rather continue to play with Shafiya."

Shafiya, who would normally stay quiet until that point, usually added, "Bro, that's a bit chauvinist but I get it, these two just love to rattle your nerves for the heck of it. Never mind them, let's go another round of target practice."

"Nah, let's run. Usaine Bolt (me) versus Dalilah Muhammad (you)."

"Deal! You won't win this race though." Shafiya would concede before a challenging race between the siblings.

"*Winning isn't everything*. I'm used to not being in the spotlight Sis. How about you?" Malik prodded.

Shafiya replied with, "Loser gets to do more research on past Muslim civilizations to share during *halaqa* time." The siblings laughed and sat off for a very competitive run.

Malik lost and he had to dig deep and discovered things he had never imagined even though their parents had taught them a lot. Knowledge was something that always expanded and made you feel like you only know the tip of the iceberg. So Malik discovered that the twenty first century saw a Muslim era that was very much reminiscent of the Muslim golden ages in Cordoba from the ninth century to the thirteenth century. Muslims in general set off on a journey to claim their narrative; their *Lost Islamic History*. The Islamic past of Africa and especially of Timbuktu in the Malian Empire was revived and became recognized around the world. The Muslim community of the twenty-first century, like the Muslims in the apogee times of Islam, believed that modernism and Islam went hand in hand. This generation of Muslims made significant changes in technology, fashion, science, the food industry, daily life, politics, you name it; they advanced many areas of this worldly life because Islam wasn't only about theology. In fact, it was about living a balanced way of life. The way this generation spread Islam was ground breaking and the first of its kind.

In the first early years of the religion, Islam had spread mainly through business, i.e. commerce. The twenty-first century Muslims decided to use a more effective way to spread Islam: the internet. E-commerce flourished and so did Muslim businesses. Muslim business owners and scholars became globally known due to their social media presence with hundreds to thousands to millions of followers. Several Islamic movements sprouted in the e-Ummah and *dawah* efforts were successful. Many people came to Islam as the collective Muslim generation told their own stories that had been hijacked by either non-Muslims who didn't know Islam or the Fundamentalists and the Zulmists. The influence of these three groups had decreased as many people became more enlightened and knew how to discern the right Islam from the propagandas also advertised electronically, either by the media or other instigating sources.

But a new kind of war emerged: internet war. These *jihads* weren't on land anymore but in the electronic sphere. In these electronic wars, disagreeing parties would go on never-ending discussions or send deadly viruses to each other which exploded computers the minute the Trojan message had been opened. This caused injuries, deaths, and the loss of properties. The age where people would block or unfriend parties that didn't agree with them was over. People you didn't agree with could target and end you and vice-versa. It was truly a new era of *dawah*, learning, and digital warfare.

On the bright side, Muslims didn't have to travel to Timbuktu's prestigious schools of the Empire of Mali like people did in the early years of Islam to learn the religion or to Mankono, one of the first Islamic centers located in the Ivory Coast, to learn the religion. They also didn't have to go to Egypt to become a learned scholar at Al-Azhar University. They could simply register at online Islamic Universities from the comfort of their homes. *Masha'Allah*. Muslim blogs were very popular and well-rounded too. In all, the e-Ummah was self-sufficient and blooming. And one particular blogger stood out the most. Her pen name was Rasheeda From Bagdad. She named her website after the original House of Wisdom (Bayt al-Hikma) in the same city during the Islamic Golden Age. If the past had taught one thing to Muslims it was that they needed a backup for everything they created to avoid their achievements being burned or drowned in water like the Mongols had done. Everything authored by a Muslim was listed on her site. It was a very consolidated resource, which was centralized and easily accessible by anyone in need of a Muslim service geared to Muslims. Muslims created these things not to copy non-Muslims but to improve their way of life. They understood their struggle better than anyone so inventions were ripe. This created jobs and a strong economy because Muslims were consumers and producers in the same market; they had buying power.

Librarians were hired and donations flowed in easily because business was good. The Librarians hailed from all parts of the world because Islam had always been universal and not only Arabic. These Librarians added collections and achievements of Muslims daily and in real time. Muslims were aware of their racial differences. They weren't color-blind because the words of the Lord of The Worlds had made them embrace each other regardless. *"O mankind, indeed We have created you from male and female and made you peoples and tribes that you may know one another. Indeed, the most noble of you in the sight of Allah is the most righteous of you. Indeed, Allah is Knowing and Acquainted."* (Quran 49:13)

And for a while Muslims were global citizens and had put nationalistic views aside and had united under the common banner of Islam, for the beloved Prophet *sallallahu aleihi wassalam* of Islam had said, *"All mankind is from Adam and Eve, an Arab has no superiority over a non-Arab nor a non-Arab has any superiority over an Arab; also a white has no superiority over black nor a black has any superiority over white except by piety and good action."* (Al-Bukhari, Hadith 1623, 1626, 6361).

Muslims had finally realized that politicians in Europe had used nationalism, also known as xenophobia, to divide the *ummah.* And they had succeeded. That said, it took a lot of eye-opening experiences for many non-Black Muslims to see the plight of their black brothers and sisters in Islam around the world. While the discrimination was clear to many non-Blacks, many of their counterparts were still veiled about the racism and double-standards the oppressors inflicted on the Blacks.

Many Muslim activists and scholars of all races raised awareness for their brothers and sisters in Islam and brought about a change. Muslims were once again a world educated and enlightened power after the times of the rightly guided Caliphs, the Ummayads, the Abbassids, the various sultanates, and the Ottomans. The internet made it possible for the e-Ummah to stay united and be linked.

However, as with everything previous, the strong leading Muslim nations' decline had to be predicted. The descendants of the pioneer movement of the twenty-first century didn't have the drive of their parents to blog about Islam or be inspiring. They had no time to be and stay good Librarians. After all, they were born with silver spoons in their mouths. They preferred to live a life of decadence instead. Their parents had worked hard to make life better for them but not in the intent that they turn around and lose focus of the end game and become lazy. No virus checks were made on the House of Wisdom website. Emails weren't checked as often as they should. Passwords weren't updated regularly. The House of Wisdom became the online abandoned park because after so many complaints, people left and tried to start their own support system. The lack of a centralized support contributed to their eventual failure. This generation was too self-absorbed, unfortunately. This created the perfect opportunity for the centralized Muslim web tool to be targeted and hacked. And just like that, overnight, another Muslim era's achievements was wiped out of the system. It felt like the Stone Age when the descendants awoke one morning and they were being overthrown by the Seculars and the sister movement of the Seculars; Nationalism.

Non-Muslims as well had used the House of Wisdom because a lot of the services tailored to Muslims followed ethical rules and the concept of being green. Thus, such a centralized database was very valuable in terms of economics. But when disinterest plagued the organization, the multinational users wondered why they had to be loyal to Bagdad's House of Wisdom, which had earned the twenty-first century Muslims interest because it of the revival period. Then, the descendants thought that allegiance to their own nations was better than allegiance to only one country which has only a piece of Muslim History. This was the beginning of the decline. It was a sign of Muslim disunity. It was no different than the *Taifa* times. History was repeating itself indeed. The once-united *ummah* blogged and went live on social media advocating nationalism while the House of Wisdom contributors didn't do their job to try to reunite the *ummah* under one banner.

CHAPTER THIRTEEN : THE KÔRÔKÔS

Hanifa

Timeline: The second day of school in Brazil

AFTER THE *FAJR* PRAYER, as usual, Hanifa had set out on her mechanical horse, Buraqa, she had designed in her father's engineering lab to replace her real horse that had died in another country. She was wearing her favorite yellow *khimar*. From the top of the valley, she could see the school stadium a few miles away. The bright lights were still on, but not for much longer. She reached for her HD binoculars to have a closer look and gasped at the sight of naked girls and women sleeping amongst naked men and unclothed ex-machinas. She could spot something that looked like red-painted drawings on their bodies. Clearly a group play had gone on there. *What a life of debauchery,* she snickered. Because looking at the *awrat* parts of others is not advised, she quickly shifted her gaze, only to find herself faced with an even more troubling scene: the severed body of a girl in the middle of the stadium. She was in a blood bath.

Subhanallah, what did these animals do to her? She vowed to investigate these events to satisfy her own curiosity by returning to the scene of the crime later that night. Normally, she would run and tell someone but she knew that chances that anyone cared about the decadence of such gatherings were close to nil. On the heel of that thought, the naked girls began making their walk of shamelessness out of the stadium to home or whatever abode they lived at.

She continued perusing the place from afar and realized the state of chaos the stadium was in. There were medieval chalice-like drinking cups scattered all over the place. Many had a red fluid leaking out of them. *Wine or blood? Or both?* Her questions were answered when she saw a naked participant sucking blood out of a human limb. He took a huge bite of it then threw it carelessly behind him as he headed towards the exit. Another one chugged a small barrel of wine like the ones she had seen at the grocery store before he also contributed to the littering of the place.

Highly disturbed, shocked, and surprised by the graphic images she'd seen and shaking out of rage, Hanifa wheeled Buraqa around and galloped home to get ready for school.

***

I'm old enough to do what I want, Hanifa thought as she walked to another class alone since Ana walked out of the other one she had.

Respecting her parents and keeping her word were a struggle. She didn't understand how they could stay silent and take the Seculars' treatment. They were hunted and persecuted. Sir Landry Big's speech at the auditorium earlier that day was another testament that the rebellion and the believers were at utmost risk. *I want to make a difference! Allah and his angels will ask why, as oppressed people, we didn't stand up for ourselves.*

Her parents would have said, "And the same scripture said that they will ask why we didn't move to go to a persecution-free area as Allah's earth is wide and spacious!"

Hanifa sighed. *Maybe I'm analyzing the scripture to my own advantage.* But she was tired of running. Her mind drifted off to old, peaceful days in a safe haven.

***

In her old safe haven, Hanifa had a ritual. After the morning prayers, she would hastily put on her backpack and leave the family house. Once outside, she pressed the white star button on the black, crescent-shaped device strapped to her hand. As if by magic, a black horse appeared and Hanifa mounted it with little difficulty. Gently, she pulled on the reins and the animal took off in a canter. She rode it around town, finally resting next to a creek. The horse feigned grazing as Hanifa listened to the majestic, soothing sound of waterfalls.

When she had taken in enough of the serene and natural surroundings, Hanifa was ready to head back home, but first she decided to bring treats to her family. She knew the perfect stop to make.

Hanifa descended from her ride and secured the reins of the stallion on an automatic parking meter. She looked at the Greenwuhud's sun high in the sky, smiled, and entered the bakery shop. The electronic notifier tinkled and the sweet, velvety aroma of dessert filled her nostrils.

"Assalamu aleikum," the bony old woman with creases around her eyes said to Hanifa, giving her a full smile. The white woman's wrinkles were barely noticeable with her gray scarf wrapped up so close to her face and secured under her chin. She'd tucked the loose ends of her scarf behind the flowery apron she wore.

I want to be as pleasant as this woman in my old age, Hanifa thought as she quickly glanced at the shop owner. She perused the different sweets behind the clear glass while the woman slowly got up from her stool to attend to her.

"*Wa aleikum salam*, auntie Dawn," Hanifa replied, sucking and smacking at her lips hungrily after a small delay. She gaped at the sight of the pastries and elaborately decorated cakes before her eyes. There was so much to choose from. When Hanifa was ready, she put in her order. The old lady pushed up the long sleeves of her black *abaya* to her elbows and deftly grabbed a pair of tongs. Then she placed some *baklava*, chocolate cake pops, croissants, and cherry-filled Danish pastries in a hot pink box that read *Dawn's Delights* on top. Hanifa gave her the money as Auntie Dawn handed her the box of sweets.

"Don't forget to send my *salams* to your family," she said with a crisp voice.

"*Insha'Allah*," Hanifa responded politely. She left the shop with a satisfied smile. "Come on, Buraqa, let's go home," she said as she untied him and strolled down the street lined with other small successful business shops. She had named the replica horse after her first real horse Buraqa. The smell of flowers and freshly cut grass wafted in the cobblestoned streets. She gulped some fresh air and exhaled happily. Hanifa felt blessed to be living in such a paradise on earth, away from persecution. The family's last incident had resulted in the loss of her dear black-and-gray maverick horse. A pang of sadness opened in her heart at the thought. She knew Malik, as a highly spiritual being, deeply missed the horse too because he often had deep soundless conversations with Buraqa.

Greenwuhud was a safe haven for a multitude of people that believed in embracing the past while living in the present. They were called the *Kôrôkôs*. The term housed every shade of Muslims, from Muslim hipsters-mipsterz to really conservative Muslims. As believers of a higher power, Allah, they also welcomed other faiths that believed in Him. Christians and Jews in Greenwuhud were their friendly neighbors who paid their taxes and knew their boundaries like their host, the Muslims. All believers weren't *Kôrôkôs*, but all *Kôrôkôs* were believers.

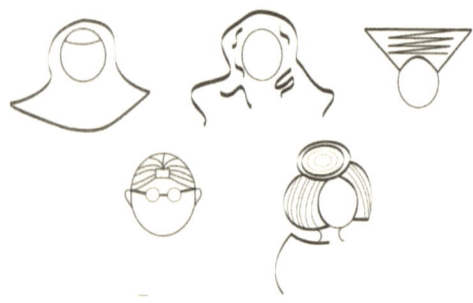

The town was lively, prosperous, and safe from the outside world and the Seculars. The town's people had lived there peacefully for a hundred years—until the Seculars, a legacy of predators, found a way to invade and enter the city under false pretense. They burned it to the ground and imprisoned many. It turned out that the town collapsed because Greenwuhud had spies that let the enemy in. A few families survived the ordeal by running clandestinely or by having a Secular vouch their non-religious ties. Hanifa's family was one of these families with the help of Uncle Abu. After that, they left Greenwuhud in America and traveled to Pretoria in South Africa.

***

Hanifa stopped daydreaming about Greenwuhud and decided that she needed to talk to her Uncle Abu in the Secular government as soon as possible to pick his brain. *He made it okay by being undercover; maybe becoming a Secular officer isn't such a bad idea after all. I just have to take care od that big boulder ahead—the family.* She sighed and put her thoughts aside. She really needed to think things through before acting, but the images of the soccer stadium at dawn had haunted Hanifa throughout the day. She couldn't wait to get home and sneak out of her room when everybody was sleeping to find out more about the cult's activities.

When she got home, she rushed to clean up, pray, and eat. She told her parents that she was exhausted and had to fold up early. Unsuspicious, they believed her story and she scampered up the stairs to her room. She then filled her bed with clothes so that anyone checking on her would think that she was lying down.

She jumped out of her window, put her bag diagonally across her body, and activated her travel-safe mode that she dubbed Niqabaya 1.0 : a combination of a *niqab* and an *abaya*. The stealth guard acted like an invisibility cloak. These days, it was the only way an unaccompanied woman could travel safely. Plus, she didn't want her parents in their routine after-dinner walk around the neighborhood to spot her without the cloak on. She would be grounded if she was caught sneaking out at night without their approval.

Only a select few could detect its presence. The Seculars had tried to capitalize on the app and develop the technology into a weapon against believers, but hey hadn't caught a breakthrough on the technology yet.

***

Hanifa made it safely to school on the SSS and alighted without being noticed. When she'd given Hanifa a tour of the school, Ana had also mentioned something about parties being hosted every day of the week at the coliseum. While it was by serendipity that she found herself at the stadium that morning, her trip to the stadium that night was on her own accord. So Hanifa made her way to the likely venue for the next party; the stadium and found a good vantage point from which to observe the party. *Let's see if they repeat what lead to what I saw this morning after the morning prayer.*

"Well, I'll be damned," she said at the sight of Sylas dressed in white and gold getting ready to address the crowd of mostly naked participants.

Some males and females wore a thin piece of white fabric to cover their genitals and butt cheeks, leaving bare their outer hips and thighs, like an ancient loincloth. Their bodies were either oiled or covered in gold glitter. Other males and females wore white and gold two-piece swimsuits. Some men, like Sylas, were bare chested and very muscular. The view made Hanifa a little uncomfortable. Reluctantly, she looked away from his oiled-up, muscular chest to examine the rest of the party. She felt naughty about the longing feeling that crept into her.

Sylas started his speech. "Magic starts with arousal and excitement. As we set to dance with the devil in a group-play fashion, I want to take the opportunity to wish you again a good *school* year." He paused as the crowd laughed and cheered.

His words seem unoriginal, and it's now clear to me that school is definitely not the reason why they attended Castle 5; it is more to increase their worldly numbers so they could continue their satanic and pagans rituals. How ironic. They despise the idea of any religion with divine intervention and claim to be Secular. Yet, they worship the devil. If that's not a twisted religion, I don't what is.

***

"Where were you?" Malik demanded as soon as she jumped back through her bedroom window.

"School," Hanifa defensively blurted out.

"We were worried sick!" He glanced at Shafiya, who was standing next to him. "We came to tell you about Shafiya's day and encounters, but we had to put that issue on the back burner because you were missing."

"I went to school," she let out flatly. "Get out of my room. I know what I'm doing."

"Either you tell us what's going on or we'll tell Mom and Dad," Malik warned.

They all stayed quiet for a bit before she spilled the beans on Sylas's party and the dead bodies she had seen. She refrained from telling them about her future plans.

She could see in their faces that they hardly bought her story. As Malik and Shafiya left the room, staring deeply in each other's eyes, that familial, conspiratorial look they shared made Hanifa uneasy. These two hardly had to talk. They could just look into each other's eyes and understand each other. She felt a ping of jealousy in her heart and wondered what they were up to. She just hoped they didn't tell on her.

CHAPTER FOURTEEN : SPIES

Ali

Timeline: The second day of school in Brazil

NO NEWCOMER ESCAPED ANA's watchful Eyes. This intruder certainly didn't. She quickly identified him as Ali, a rebel working for the Resistance with the help of the secret database she called "Eyes." She could hear his thoughts, too. All she had to do was send a speedy mosquito-like bug to bite the back of her target's neck to implant the Mind Reader.

When Ana's bug hit Ali's neck to implant the Mind Reader, he had cursed, "Damn mosquitos!" and slapped his neck. She giggled because it was always the same reaction she witnessed when she tracked people.

It always amazed Ana that Sylas didn't need such mechanics because he had capabilities that allowed him to hear people's thoughts. *Details.* Ana's Eyes watched Ali's hands form into fists—he was listening to Sylas and the president of the Seculars address the crowd in the gathering room. He stared at Sylas' white uniform, seeming to linger on the big "S" plastered on his chest.

"There'll be other times to take this oppressing regime down," Ali said under gritted teeth, following the other Secular officers to the vast soccer stadium, the place where they normally regrouped and held events. As he walked toward the stadium, he looked back at the school towers and their imposing steepness. He still had to get used to the school with its futuristic castle vibe and the different towers.

Ali mimicked the way the other Secular officers and followers marched to the stadium in an orderly fashion. *I wonder if they will know I'm an outsider. It was really easy to disarm that bozo Secular follower and wear his clothes, but that was the easy part. The hard part is yet to come. Good thing they didn't have badge numbers on these uniforms. All I need to do is remember my Secular officer number and find the prisoner and report to Dawud—The Insider.*

They don't know who they're dealing with when it comes to me. The coup failed but we still have a chance; this place recruits more followers than any school around the globe. I just need to blend in by registering post-mission for a few classes. That way, I can have access to the students easily.

When they got to the stadium, Sylas took the voice enhancer and addressed the crowd. "Hail to the Seculars! The world will never end!" He saluted the crowd of followers.

The stadium looked like it had uncharacteristically snowed in Brazil, with rows upon rows of soldiers dressed in white uniforms and helmets.

"Hail to the Seculars!" The soldiers replied on cue, getting up in a swift movement before sitting back down. Just like androids. Ali followed, copying each movement.

"The Resistance almost had a successful coup," Sylas continued. "And this was possible because we still can't shut down their main herald source—*The Muezzin*. They have devious hackers who made the circulation of this e-zine hard to trace. We need to recruit better hackers than theirs! If we're able to shut them down, Sir Landry Big will personally congratulate us in front of the whole world. Go get them!"

"Hail to the S!" the crowd of followers chanted abbreviating their creed.

Good luck finding The Muezzin's source, Ali thought, grinning under his helmet.

***

After the stadium meeting with Sylas, Ali stayed behind the group of men and androids. When he was sure they wouldn't notice his detour, he whipped a tablet out of his uniform and looked at the mission's directives. On a hunch, he decided to go northeast from the stadium before setting up to rescue the prisoner at night while Sylas had his party. *Security should be minimal then*, he thought.

While walking, Ali spotted a girl sitting in the school gardens dressed unusually—*could she be a Kôrôkô in the flesh?*

Word had it that they were extinct. Before he could approach the girl, who seemed dazed in her own thoughts, another officer approached her. Ali stood still, watching them from a small distance as he gently pressed the recording button on his helmet.

"Hello Miss," the officer said to her in Portuguese.

"Hello." The girl squinted her eyes to examine her confronter.

"Do you have a permit to wear such a traditional and ancient head covering?" the guard asked, wearing a wolfish grin.

"I do. I'm a fashion major so old artifacts appeal to me," she replied calmly and fished for the pendant under her shirt.

The guard leaned over to read off the silver digital permit. He seemed taken off guard that she had one, but he regained his vertical standing position quickly. "Well, that doesn't mean anything. It could be a fake. You're going to have to give me further proof." His face contorted in disapproval, and he pointed his nose in the air.

The would-be victim shifted in her seat for a minute, cleared her throat, and said, "I'm sure I can make that happen. I have my uncle on speed dial just for these daily hiccups within your ranks," she said in a sarcastic tone. Ali picked up on it but wondered if the officer did as well.

"Really? That won't be necessary." He yanked the scarf from her head and grabbed her arm. "You're coming with me!"

"This isn't fair!" she cried out.

Ali debated on whether he should intervene and help the girl, but an inner voice kept reminding him that she wasn't part of the mission.

The girl's complaints escalated as she and the officer entered into a physical struggle. He tried to handcuff her with a set of magnetic, glowing loops that seemed individual but had an invisible linking mechanism. He managed to secure one onto one of her wrists as she put up a good fight. At the clink of the loop, she raged furiously and punched him in the nose.

Good girl, Ali secretly cheered.

Then the officer mercilessly tased her on the neck and her body brutally jolted like a fish out of water. Her face twisted in pain and she let out a piercing cry.

Stay out of it, Ali reminded himself again. But he couldn't stay indifferent to the gruesome sight and the goosebumps that he felt raising on his skin after her piercing, shrill cry.

Ali darted in their direction. "What are you doing, man? Don't you have a sister or a mother? You shouldn't hit or hurt women." Ali wrenched him away from the poor girl.

Haughtily, the guard dropped the taser in the grass, wiped his bloody nose and replied, "In case you weren't here when we started this, *officer*, she hit me first. She might as well be a man with that strong fight she put up!" He spat, disgusted.

"I was here when it started, and I recorded it. You have no grounds to retain her. She showed you her pass. Let her go. These are the rules." Ali tried to regain his breath from sprinting to reach them.

"Excuse me? I didn't catch your name. Identify

yourself, officer," the bully ordered.

"I don't have to."

"Yes, you do. What tells me you're really one of us? Once again, I demand your identification."

"Nothing does." Ali lowered himself to the girl's level and helped her up after removing the cuff from her wrist—its unconnected twin hovered close by its other half.

"Just give it to him so he can leave us alone," she said, breathing hoarsely.

"Good call, you can trust me," Ali said as he recognized a mixed air of confused and safe on the girl's face.

"Thank God, you're different from the others," she said.

"SO#1-11-Goliath." He was glad Dawud had provided him with the identification.

"Duly noted. You can have her," the guard snarled bitterly, dabbing at his bleeding nose. "But she attacked me, as you will see on the video." Unexpectedly, he patted Ali's back, making Ali wonder if this guy had been possessed by a *djinn*.

How else could he suddenly become so friendly with a stranger he clearly didn't like?

Come on, the pat is fake. It's textbook. Think about it, an inner voice warned Ali.

The bully stepped back and added, "Besides, they're plenty more around school and town to torture. You can't trust anybody these days. There was just a coup! Everybody dresses 'funny old' these days. Ancient, to say the least. And when they're questioned, they say they're into fashion or arts or something nonsensical in the same trend."

It was the sad reality. The Secular officers, like the Nazis before them, grew by the number daily. They terrorized the students on campus, scrutinizing everybody. And when they graduated from their current military rank, they would be allowed to flood the outside world and apprehend any believer of a divine presence and chastise them any way they saw fit.

"I'm Safi," said the woman. "Thank you for helping me. I don't know if my uncle was going to be able to get me out of detention this time. He thinks his Secular colleagues are starting to become suspicious of him now."

"You're welcome, don't mention it. I'm Ali. Nice to meet you."

"You're different. There are only a small handful of officers around the campus that stand up for what's right. And you seem like you're one of them."

"You're some sort of a beacon…in a good way, I promise," Ali confessed.

"I know," she replied shyly, blushing from the compliment.

"You're different, too. And you owe me an honest answer after all this. I promise I won't judge you," he continued, smiling as he spoke these words.

"Sure, anything," the young girl said.

"Are you a *Kôrôkô*? If you are, you can trust me with this secret. I promise I won't tell a soul," he reassured her again.

She stayed quiet for a moment, eyed him for another bit, squeezed her chin in her hands, and confessed, "Yes, I am.

I'm also telling you because of what your name implies."

He grinned. "I knew it! I'm undercover, sister. Your secret is safe with me, Safi. Come on, let's talk."

They smiled at each other and made their way back to one of the garden benches to get to know each other more.

"You know my deepest secret. What is yours?"

"I have many because I'm always on secret missions. But above all of these, I want to avenge my family and relatives' deaths," Ali said.

"Hmm, revenge is tricky and not advised in Islam."

"I know. I'm human," Ali said.

"We all are. May you find peace," Shafiya prayed.

"*Ameen*," Ali replied.

"What's your weapon of choice? I hope not a taser like this jerk who assaulted me?"

"A bow and arrow. Archery is a *sunnah* sport, and I believe in its powers. I like to buy the latest versions for sport," Ali confessed.

"Nice, me too at times. But I prefer a sword like my

brother. You can't dodge bullets the same way, but I like a gun and a sword in each hand to fight off my assailants," she replied, craning her neck up with a serious face, a tiny smile on the corner of her lips.

"Hmm, a multi-tasker. *Masha'Allah*," Ali complimented. "While I respect our talents, I feel like it's sad we had to learn to protect ourselves at such a young age because of an oppressive regime."

"I totally agree with you," Shafiya said.

They talked until Safi had to leave. Then Ali wandered around the vast school until he retraced his steps back to the stadium, where he got hit with a vision.

This girl is truly amazing, and she has the gift of motivating crowds, something I am too shy to overcome. And she is truly classy; her outdated and modest clothes got me at first glance. The entrance she pulled with the horse was also brilliant, a Coreishy woman-wannabe in a good way. A smile crept on Ali's face at that thought.

Her round face accentuated by her almond eyes and skin tone won me over. Maybe I still have a chance to find a Muslim companion in these times after all. Maybe joining her cause will help me know her better. Being a lone ranger is starting to take its toll on me. Since my family was slaughtered by Sylas' kind, I haven't had any attachment or engagement to fulfill. I don't even regret taking this infidel's life because he has no respect for women. Besides, it was a necessary evil. I either eliminated him or they would have lynched her.

Eyes and the Mind Reader recorded the slideshow of images from Ali's vision. And the beauty of the human mind fascinated Ana even more at that moment. *If there is no God, then who created such a complex being?* Ana pondered and continued, "And I always knew the girl would do great things, the minute I saw her. It was written all over her."

Ali's vision continued. "The offer is very tempting, but before we go, some of us need to talk to our families," a male voice in the crowd said, bringing Ali's thoughts back to the real world. He believed he had just had a strange vision he couldn't decipher yet.

When Ali snapped out of it, it was 8:30 p.m. He found himself seated at the stadium witnessing, for the first time in his life, a full Secular party in progress. He needed to carry on with his mission, but he was transfixed by the nearly naked girls and boys, men and women, and android ex-machinas crawling all over the place. They wore outfits very similar to white and gold two-piece swimsuits for women. The males had their chests bare, as did some of the women, but wore white briefs hemmed in gold. It was like a toga party, but the theme was definitely naughty and rated X. Ali started to feel out of place; his uniform was too covered for this party. He decided to set off on his mission.

You're right, get on with it. I should probably report this but let's see how this plays out. Excitement is just around the corner, Ana thought.

CHAPTER FIFTEEN : THE PRISONER OF MIHSSER

Ali

Timeline: The evening on the second day of school

MIHSSER SHOULD BE RIGHT about here, Ali thought.

The Eyes robot exclaimed, "Intruder! Intruder! Intruder!" but Ana didn't react to the distress warnings, and Ali proceeded, unaware of the extra pair of eyes on him. Ana was in a coma after her assault, and Eyes' feeds appeared to her in dream formats. Her body cells were synched with Eyes.

Ali swung the silver sphere in the air and it bounced up, almost dropped to the floor, and rose back to Ali's chest level before emitting a fluorescent blue laser in the dingy alley he was standing in. Before long, a sequence of numbers appeared in the air, comprised of the blue laser rays, and then a cell appeared. The sphere continued spinning before he heard an unlocking buzzing sound. A gray door appeared and opened.

Cautiously, Ali stepped in and scanned the room. It was more of a suite than a prison cell. Then he heard a voice yell, "Judas, I already told you, I'm not telling you anything even if you strip me of everything in this room. I really don't care. I told you, don't do me any favors just because my sister works for you."

"Tim? My name is Ali," he yelled back.

"Oh! The Resistance got my SOS message!" Tim yelped with delight before shifting to a whisper, "I used my regular prescription glasses to communicate with the outside world. That's the only thing they didn't take from me since I need them to read. My glasses have a memory card instilled in them. The only person I can't reach is my sister Ana because they monitor her closely. Can we find her?"

But I can see you Brother, Ana's mind said.

"It's not part of the mission," Ali countered.

"She's the only reason I haven't been tortured. I can't leave her with them."

"Nope, can't do it," Ali said, remaining firm behind his words. *My helping quota for the day has been met after helping Safi*, he thought. *Besides, if Ana works with the Seculars, she'll be fine.* His conscience rationalized his decision. *Obviously, she's of some kind of asset to them.*

Not completely true, Ana's voice said again to no one in particular.

"Fine, quick, we need to hide before the camera sees you. They monitor me continuously, but the system has loopholes," Tim said.

But Ali only stood there, contemplating the prisoner

like he was an exotic creature. *Who didn't he want to sleep with to get locked up here?* his conscience remarked atypically. Tim's pearl complexion, his well-groomed, growing beard, his white tunic and ankle-length pants were truly mesmerizing to Ali. Indeed a beautiful man stood there before his eyes. The image of the prisoner that the rebellion had given Ali didn't do any favor to the man he was saving. He thought again and suddenly felt ashamed to be blown away by the looks of another man. He quickly looked away.

"Thank you for coming to save me. You know the most ironic thing about my imprisonment?" Tim asked.

The voice pulled Ali from his short amazement. "No, Brother Tim," Ali replied, focusing back on his mission.

"I go by Tariq Larayba now," he corrected, adjusting his rectangular glasses on his thin nose. "Anyway, this place is called Mihsser. In Arabic, which I'm still learning, Misr, which is much closer to the name of this damned place, is Egypt! Like Prophet Joseph (May God be please with him), I could be called the 'Prisoner of Egypt.' I mean, Joseph was." Tariq beamed with excitement, obviously proud of the link he made between himself and a handsome Prophet who lived centuries ago.

Suddenly annoyed, Ali regained his normal state of mind. "You're a pretty boy for sure, but not that pretty. According to the scripture, no one's beauty comes even close to his. So relax, okay? Now, 'Piercing Star,' we need to go! Like yesterday!"

Trembling, Tariq shielded himself from the harsh words and scurried out of Ali's way. He obviously hadn't expected the rageful outburst from his savior. "Okay… Gawh, I was just joking. Maybe the place was named to denote the 'missers' of free life that are being jailed here," he quipped again.

"I don't care, man. Stay quiet so I can think of my next move to get us out of here. You're very distracting."

"Fine, I don't mind being caught. I live here peacefully, so I'll just let Judas catch us."

At Tariq's words, the security breach siren started

ringing. Ali cursed while the man previously known as Tim grinned at his accomplishment. *Could this have been a trap?* Ali thought, not knowing what to think anymore.

He moved to grab Tariq to leave by force, but like magic, the Secular officers flooded the jail room, circling the two. Judas entered the room last.

"Well, well, what do we have here?" Judas asked, looking pleased to have caught a trespasser.

"This guy is lost. I don't know him," Tariq quickly uttered.

"One thing he is *NOT*, is lost. You just don't stumble on hidden cells around here. Officer Ata, is this the officer you met this morning in the gardens?" Judas asked as the bully made his entrance into the room.

"Dang!" Ali said through gritted teeth. *What to do now? Think quickly.*

"Yup, that's him. I put a tracker on his shoulder this morning," Ata gloated. "See, I looked up the number you gave me, and it's not assigned to a human being. When I realized that you were sporting an android uniform, I had to let Judas know," he finished, proud of himself.

"Good catch," Judas said. "You'll be generously rewarded by Sylas when he hears of this after his party."

Ali rolled his eyes. This is why the shoulder rub had felt wrong and awkward to Ali earlier. The slime ball had bugged him. Ali fumed, but before he could lose it, Judas signaled one of the officers. With a straight face and matching posture, and an impeccably disciplined march, the officer came forward holding a bag in his right hand and his weapon in his left, resting on his left shoulder. He approached the middle of the circle where Tariq and Ali stood before dropping the bag at the feet of the trapped men. The bag opened, revealing the severed head of a blonde girl.

Tariq shrieked in horror, losing all composure. "Ana! ANNNAAAAaaaa. No! Nooooooo. No! What did they do to you?" he cried out.

Shit! If that's Ana, this is bad, Ali thought. Then an idea hit him. Ali elbowed Tariq, who had fallen on his knees to grab the head, and punched him in the face, knocking him unconscious to calm him down. This move took the soldiers by surprise. Then Ali dropped to the floor on one knee and pressed the inside of his right boot. A small rectangle abruptly levitated in front of him and quickly expanded to a quiver full of missile like high-tech arrows and a bow. Ali deftly swung it across his back and drew the bow back, shooting the arrows rapidly, one after another.

He skillfully shot arrows at the officers' legs, quick as lightning. In the blink of an eye, the circle of officers was broken and they were moaning in pain. He had spared Judas and Ata, whom he'd grazed at the hip and shoulder respectively because he only aimed to maim in those instances, which was unlike him. *I have been too generous today.* Then he turned to Tariq's body, which lay on the floor next to the bloody bag and the severed head. *I really hope this is a fake,* he thought. He quickly lifted the body and lodged it across his shoulders before pressing the teleporting device strapped to his wrist like a watch. And like a magic trick, they disappeared with just a click before the eyes of their assailants.

Ana had never prayed in her life but she made a silent prayer for her brother that day. "Dear God, if you truly exist, please keep your eyes on my brother. I'm no longer human, and I need to keep a low profile at the moment. He was safe where he was up until now. Now they will hunt him down, and he will remain a fugitive for the rest of his life." She finished her words with a deep sigh. While her body was inactive because of Sylas and Judas' assault, her mental capabilities were thankfully intact.

CHAPTER SIXTEEN : THE INSIDER

Dawud

Timeline: The second day of school in Brazil

DAWUD SNEAKED UP BEHIND Secular officers to listen to what they were talking about. As an eleven-winters-old orphan boy, he secretly followed them everywhere, gathering intel for the Muslim Resistance as The Insider. As Ana's Eyes robot recorded everything, Dawud bumped into a gigantic officer and quickly apologized. The soldier leered down at Dawud—the pest that had dared to touch him. That gave Dawud enough time to put a small video camera tracker on the officer before getting out of the beast's way. Then he ran in the direction of the library.

Just before the library's double doors at the end of the hallway, Dawud stopped and quickly surveyed the area. The school cameras didn't cover the small angle of the corner. When he saw no one, he placed his right hand on the wall, making a circle with his thumb and index while his other three fingers stayed erect. An electronic pad appeared and read the hand sign denoting "God" in Arabic and let him in.

The place was empty and smelled nice, as usual, with the strong, pleasant odor of *bakhour* incense. He took in the woodsy smell and kicked his shoes off by the door once he was fully inside. He rushed into the empty secret place to sit on the carpeted floor; a golden minaret was repeated on the carpet like a plaid pattern. He quickly removed his backpack, bringing it in front of him to dig out his tablet so he could watch the video from the guard's view.

Dawud watched Sylas address the crowd, surrounded by a display of the symbol of the Resistance on the digital screens all around the modern-day coliseum: a golden minaret on a dark green flag. Through the beast he'd tagged, Dawud listened to the speech.

Dawud internally responded to Sylas speech before tuning back in. *No, you aren't going to bring us down unless the Almighty wills it. Updating our servers and coming up with new ways to counter-attack you Seculars comes easily to us believers because we're dedicated to a just cause. It's nazif for us. We still pray five times a day, if not more in these treacherous times, and that's true dedication. Working for the Almighty is an intrinsic thing for us.*

"Don't forget to come to the party tonight. The admission fees for the parties at the beginning of the school year are on me. If you prefer real girls, there will be plenty. But if you're into the latest ex-machina type, there will be plenty of them too." Sylas sneered, winking as the crowd cheered in approval.

From his computer, Dawud zoomed in on Sylas' face. He rolled his blue eyes at Sylas's vulgarity. *Ew, grownups, always so horny.*

Dawud snickered then remembered he had to run a program to cover up the arrival of that new Resistance guy, Ali, they sent over to the stadium. *The quick seconds that yahoo of Ali disarmed the android soldier could still easily be caught by Judas's IT team.*

On the heel of that thought, his computer started beeping alerts off the walls.

Darn! We have a situation.

***

Judas stood outside the library with a good number of Secular officers. *Something must have led them straight to me*, Dawud thought as he saw them standing a few feet away, oblivious that he could see them from the inside, like possible with a tinted window.

Dawud hadn't run the program yet, so he couldn't understand how Ali's arrival could have been traced to the *masjid*. His mind continued to race for more answers. He then activated the stealth program to make the *masjid* invisible just as one of the officers started scanning the walls. *Jabal Thawr X.O* successfully did its job and Dawud blessed the inventor under this breath. "This Mustapha Kreedor is a genius. I hope I meet the guy one day *insha'Allah*. It's simply brilliant. And naming the program after the Cave of the Bull…" Dawud shook his head in awe.

Outside, the officers argued over the unfavorable scan results. "Are you sure you tracked the location of the hacks to here, sir?" the guard with the scanner in hand asked. He scratched his helmet.

"I'm a good tracker. I've never failed to capture believers, hackers, non-denomination folks—you name it. It goes without saying that I know well my art of tracking!" Judas snarled.

Dawud couldn't believe his eyes. It felt like a déjà vu moment. *Of course! The scene in The Message where the Prophet, sallallahu aleihi wassalam, and Abu Bakr, radiallahu anhu, were being tracked and took refuge in the mountain. Then Allah covered the entrance of the cave on Jabal Thawr with a spiderweb while a bird lay there in a nest, making it look like no one had entered the place in eons.*

Now will a snake appear? Dawud dreamily thought. *Of course not. Snap out of your awe! Get out of here before they decide to break this wall and find you!* a voice inside Dawud's head warned. He grabbed whatever necessities he could find—computer and tech stuff—and bolted out of there. He decided to use the sisters' entrance since the brothers' entrance was out of the question.

When he appeared at the other side of the portal, he immediately regretted not taking his feminine disguise with him. The sisters' entrance located inside the women's restroom was not empty as he had hoped.

"Ahhhhh, little pervert!" a group of teenagers shrieked when he appeared in the girls' bathroom. Not only did he not have a wig on his head, or girl outfit to warrant his presence in a girls' bathroom, he also had all those computer and tech supplies, making it seem as though he was guilty of filming or watching them!

"Why on earth did this have to happen, today of all

days? People barely come to this library and even use this bathroom!" Dawud grunted under his breath. Then he darted out of the restroom before the "opera girls" attracted more attention to him with their screams.

He needed to warn the other users of the mosque that the location had been compromised. Right at that moment, Dawud realized they had never exchanged contact info. They needed to come up with an emergency way to warn each other ASAP!

Crazy, but cute kiddo, Ana always thought when footage of Dawud showed up.

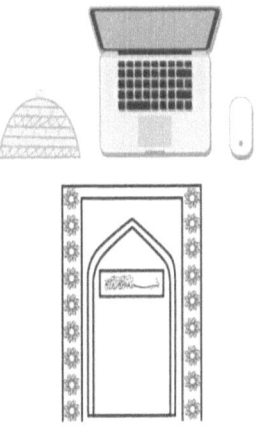

CHAPTER SEVENTEEN : A TASTE OF REBELLION

Hanifa

Timeline: The third day of school in Brazil

THE PLACE WAS DESERTED. No one walked in the alleys or studied in the library. At least none that Hanifa could see through the transparent glass doors.

Where the hell is Ana? Hanifa thought, steaming inside; she had been waiting for Ana for fifteen minutes. As a punctual person, she couldn't stand tardy people. *Flirting with Sylas again? Ew, why do I even care if they flirt?*

Ana's electronic message had said she would meet

Hanifa in front of the library the third day of school so they could walk to class together after breakfast. Hanifa stifled a yawn as her internal thoughts continued to race and her irritation grew.

This is perfect! Darn perfect! I could have slept a little more this morning after fajr. With gritted teeth, she pinched her thumbs to her indexes, mockingly making the "OK" jester. She was going to be late to public speaking class thanks to Ana Fashionista. She paced before the library and then turned around to face the wall between the end of the hallway and the library. She lightly banged her head again and again as she repeated, "perfect," her hands still fixed in the gesture and resting on the wall. Suddenly her entire body felt as is something was sucking or pulling her...*through the wall?*

"Hey!" she screamed, trying to make sense of what was happening. She tumbled into what she thought was oblivion, landing on a carpeted surface on her hands and knees. Quickly, she scanned her surroundings.

Hanifa immediately smelled incense. The delicious

woodsy incense was familiar. She kept her eyes closed for a moment and it came to her. *Of course! Grandpa brought the same kind!* Before she could further enjoy the comforting smell of the *bakhour*, a young, excited voice yanked her out of her reverie.

"How do you know that sign?" a young boy asked her.

"What sign?" Hanifa's tresses bounced on her neck, pouring out from her crocheted, slouched hat. She opened her eyes and scanned the room. "*Takbir!* A freaking mosque! This is unbelievable!"

She beamed with excitement, swirling her head around to admire the ceiling, the hanging lanterns, and the beautiful calligraphy on the walls. The figurative art was of the best she had ever seen. The calligraphy of the golden Arabic letters was exquisite. It adorned the mosque beautifully. She quickly removed her sneakers and started walking in all the directions, looking closely at the details.

"You know what this is?" Dawud asked, surprised.

"Of course I know what it is. It's a *masjid*, a mosque.

Wait a minute, are you a Secular?" She reached in her skirt pocket with a defensive stance, enclosing her hand around the taser with firmness and got it out. She was ready to deftly tase him or even erase his memory if necessary. As much as she hated the second option, her survival instincts came first.

"No way! To find Muslims in this school that just happen to be standing right in front of the sealed brother's entrance is a rarity. We're all covert crypto Muslims and only a few dare coming here to pray during the day. "I'm Dawud, by the way. Nice to meet you," he said, throwing one hand up and showing her the front cover of the Quran.

"Were you reading just before you vacuumed me in with some type of remote control, I assume?"

"Yes to both," Dawud replied.

"You're probably starting to regret bringing me in so impulsively with your gadgets now, huh?"

Dawud nodded.

"Alright, it's cool. You must have enjoyed my dumb face when I tumbled into oblivion, huh?"

"It was priceless!"

"Well, that's what you get. Now, we're even." Hanifa lowered her weapon.

"Whew!" Dawud let out.

"I'm Hanifa. I'm Muslim too. *Masha'Allah*," she said, relaxing her facial features.

"I knew it! That's why you did the Allah sign," he said and connected his thumb to his index finger, making a hole while his other three right fingers stuck out.

"I didn't purposely make the Arabic Allah sign with my fingers. I know what it is but I didn't. I was waiting for a friend so we could go to class but she's late," she said, continuing her meticulous dissection of the beautiful mosque.

"Yes…you did," Dawud said, eying her amusingly. Then he mimicked to her the exact movements she made as she paced in front of the *masjid*.

"Oh!" was all she said, recalling the details, but unsure of the connection. "But how the hell is this possible? Who else knows about this place?" She was still marveling at the place.

The last time she saw a real mosque like this was when she was back in Greenwuhud, USA. Her eyes glinted with joy and delight.

"Welcome to *Masjid Al Makhtum*—The Sealed Mosque. Not many people know it. Apparently the architect is a crypto-Muslim. He's incarcerated at the moment and we're trying to free him from the Seculars."

Then he explained to her how *The Muezzin* and word of mouth helped them bring the small community together at the school. "I run a background check on everyone that shows up at these doors and I cross-reference it with the Resistance database. For you…my gut tells me I should just trust you because something about you screams spirituality. Even thought, I'm a child, I'm very perceptive, truthful, and intuitive."

"Good for you! *Masha'Allah*. Are you the keeper of this place? How old are you, about ten?" Hanifa asked rapidly all at once.

"Something like that—a keeper. I'm eleven-winters-old.

I do almost everything hidden in here because they kidnap children here at the school. Crazy, right?"

"Very. *The Muezzin* and this new girl I met said the same thing. They both mentioned devil worshipping with the abducted children." She winced at the words even though a voice deep inside kept telling her that the information could have been farfetched.

"Anyway, we don't disclose secret passcodes or things like that in the e-zine. Just news about the Resistance and persecuted believers. All types of them. I have a cat."

"Right. It would be too risky. Wait, what? You have a cat here? I like them, but I sneeze so much around them. Anyways, the Seculars are onto the Resistance. And with the recent failed coup d'état, things are tighter. My parents don't want us anywhere near *The Muezzin*; it could blow our cover. I mean, it's a clear sign of rebellion if one is caught with it. We were on the run because of me."

Dawud gave her a puzzle look and she continued.

"Yeah, I know…and my computer-savvy uncle had to

be very crafty to provide us new identifications," she confessed.

"Everybody needs a connected uncle like yours *masha'Allah*. And no worries, my cat won't bother you. She stays inside the walls most of time via her secret door to her cattery. Muezza only comes out when she wants more food, cuddle or something."

"Great!" Hanifa said, relieved that her allergies would stay at bay and Dawud changed the subject.

"But for real? Were you featured in *The Muezzin?* Your uncle seems very cool! Do you think your uncle is better than me?" Dawud blasted her with questions like a normal kid would.

Half-distracted, she replied, "Egomaniac, huh? Anyway, I don't know if I was, or we were, featured. I'll tell you about my uncle one day, but I can't compare you two even if you seem very technical with all your gadgets in the corner over there. I just met you."

Then, Dawud candidly debriefed her on the mosque.

He explained how he had almost been compromised the day before when Judas showed up at the sealed door with a team of officers, and about his future decisions as the keeper of the place. His goal was to try to find another place to work and perform hacks on the Secular system. Hanifa promised to lend a hand in the search of such a place.

Then, extreme fascination took over Hanifa all of a sudden. The place and Dawud's tales revived feelings inside her she had long suppressed.

CHAPTER EIGHTEEN : BORN A REBEL

Hanifa

HANIFA CONTINUED TO ATTEND the mosque, without non-Muslims noticing her ins and outs, for the next ten days. In that short time period, she met other Muslim sisters who came regularly to the *masjid* to pray. Tahany was a friendly Egyptian sister with beautiful eyes embellished by that now-rare *kohl* from the old orient. Romeehna Torales was another native Brazilian sister; she was bubbly, a breath of fresh air. Hazera, a Bosnian girl, also attended the *masjid* religiously but used to be a Secular Muslim like the rest of her family—her family still didn't practice.

Hanifa became friends with them all and looked forward to leading the prayer with them at her side. She was immensely happy to find her sisters in Islam. Since she couldn't share this exciting discovery with her own siblings, for fear that they might worry she was once again putting them at risk, she guarded her knowledge of the mosque on campus with a cautious zeal.

One day, she said to Dawud, "I have an idea. We need to take over this school. This school has everything you need to study but no one takes advantage of it. Ever heard of a female scholar and community-driven person called Fatima Muhammad Al Fihiri Al Quraysh?"

"Nope! It's too long of a name," Dawud said bluntly.

"Okay, she's one of my role models. I want to be like her. We're taking over this school to educate the masses and to make a stand against the Seculars," Hanifa insisted.

"I-I-I don't know how we're going to do that." He pivoted, abruptly swirling around with his arms extended to emphasize how empty the space was. "Even if you and the few people that come here agree, plus that Resistance guy who is amiss, it will be very difficult to convince them. It's insane! Think about it."

"I know, but I have faith that it will be just fine. I can sense it. Besides, I thought you were working with the Resistance. Don't they have the same end goal?"

"Yeah, but their plan involves more spying and less action. Kinda like ruining the foundation of the house like mites do and then let the house crumble on its own. The same way many great empires fell." Dawud narrowed his blue eyes at her.

"We need to recruit more students and we need a sign to recognize all the believers and the non-believers that want to join," Hanifa wagered again.

"Hmm, grownups. They're sillier than us young folks. Let's say you can convince them. What's the plan to take over?" Dawud quizzed.

"I'll have to reconsider an opportunity that I had

formerly rejected." She winked.

"In that case, how about a small 's' for our insignia?" Dawud proposed. "It could easily be taken as a Secular sign; only Muslims will know it denotes Sunni or Shiite."

"Great idea!" Hanifa agreed. "I also want to lead an expedition to find the cave mentioned in *surah* 18 of the Quran, after we have this place under control."

Dawud didn't comment.

***

Timeline: Two weeks into school

Hanifa followed a tray of food downstairs to the basement. As she made her way down, the wooden steps creaked, indicating its old age. The wood used for the steps had been in her family for centuries. It had survived many attacks, and the family made sure that the wood, along with any family heirlooms, was retrieved and kept. Uncle Abu always made sure of that. The cool breeze made goosebumps appear on Hanifa's arms. It was such a contrast from the warm air upstairs.

Once down, she stopped and so did the tray. The bathroom door on the left was slightly ajar, with the light turned off. She looked straight ahead—the two rooms facing her were both shut. One served as a prayer room and the other as a guest room.

"Who's there?" Mustapha asked distantly, coughing.

She tilted her head, aiming her ear to pinpoint his location. The prayer room and the guest room were wall to wall, so she couldn't differentiate where his voice was coming from.

"It's Hanifa, Grandpa," she said, dropping her gaze. She bit her lip as her eyes went from the glass of water to the sourdough flatbread with the ten dollops of different vegetables and two boiled eggs on it. It was a rainbow on a plate indeed.

He emerged from the prayer room, and Hanifa caught a whiff of the familiar incense he brought with him. She inhaled deeply to fully take it in.

"Oh Hanifa! Come," he said, leading her to his studio

room. She smiled, pressing her thumb down on the flat, oval-shaped remote in her hand; a tray of food landed on a wooden mahogany table, the only table in the room. Another family heirloom they'd kept preciously over the years. Unlike the tables of her time that stood above the ground due to an invisible magnetic field, this one had a trapeze trunk in the middle, between the surface and square piece that grounded it to the floor. She pulled one of the three chairs and slumped in it as he walked past her to reach the sink.

"Smells delicious. What do we have? Hmm, lentils, collard greens, spicy tomato sauce, many more delicacies," he said, peeking at the plate. "Who cooked?" He turned around, starting to wash his hands.

"Mom," she replied flatly.

Mustapha narrowed his eyes at the tone of her voice. He wheeled around again and yanked the white towel hanging on the silver fridge door. He dried his hands and sat next to her by the table. Mustapha didn't need to use his wheelchair since the distance was small and manageable.

He pulled the plate closer to him. "Is everything okay with you?"

"It depends."

"On what, young one?" He raised an eyebrow as his chubby fingers dove into the shredded beets in front of him. He squeezed his round eyes shut and savored the taste for a moment as he waited for her answer.

"If it's health and social status, I'm okay *alhamdulillah*," she said. "I'm pleased with what the Almighty showered us with. However, if you're talking about life goals and achievements, I'm not okay. I feel like I was created for a higher purpose, something bigger." She banged her forehead on the table and held her head in her hands. Eyes shut closed, she breathed in and out slowly.

"And what's stopping you from achieving that 'something bigger'?" he demanded, shoving a handful of spinach and *injera* bread into his mouth.

"Mom and Dad are. You know that," she said, rolling her eyes. *Darn it, Grandpa, your Alzheimer's is getting annoying.* But she checked that impulse to speak her mind. It was cold, disrespectful, and she knew it.

"Right, sorry," he said. "But if you want my honest opinion, you can do anything you set your mind to. Besides, don't they know that you can't force teenagers to be what they don't want to be?"

Hanifa got up with a pivot, trudged to his bed, and sat on the beige cotton sheets. "What's the rebellion like?" she asked with a hint of doubt. She cupped her chin with both palms and pouted.

"Your parents wouldn't approve of me telling you these kind of stories. Come eat. You look thin and too preoccupied. Feed your soul and you'll be happier. Besides, those big cute dimples on your face are disappearing," he said, laughing.

She gaped at her grandpa in horror and shook her head to decline the meal invitation. Then she jetted to the mirror a few steps ahead of his bedframe, next to a back door. She tossed her face left and right in front of it, trying to see how bony her face had become so fast. She'd intensely studied and trained unarmed combat techniques and stealth attacks for her military techniques class in a span of two weeks. She was trying to keep her mind off things like saving the world and leading armies by staying busy in school.

"You eat or I won't tell you anything about the rebellion," said Mr. Kreedor, studying her intently.

"Bribing? Really Grandpa?" she threw up her hands in the air and then proceeded to wash them in his little sink so she could hear his tales before he changed his mind.

"I'm not going to tell you all this so that you can have ideas. I just want to satisfy your curiosity and that little rebellious side of yours that you try to inhibit. You know...you take after me with that." He winked and waved his index finger in her face.

Hanifa nodded and took a seat next to her Grandpa as he started explaining his past dedication.

"The rebellion has always been divided into four groups: the Sunnis, the Shiites, the Fundamentalists, and the

Zulmists. Though we were interested in getting support from the NOI, we never reached out to them. Anyway, the first two, as you may suspect, are harmless to some extent while the last two are bad news."

"Did you ever have to work with the bad guys?" Hanifa asked as she shoved some lettuce in her mouth, her eyes fixated on her grandfather's face.

He sighed and shifted uncomfortably in his seat. "Yes, as a member of the Sunnis' rebellion, we have a common enemy: the Seculars that persecute us day in, day out. So, all four groups tried to come together to try to take Sir Landry Big out, but the coup failed even though all the odds were on our side. We had a good number of soldiers, a-state-of-the-art military plan, and more than enough ammunitions with the latest technology," he cited, curling one finger after another in his left hand. "Some of which I engineered and pioneered. It was a beautiful plot," he finished dreamily.

"So why did it fail?" Hanifa asked, putting a piece of *injera* in her mouth.

Mustapha searched for words then paused. He reached for the glass of water and hydrated himself before finding the right word. "Discord."

"I know what Sunnis and Shiites are about. What do the Fundamentalists and Zulmists want?"

"They're blood thirsty individuals who love power and share our religion. They are also very intolerant toward the non-denominational population that is neither secular nor religious. Soon after we all united, Fundamentalists and Zulmists got ahead of themselves and made plans on Sir Landry's seat. Sunnis and Shiites lost many members to the last two groups as a result of brainwashing."

"Don't count your chickens before they hatch," she said, swallowing a boiled egg. "Do the last two groups even get along?"

"Of course not. Putting four strong, opinionated leaders at the same table is a daunting task even for a neutral party like myself. They criticize each other's leadership. All they did was throw the word '*takfeer*'—infidel—around the table as soon as a disagreement surfaced. Soon, every brother or sister used that word to fend off arguments. It got real nasty." Mustapha twisted his face in disgust.

"Sorry to hear that. Maybe it wasn't meant to be," Hanifa reasoned.

"Maybe. If you realize your dream to lead one day, make sure you have a united front. Okay?"

"Yes, Sir!" she said, straightening her chest and back in one upward movement.

Hanifa continued asking questions as they ate and laughed. She also learned that Sir Landry had been her grandpa's classmate in the old days. This discussion also opened a can of worms about the supernatural and sci-fi dimension. And Hanifa was eager to have her questions answered.

"Grandpa, do vampires and clones really exist?" Hanifa asked candidly. Her stomach twisted. Though she had seen it for herself in the stadium the other day, she hoped her grandfather would have some simple explanations to explain it all away.

"They do," Mustapha said and Hanifa could hear the change of tone in his voice. It was more serious. Hanifa deflated. "And usually rich Seculars have access to them because they want to be immortal. Controversial methods like cloning challenge and disrespect the holiness of the creation. They also deal with the unseen, commonly known as *djinns*, to create vampire that they genetically engineer later. Watch yourself out there, and be extremely careful around rich Seculars. Many will not stop at anything to be immortal, dear. Promise me you will be careful."

"I promise."

"Great, let's open my portable lab later and work on some engineering projects and cool inventions to help the *ummah!*" Mustapha said, glancing at the gray triangle remote a few inches from them on the table as Hanifa grinned widely. *That's what I'm talking about!*

***

In Hanifa's South African high school, she had longed

to have a club again but this time she wanted to achieve everything on her own and not involve anyone. So she saved her monthly allowance and tried to sell sweets she baked herself at fundraisers she organized all on her own. Auntie Dawn, whom she had done community service for plenty of times, gave her recipes that came very handy. Her mother did too.

Her new school was more secular compared to the one in Greenwuhud. She applied for a student exchange program to go to Turkey, hoping a third party would fund the trip.

"No, there is no extra money right now to allocate to this program," the staff teacher had told her. "You can self-fund, though—just make sure your parents approve and be sure to have an e-visa to enter the country. Here is the application and required information you need." He handed her a multitude of e-links to read on a tablet.

After she weeded her way through the dizzying links and their texts, she sat at the embassy for her visa request. *We always like to do things the hard way. I could have applied for a visa online and got my response right away*, she thought—but another voice countered: It leaves a trail.

They are going to do the same thing here, apply for me electronically.

Well, at least it won't be from your home computer where you could be traced.

But I'm on camera all over the place here. Hello!

As she continued to snap back and forth with her inner voice, she heard her name.

"Hanifa Ducktrinor," said an agent who had come out of an office.

"Here."

"Follow me," the middle age woman said. She had a beautiful brown skin and wore a very nice, professional navy-blue suit. "Please verify your name."

"Hanifa Kreedor—no, I mean Hanifa Ducktrinor." Hanifa wiped sweaty palms on her jeans skirt. Then she let out a nervous laugh.

The middle age woman examined her with squinted

eyes and proceeded. The interview was a success and Hanifa received her visa. She went home, running and skipping. Turkey at last! She recounted every tiny detail of the interview process to her parents.

"When I said Kreedor instead of Ducktrinor I thought I was done for," Hanifa confessed with worry. "She looked at me suspiciously but still gave me the visa."

"You slipped up our old made-up last name?" her father asked.

"Yes, it's no big deal. The proof: I have the visa."

"Oh no, that's what you think—or they *make* you think! Trust me, these people are trained to analyze every little details, and right now, I'm sure they're preparing to come arrest us with the whole shebang! We've got to get out of this country like yesterday!"

"But Mom and Dad, you're overreacting. I promise you we aren't in danger!"

"Kreedor is not a name you utter lightly, my dear. I'm afraid you don't understand or see the bigger picture yet. We're in danger now. We're in code *fitnah*. Get to packing right now!"

Temporarily paralyzed, Hanifa watched her father call her uncle Abu to verify that there was a planned hit on their heads. And there was one.

She watched her family members run around her like headless chickens, grabbing any necessities from their South African home. Everything else after that was a blur to Hanifa. When she came out of it, they were safely in Brazil and she was not allowed to speak to anyone outside of their home. Additionally, she wasn't allowed to share her desires and dreams to anyone. They were simply too inflammatory. "It's those crazy ideas we let you nurse all this time that landed us in these hot waters. If we had nipped it in the bud, you wouldn't have wanted to go to Turkey in the first place," they had vehemently said.

CHAPTER NINETEEN : SUSPICIONS & RECRUITMENTS

Hanifa

Timeline: Three weeks into school in Brazil

HANIFA SAT ON THE gray bench designated for people waiting outside of Sylas's office. She nervously tapped her sneaker-covered feet on the floor, and her thoughts raced. *Did I really think this through? The guy is sadistic, satanic, and more.* She nervously bit her lips until Sylas came out. A manly musk that seemed to cling to him immediately captivated her senses. Getting up from her seat whilst tightening her grip on a strap of her backpack, she realized his odor was redirecting her thoughts to a sudden inexplicable and fleshy desire.

"Well, well, what a surprise!"

He's a villain. Pull yourself together, she admonished herself and stared down at her feet, feeling embarrassed at such scandalous desires. "Can we talk?" she said, collecting herself.

"Sure, come in," he said, stepping to the side so she could enter his office.

She traipsed into the room and scanned it slowly. Then her eyes set on the beautiful view of the sunny morning outside the spotless glass. She stood still for a moment, admiring the calm of it all.

"Beautiful, right?" Sylas said, pulling her out of her daydream. He walked around her and stood a few inches in front of her.

She looked away from his searching eyes. In that quick second, she noticed that his irises weren't red but a beautiful green.

"Indeed," she replied as her mind raced further. *How is*

it possible to go from red eyes to green? Is he a clone? Something is strange with this guy.

Hanifa would have given anything for a third person to be in the room so that her temptation could be monitored and controlled by the buffer chaperone. Even if it was just the sketchy Judas and his rotund belly. She just felt too attracted to Sylas.

"Have you thought of my offer?" he prodded.

"Y-yes!" Hanifa was once again yanked away from her reverie with another of his questions. "I'm here to join your army."

He beckoned her to sit on the lavish ottomans floating in the air just slightly above ground, like enchanted carpets. Then he sat next to her, flaunting his class and distinct manners, his right hand palming his right cheek while his elbow gingerly rested on the armchair.

"I knew today was my lucky day!" His green eyes scintillated seductively.

A sultry feeling overtook Hanifa and she breathed out

to reject it and refocus on her plan.

Then she silently made the quick *dua* of surah 60:5. *Rabbana la tajAAalna fitnatan lillatheena kafaroo waighfir lana rabbana innaka anta alAAazeezu alhakeemu. Ameen.*

O Our Lord! Do not make us prey to those who disbelieve (lest, in overcoming us they think their unbelief to be true and increase therein). And forgive us, our Lord (especially those of our sins that may cause us to fall prey to those who disbelieve). You are the All-Glorious with irresistible might, the All-Wise. Ameen.

After that, she harrumphed and continued, "I'll join your army—on one condition."

"Anything! I'm glad you changed your mind," he replied, excited.

"I want to recruit talented students to form an elite Secular team, after the first day of training I spend with your officers to get a feel for what I need to do," Hanifa proposed.

"Why? It'll be a subgroup of a subgroup. Decentralization causes problems in the long run. That's why I'm everywhere and keep a tight leash on the Seculars in this school."

"You said *anything,*" Hanifa reminded him.

"That I did. Okay, fine. Give me their names when you put your list together," Sylas said.

Hanifa nodded and they continued talking about Secular business. Her muscles tensed up when she realized that she would have to arrest suspicious citizens—even end their lives when ordered.

"Do you think you have the stomach for it?" Sylas asked, studying her intently.

She nodded. "Piece of cake." She suddenly felt dirty from the lies she'd uttered. *Since when is it okay to waste a sacred human life to fit in?* As conflicted emotions and thoughts slightly distracted her from the meeting with Sylas, she made an extra effort to look normal.

Next, they talked about uniforms, and he instructed her to get in contact with the design and supply team since she wanted to make a few tweaks to the way they looked for her special team.

After she left his office, Hanifa heard him call Judas in.

***

The next day, as soon as Hanifa got to school with her siblings, she went her way as usual. As she walked, she felt the looming presence of an invisible shadow tracking her. She turned her head a few times, but didn't see anything. After incessant head rolls with no pinned culprits, she went to the library's restroom to change into her Secular uniform. She removed her knee-length orange tunic and white pants. After that, she tore off her knitted hat and folded all her clothes neatly before putting them back into her backpack.

Then she replaced her clothes with the white uniform, rocking a small "s" on her chest just as she had instructed the design and supply team to make. "Since the elite team is a subgroup of a subgroup, a small 's' will be fine," she had explained to Sylas. If only he knew what it truly meant for Hanifa.

The uniform was loose. *What an efficient and speedy design team*, she thought. She'd told Sylas that she didn't want to feel squeezed in a tight uniform where she couldn't breathe. She was grateful that they made her a medium-sized uniform even though a small could have worked perfectly. She carefully examined the uniform to make sure neither Sylas nor Judas had bugged it.

Let's start right with the undercover process, she thought. *All my routine moves stop today. He clearly stalks me.*

After she got dressed, Hanifa walked out of her restroom stall and looked left and right. When she saw no one, she mumbled *bismillah* and pulled down the baby changer that seemed odd in a place like a school. This clandestine addition to their interior design could have been a dead giveaway for the Seculars, but fortunately they hadn't noticed the oddity.

A blank, glassy pad appeared on the wall inside the changer. She pinched her right index to her right thumb, making a circle, while the other three fingers stuck out erect. The pad immediately came to life and, like lock and key, fit together. A door opened in the wall next to the baby changer. Hanifa walked into the mosque—a sign in front of her read

Sisters' Entrance. She smiled. The last time she had seen such a sign outside of Brazil was in her dear Greenwuhud. While it was a happy moment for her to feel alive again at the sight of this house of worship, she still felt a pang of sadness in her heart for her home that had been burnt to the ground by Seculars. At that moment, she envied the first Muslims who had been driven out of Mecca out of persecution, but eventually returned to their home—Mecca still standing and ever more beautiful and powerful as their numbers had swollen.

"Tell me why I shouldn't obliterate you right now. I trusted you and never even ran a background check on you!" Dawud said as he aimed a laser gun at her. He pulled her out of her haze with his threat.

"DON'T SHOOT! This is the plan I was telling you about. I'm undercover." Her hands high in the air, Hanifa approached him slowly. "You can trust me. I'm not a real Secular officer. Please put that thing away, it's dangerous. Remember we talked about a small 's' sign to distinguish between Seculars and Sunnis/Shiites?"

"Kinda. Explain quickly before I lose my patience. And stay where you are," Dawud told her, still leering at the sight of a Secular's uniform in the mosque, clearly unsure of what to believe.

"I have successfully infiltrated the Seculars' organization. Well, I was offered the position because I aced the test. I wasn't interested, but Sylas stalked me and popped out of nowhere every time I was on campus. I said no each time, until I found this mosque. This place restored my faith in my goals and dreams of using the school to help educate and lead an expedition to Tarsus."

"What goals and dreams?" Dawud asked, perplexed.

"I told you! Fatima Al-Farihi. The Cave. Gog and Magog…" Hanifa rolled her eyes, annoyed.

"Oh," he said finally, lowering his weapon. "You joined so that you can recruit others like you who are fake Seculars…who joined to remove any doubt about their true religion from anybody's mind?"

Hanifa nodded proudly, amazed by the sharpness of the kid at last. "There must be a lot of crypto Muslims out there. It came to me last time when you said that only a few Muslims took the risk to come pray here during the day. Many people don't advertise what they are for fear of being persecuted. They'd rather blend into the crowd and not attract attention to themselves."

"It's true!" Dawud said. "I don't know why I didn't think about it at first. It makes so much sense! Do you have concrete plans to recruit this select group of crypto Muslims? I don't know if the girls will happily join."

"I do have a plan. I just don't know if the girls will fall for it too. To brief you, it's going to be a Secular elite team and that's where you come in. I want you to find a group in the Secular database, a group of boys and girls that performed really well in the religion aspects of the Secular Army test—and I'll try to recruit them after I get a feel for their mental fabric. I already have names picked out! $(CO)_2$—Courageous Coreishy and the Sahabas X.0!"

"Hmm, like a mommy picking out names for her future babies. It's like a Dad's Army, only you're the mom. Anyway, your plan seems dangerous. How did Sylas even allow you to have your own elite team? Surely, he isn't dumb enough to not keep an eye on you…"

Hanifa wanted to laugh at his remarks of Dad's Army; she didn't understand how he knew about such an old thing, but the feeling dissipated quickly. As soon as he said "eye on you," Hanifa's demeanor changed. The hair on the back of her neck stood up and her body temperature dropped. "Talking of tracking, today I had the strangest feeling ever. I felt like I was being followed by something or someone. The feeling disappeared once I entered the women's restroom," Hanifa said.

"Well, good thing I gave you the sisters' secret passage to the mosque. Besides, it looks like your follower wasn't a pervert after all. Most cameras or drones that spy are made in a way that they don't invade your privacy that way." Dawud held his tongue in his cheek, rolling his eyes halfway.

"Ha! Okay, you think you can handle that task I asked you to do?"

"Of course!"

"Alright, don't get caught and see you later," Hanifa said before praying two *rakats* in her uniform, which she had untucked so that it covered her behind. Then she left the mosque the same way she had come in.

***

"Hey girl! What did you eat last night? You took forever in that bathroom," Judas said, his back resting on the wall outside the bathroom. He fiddled with a small black helicopter in his hands, juggling the thing up and down in his palm.

"Eww, none of your business," Hanifa said.

"Did you wash your hands?"

"Judas, if you didn't notice, I was changing into my new clothes," Hanifa told him, pointing at herself. "Wait a minute. Are you following me?"

"No!" He said the word like it was an insult, like she

had insinuated something along the lines of him loving her. "Pffft, I just saw you coming into the library and wanted to wish you a good first day with us."

"Is that so? Well, the time I spend in the bathroom changing is none of your concern!" What had he seen or heard? Sweat beads formed on her face. She needed to distance herself from him quickly.

"Relax, psycho, I was just trying to be nice."

"Sure. You're gross; please stay out of my way," Hanifa said, leaving the library to attend her classes. Then the memory of being here last time with Ana crossed her mind. *I wonder what she's up to.*

***

Hanifa's first mission as a Secular officer started with a patrol of the school with other Secular officers. She'd watched the training videos and done the practice exercises with the weapons after her meeting with Sylas, so she knew how to proceed. Any student who openly displayed religious signs or wore an obvious religions garment had to be arrested, interrogated, tortured, and possibly killed.

She started the day apprehensive, worrying that her siblings might find her out as she strolled around the school whenever class wasn't in session. Then she realized that she had a helmet she could use to hide her face. Very quickly, she put it on and felt better disguised.

As she walked, she studied the clothes of the students. They were colorful and mostly made of fishnets or sheer fabric. All body parts were exposed except for the opaque material that covered the bosoms, genitals, and butt cheeks. The memory of her first days at Castle 5 came running back to her again.

She sighed at the view of their *awrat* parts hanging out so freely and averted her sight to wander even more. "So when do you get time to rest if we patrol between classes?" Hanifa had asked.

"We sleep through class or mostly skip it," the Secular officer replied, shrugging. "Besides, I don't need school. I'm doing exactly what I'll be doing when I graduate from here."

"Okay…" Hanifa said, pursing her lips.

To the left of the pathway, one officer addressed a couple of religious rebels wearing the *hijab*. "Remove the scarves or I will taser you both," he warned the two girls wearing dusty pink and coral headscarves with full-length black dresses.

The girls didn't comply so the officers arrested them.

Then more Secular officers patrolling with Hanifa arrested a young man wearing a Jewish hat standing to the right of the pathway.

"It's my freedom of speech!" the young man yelled in Portuguese as the officers tackled him down.

Hanifa felt a pang of sadness for the torture and death the arrestees could possibly face for being so open in these *fitna* times. She admired their courage but thought they were fools for not having more sense of self-preservation. *And you do, with all your jihad plans?* A voice inside her quipped. *Touché.*

She planned to avert her eyes from anybody that looked remotely religious, whether they were Jewish, Christian, or Muslim. *If you see anything religious, look the other way and pray for their safety.* As she rehearsed that plan in her head over and over, Lucas, another Secular officer, interpolated his orders.

"Yo, SO#6-16-Duckies, don't just stand there. Get to work! Look at 2 o'clock, easy target!"

Hanifa stopped abruptly, feeling crushed.

CHAPTER TWENTY : TESTS & RECRUITMENTS

Hanifa

Timeline: Three weeks into school in Brazil

I GUESS I CAN'T pretend to be blind after all. She looked at the target to her right and realized she was wearing a *burqa. Seriously? You don't watch the news?* Hanifa thought, incensed as she approached the target.

"Stay back or I'll detonate the bomb," a feminine voice said under the black robes.

"Target is armed!" Hanifa yelled and stopped walking

as sweat beads formed on her face under the helmet. *Snap, what do I do in this case?* She tried to recall her training. *Forget it! Improvise!* So she went for it. "Sister, my name is Hanifa. You'll be taking a lot of innocent lives with you, dear. Doesn't that strike you as unjust?"

The girl scoffed under the veil. "Well, my name is Latife, and I don't have anything to lose. You want to talk about unjust when you people arrest us religious folks on a whim or out of spite and dictatorship? You oppress us day in and out. You kill us and our families! You should really think before you talk."

"Just shoot her! It's standard procedure!" Lucas yelled from behind Hanifa.

"I got this!" Hanifa wagered.

"You're not a diplomat! Neutralize your target!" Nate said. Other Secular officers were becoming alerted of the situation.

"Secular Officer#6-16-Duckies, control your target ASAP or we will!" another officer in the foot-patrol training group she was part of warned behind her.

But before she could say another word, the girl lifted her hand in the air like she was about to press a detonator. *You leave me no choice*, Hanifa thought, defeated, as she pulled her laser gun and shot the girl.

The target slumped to the ground, graceful as a feather. Then her palm unrolled, revealing emptiness. It had been a bluff.

Hanifa fell to her knees. *I killed an innocent person.* Tears welled into her eyes and she started sobbing quietly and without theatrics. There was no coming back from killing an innocent person. It was a point of no return.

"Well rookie, you're initiated now!" the officers behind her cheered as they gave her pats of encouragements on the back.

"She was bluffing! She was bluffing!" Hanifa kept repeating like a mad person, fighting their hands off of her.

"We know. That's why we took you on this route today; it never fails. Her suicidal daring kind always make a show in this area." The group of officers made a cacophony of sounds, puffing in laughter. Proud of themselves.

Hanifa felt furious. She had taken a precious life. What had Latife meant by she didn't have anything to lose? That was suicide.

A gloomy fog followed Hanifa all day after that. If she asked to be released early or give up on being a mole, this girl's untimely death would have been for nothing. She needed to make things right and suck it up! While she felt at the lowest by ending someone's life, she felt even more determined to ask for forgiveness from God and the parents of Latife, whom she planned on visiting secretly. She reckoned the parents would surely hate her for killing their daughter, but she would try to contact them if there was any next to kin available. Now more ever, she needed to ride solo or seriously recruit her own army like she'd originally asked Sylas to avoid the same incident to repeat itself.

That awful wanting-to-die feeling didn't desert Hanifa as her siblings brought up the incident at home later the same day.

"This is sad and messed up!" Shafiya said heatedly.

"Very," Malik added.

Unable to tell them why, Hanifa just stormed out of the room, once again enraged and balling her eyes out. They had looked at her with quizzical looks as she stormed out.

***

A week after Latife's death, Sylas called Hanifa into his office.

"How was your first week?"

"Fine."

"The other officers don't like you. They find you hard to read, distant, and cold."

"I didn't join the Seculars to make friends," she shot back.

"Whoa, easy girl. You have the right attitude, but if it's too much on you psychologically, you're free to resign." Sylas held her gaze.

For a minute she saw the ghost of a compassionate

smile on his face. *Who knew?* "I can handle it."

"Great! I knew you could. Please report to me in another week."

"That soon? Aren't you too busy to track all the officers weekly?" she asked.

"I'm busy, but your high performance will reflect better on our school numbers when we meet with Sir Landry Big himself."

"Okay." Hanifa left Sylas's office and continued being a secret Secular officer.

Her daily routine bored her to death. All day long, she repeated the same phrases.

"Give me your scarf or I'll taser you."

"Give me your *kipa* or I will punch you in the face."

"Wipe that red dot off your face or I'll wipe it with bleach."

As boring as her new job was though, the second week went by fast and before she knew it, she was back in Sylas's office.

"That's it?! You only made confiscations of religious garments? No arrests or death sentences?" Sylas's voice roared in the room. "And you want me to give you a team when you're underperforming on your own? That's strike two!"

Hanifa knew this would happen so she was ready to take it. She pretended to make herself small in his presence. *Oh yes, please continue the show. You're a very powerful man, and I should be "ashamed of my performance." While I want this team badly, I won't sell my soul for it.*

"You suck at this job! Theory and application are clearly two different things. If I didn't need the numbers, I would have fired you."

"I will deliver," Hanifa reassured him.

"You better, or you can forget that little team of Secular officers you want to lead!" Sylas screamed, and Hanifa covered her ears from his loud tantrum.

When the third week came along and there was no progress on Hanifa's part, she began to see him everywhere. Once, she found him waiting for her outside the women's restroom. Her heart dropped. *What if he went after me in the restrooms and saw me going or leaving via the secret door?*

"Are you following me?" she asked Sylas.

"Maybe. And perhaps if I constantly watch over your shoulder every now and then, that will push you into making the arrests and death sentences I need. You could say I'm out for blood," he said lazily.

"I don't need a chaperone, Sir," Hanifa said and resumed patrolling.

"Sure you don't," Sylas replied, but he still followed her everywhere, including to her classes. A couple of days before the start of the fourth week, she was in the corridor heading to the library, and he was behind her. She picked up the pace, turned right, and disappeared at the men's entrance to the *masjid*.

"*Alhamdullilah,*" she exclaimed the minute she had vacuumed safely inside the mosque. "*Assalamu aleikum Dawud,*" Hanifa said, sprawled all over the *musalla*, trying to catch her breath.

"*Wa aleikum salam.* Is he still following you?"

"Like clockwork!" Hanifa and Dawud then laughed as Sylas made circles around himself trying to figure out where Hanifa had gone in a split second.

"On a more serious note, I need your help with some prisoners I arrested because he made me do it," Hanifa pleaded.

"Sure, anything."

***

When her arrests poured in, Sylas finally honored her request and officially granted her the green light to have her own Secular army. Screens all over the school displayed the same message:

If you think you have what it takes, join the Secular elite team. Simply key in your name below in the box displayed on the screen.

The prestige of joining an elite Secular team spread like wild fire through the school.

"Too many people applied! How are we going to distinguish between so many applicants?" Dawud said, freaking out. "We didn't need this. I already have the list of highest score test takers who did well in ancient religions."

"It's simple," Hanifa said calmly. "We'll compare the names on your list to the names on the application. The ones who didn't apply from your list are probably the religious ones. They obviously don't need to be in an elite team. It brings them closer to disbelieving, if I am correct in trying to think like them. Right now, they're low-key and safe in the Secular system. They don't need to bring attention to themselves." She wore a calculating expression, like a chess player, as her hand cupped her chin.

"That's brilliant!" Dawud said.

"Now I just have to have a tête-à-tête with the non-applicants. I'm also thinking about getting into contact with all the surviving families of my old town to see if they want to join. I know for a fact who is a believer and who isn't," she finished more somberly.

Dawud eyed her suspiciously. "That's cool... So...I thought playing head doctor was fun. Why are you so gloomy?"

"I'm gloomy because I broke my promise to my parents. And it's only a matter of time before they find out what I'm up to. I'm just tired of running."

***

That same night, dinner at the Ducktrinors' home was interesting. "Like having Seculars isn't enough, now they're assembling an elite team!" Malik told their father at the dinner table.

Hanifa immediately tensed up. *Uh oh.* But she remained quiet to see how the news would play out.

"Haven't you heard the Secular Army is the American ROTC of the era? They aim to recruit the best of the best and continue ruling the world in a Nazi way," Shafiya noted sarcastically as she chewed her spoonful of rice. "Thankfully, many Seculars choose to have other jobs after leaving school. I mean, otherwise we wouldn't have any doctors, tailors, bakers, farmers, etc. That said, these same people will drop anything the minute the Secular Military Corp summons them."

She's right. These people are loyal, but what's up with her tone? Hanifa thought. Shafiya wasn't the type to have snappy remarks. *Maybe she had a bad day.*

Malik shot her a look while their parents mulled over the elite team news. "What do you think, Hanifa?" he asked.

"I don't know. The elite team is up to something big for sure," she said. Then she averted her eyes and continued eating her minty yoghurt.

"I'll tell you what I think," Shafiya said. "I think they're up to something, and if we can't fight them, we might as well join them. I'm tired of starting over or getting abused at schools by them. I need to get myself some power! Uncle Abe is a testimony that it's possible to hide inside their ranks." She eyed her parents from the corners of her eyes.

Hanifa was taken aback. Something was definitely off with her sister. And she had to act quickly before this blew up in her face. "You can't just join. They pick between existing officers," Hanifa told her.

"How do you know that?" they all asked as if on cue.

"I just heard people talking about it at school," she said quickly.

The fog lifted from their faces and they seemed to grow less suspicious of her.

"Yo Malik, are they hiring at your job at the movie theater?" Shafiya asked.

"I don't know. I will ask," Malik said and their father cut in.

"Well, children, stay away from the Secular Army and the elite team recruitment. Is that understood?" their father asked.

"Yes, Sir," the children replied while Hanifa mumbled her response under her breath.

How will they react if they find out that I'm the one behind it? she thought with a divided and heavy heart. *I need to convince them to let me pursue my dreams. This is my calling and I need their blessings if I want this mission to take over the school and go to Tarsus to succeed.*

***

At a young age, Hanifa had picked up on marking celestial events. She was into astronomy. Thirty nights, recorded by her celestial abilities, passed before Hanifa could get a hold of any of Latife's relatives. Latife's parents, like many other clandestine Muslims, were getting ready for the *Hajj* pilgrimage. When they didn't see their daughter come home one day, they had a crypto Muslim Secular officer inquire and claim her body for *janazzah* and other funeral rituals before they quickly escaped Paraty to Saudi Arabia, where Muslims were still free to practice their religion. Dawud, with his tech abilities, and Hanifa with her software engineering skills, had tracked Latife's parents' biometric identities being scanned at Mecca's entrance.

After these thirty nights of searching for Latife's parents, the weather was around 77°F, and it felt like springtime even though it was still fall in other places in the world like North America. Aside from the luscious green ecosystem, the city of Paraty had also re-animated beautiful and bright flowers of all kinds; there were roses, daffodils, tulips, bluebells, and many other flowers she didn't know the names of across town. While Hanifa longed to smell real flowers, she was happy the flowers across town were fake. *At least there is no pollen to trigger my allergies. Bittersweet situation.*

Hanifa had spent her first weeks at school split between making The Supplies she would need for her future expedition in the engineering home lab, studying, patrolling, searching for the dead religious activist's parents, and hanging out with Dawud when time allowed.

They usually worked on designing more of The Supplies together. Hanifa had a vision on how The Supplies would look, what problems they would solve, and who would need them. Therefore, she worked hard to make sure she could bring them to life with her curiosity and problem solving skills.

Ana, on the other hand, had disappeared and Hanifa wished that she had a means to contact her. She missed the girl. Hanifa found it odd that they'd never exchanged contacts.

Did she guess I had an attraction to Sylas? Hanifa became horrified at the thought of Ana pegging her as a boyfriend stealer. But she decided to put the thought aside.

When *Eid al-Adha* came a few days later, Hanifa invited Dawud over to celebrate the holiday with her family, knowing that he was an orphan. Her family accepted her introduction of Dawud at face value and she was grateful they didn't dig deeper. She only told the whole story to her Grandpa whom she trusted more.

"Mr. Kreedor?" Dawud had asked when she introduced him to her grandfather.

"The one and only," Mustapha had replied.

Dawud gaped at Hanifa's grandfather in complete awe. "I never imagined I would meet you in person. Not once whatsoever."

"Is that so?" Mustapha asked, elated.

Dawud nodded and they bonded instantly, like a grandson and grandfather separated ages ago. Their shared interest in technology and electronics made the connection deeper. They planned to team up with Hanifa to create new gadgets and toys that would continue to help with the safety of crypto Muslims in their times.

CHAPTER TWENTY-ONE :
MEETINGS AND PLACES

Hanifa

HANIFA, MUSTAPHA, AND DAWUD played the video again and again in bewilderment in the Ducktrinors' basement. The portable engineering lab of Mr. Kreedor they had been working in to make The Supplies no longer held their interest. Another thirty nights or so had passed, and they had just secretly observed the day of *Ashura* with the beginning of a new Islamic year in that month of *Muharram*. They had prayed and fasted for themselves and the Muslims of their time so that Allah would facilitate living with the Seculars always on the lookout.

But things were getting worse by the day and it was predestined. On the screen of Mustapha's TV, a light-skinned man announced to the nation a new law and order passed by His Excellency Sir Landry Big.

"Effective immediately, no head garments are allowed—whether you are a fashion designer, a fashion major, an art major, or an artist. Anyone that displays or wears ancient clothing or artifacts shall be apprehended and put to death immediately. Signed, Sir Landry Big. I'm Corayto Kreedor, new Press Secretary. Thank you for your service, Secular officers."

Dawud was the first to react with words. "Your brother is the press secretary? When did this happen?"

"Half-brother," Hanifa and Mustapha corrected. This was bad. They remained silent, trying to wrap their heads around this new appointment.

"I need to talk to him," Mustapha said with a croaky, hoarse voice.

"This is madness. You need to meet these lunatics

ASAP," Dawud said as his computer spotted more flashing news from *The Muezzin* and *Radio Al Bayanne*. "Look"— he pointed at the screen of his device—"the Secular officers are massacring the masses who aren't walking around nearly naked in fishnets and see-through garments. God have mercy on us. This video is a blood bath."

Speechless, the trio witnessed men and women, boys and girls, being shot the minute they were spotted with a head scarf, a *kufi*, or just too many clothes on. Some were dragged behind hexagon cars until their burned and marred bodies billowed lifelessly. Then, they were dropped on the ground like weightless objects.

"This is unjust. Many of these people didn't even have the chance to hear the news. It's a purge and a message to us. He wants us to know that he's capable of way worse," Hanifa said disheartened.

"I agree, this is definitely a message," her grandfather vouched.

"The death toll is reaching millions across the globe!"

Dawud yelled. "It's a global purge. We need to do something now!"

"We need to think before we act," Hanifa added calmly with a glassy dazed look. "This is about more than just the deaths of fashion and design laborers in former developing countries."

"What do you mean?" Waves of confusion washed over Dawud's blue eyes.

"Fashion was the excuse used to wear anything religious for most crypto Muslims. Now the Seculars aren't buying it. And fashion has been at the source of deaths due to poor working conditions in these poor countries. Deaths related to 'fashion' strike again. But the real problem here is demonic greed."

"I see, you're making a connection with the number of deaths," Dawud said.

"Let's stay focused Hanee. Right now, we need to think of a response for the future not the past. It is not the time to think of Pakistan, Bangladesh, or any other poor countries victim to the world of fashion," Mustapha said.

After that, Mustapha made a lot of calls and finally got a trusted source on the line.

"Is this a secure line, son?" Mr. Kreedor asked calmly.

"Yes, Pop."

"Why didn't you tell us about Corayto?" Mustapha demanded sternly, his voice going up a notch.

"I didn't know. I was just as surprised as you," Abu defended himself.

"I need to talk to them. Can you arrange a meeting, son?" Mustapha asked.

"I can try, Pop. No promises—and it won't be easy. I'll risk my cover on this one. Did you try to contact Uncle Corayto directly?"

"He's changed all his previous ways of communication," Mustapha replied, sighing deeply.

"Alright, I'll see what I can do," Abe said before Mustapha let him talk to Hanifa. She asked him cryptic questions about higher parts of the Secular government that only he could know because they weren't listed in the books or Secular manuals. She sensed hesitation in his answers a few times, but he seemed preoccupied with his uncle Corayto's business, and answered her questions anyway.

After the call, the group continued to follow the news. The Seculars' electronic magazine, *The Irreligious*, had also started circulating propagandas. Undoubtedly sponsored by the government, the publication offered bigger rewards and incentives to whistleblowers. Their news also had one main goal—brainwash the masses by giving them wrongful facts about non-Seculars, such as reporting that religions with divine intervention were a hoax cooked up by great storytellers and supported by the rebellion. They claimed these rebels had all been apprehended and accounted for. So, people shouldn't worry about their safety and being forced into conversion by the rebellion one day.

At school, it became harder for Hanifa to shake off Sylas. "I'm going to take a pee break since you want to know what I'm up to at all times. You have trust issues." She rolled her eyes.

"You're damn right, I have trust issues. How do you explain the fact that many of your arrestees escaped right under our nose?" Sylas asked.

Dawud struck your database, she pinned secretly with great pride.

"Ask your head of security. The guards. Anybody except me; I just deliver them to the guards and they lock them up. How did they escape your tight surveillance? Like I said, it's a question for your head of security. Judas has never liked me; maybe he's throwing wrenches in the works for me." She knew she was being creative with her words, but it didn't stop her. Dawud had been the Master of Unlocking Cells, and she couldn't be more proud of his hacking skills.

Sylas eyed her with a cryptic look. "Fine. You got your five-minute pee break."

Whew! Five minutes is not even enough if I make wudu. I'm glad I still have ablutions. She raced through the sisters' entrance and immediately started calling the *adhan* followed by the *iqamat*; then she started the first afternoon prayer with "*Allahu Akbar*—God is Great."

"Hanifa, you've been in the restrooms for a while. Are you OK?" Sylas inquired.

"Hanifa, sorry to interrupt but you need to finish your prayer quickly. Based on the camera feed, this bozo is trying to get into the women's restroom," Dawud warned as she prayed. She could still hear Dawud's words and tried her best to not lose count of her *rakats* and focus during her precious moments of worship.

"It's been five minutes! I will come in if you don't come out in another minute. Screw it, I'm coming in."

"Get out or I will use this pepper spray on you!" Hanifa said, holding the can in front of his face. She had just appeared from the secret door and took long strides to meet Sylas at the restroom's door to prevent him from coming in.

"Please try. These red eyes are pepper-spray proof," he said in a fit of laughter.

"Are you done yet?" she asked as he continued

laughing and coughing uncontrollably.

"Almost," he replied as he held his belly.

Since orders didn't seem to have any effect, she opted for a "nicer way." "I need some privacy, please. Please exit the women's restrooms so I can resume my affairs."

"Sure, now that you found your manners. I just had to make sure you didn't vanish like last time."

"Get out, you perv!" another girl piped into their conversation from behind a closed stall. Hanifa smiled at this.

"Shut it! I was on my way out on my own accord anyway!" Sylas cursed.

"Vanish?" Hanifa giggled denying her disappearances from his regular monitoring. "You need new eyes. I was in the library. You're just not good at playing hide-and-seek, player," she said, winking.

"Are you flirting with me?"

"Ew! Get out!" Hanifa demanded, and Sylas complied.

***

After the religious garment ban, the Ducktrinors,

Dawud, and the *ummah* of Castle 5 continued to keep a low profile until school was out for vacation. *Mawlid*, the birthday of Rasoollulah *sallallahu aleihi wassalam*, came during the school's thirty days of vacation. It was an opportunity for Hanifa and her siblings to spend time outside with kids their own age, with the permission of their parents. Some weekends the family would travel in their personal red flying LOHLA car to Rio de Janeiro to relax and spend time as a family. Most beaches on the coastline were nude beaches so the family would avoid those. But every now and then, they would stumble upon an empty piece of beach where they could run and play wild until the empty, cozy place would be spotted and flooded with more naked people.

On days she was alone, Hanifa went hunting for an abandoned place she could use to train, pray, and just be herself far away from the Secular officers and civilization. After about twenty-one nights, she spotted an old and vast warehouse. It was perfect. She swept the perimeter to assure herself it was really empty and up for grabs. Then she spent the next week of Paraty's summer, which was winter for many other countries, cleaning the place and adding high-tech cameras and security gadgets she got from her father's and grandfather's labs. She made the place so homey that she had a bed and all her required necessities at arm's reach. This was all possible with the help of an application she developed—thanks to her grandfather's mentorship—that worked like a zipped file; it helped reduce real objects instead of electronic files.

The need for comfort also gave her the idea to design a tent equipped with everything she could easily move around with, in case this place became unavailable and she had to squat somewhere else. *I'm sure Grandpa will help me design it with all his engineering skills, insha'Allah,* she thought decidedly.

In the meantime, she had dubbed the warehouse Knights Inn, rationalizing the name by telling herself that she was an unconventional knight. And Hanifa was all about defying conventions, in her own *halal* way.

When school started seven days after her Knights Inn discovery, Hanifa was elated to go back to share her new discovery. She couldn't wait to see the girls and inquire about their break stories. Ana was one friend lost and though Hanifa had won another three, she was worried and really wanted to find that Shadow Hunter so she could figure out where Ana was. *I hope nothing happened to her.*

Hanifa had also spotted Judas by the mosque's sealed door a few times. She reckoned he was still obsessed with the false location for the hacks. Every day since the second day of school, Dawud told her that Judas had stopped there and stared at the wall for answers. Her fears were confirmed when she overheard him talking with Sylas.

"But the scan revealed nothing behind the walls," he told Sylas again. "Something isn't right. I'm good at these things. I know one can hide behind some of the walls of the school. Besides, we used the same technology to trap and imprison religious activists and suspected believers."

At these words, she made sure to tell Dawud and the rest of the mosque attendants to be even more careful than before, until they moved to a safer place.

Even if non-Seculars weren't caught flagrantly worshipping, if the Seculars had doubts about them, the Seculars would make people pay a huge fine and torture them if they couldn't pay before letting them go. This quickly drove many out of religion, as people's spirits became broken and they started doubting the presence of a God who would allow such a punishment on good servants like them even though religious texts are filled with devout people being tested. *Tried & Tested!* Do the people think that they will be left to say, "We believe" and they will not be tried? (Quran 29:2)

But the cold truth was, people didn't like to be tested. And with these thoughts in the back of her mind, after almost half a year at the school, Hanifa decided to go admire the *mihrab* of the mosque one afternoon. On her way, she passed the *minbar* on the right where the Imam is supposed to stand and address the *ummah*. Dawud assumed that position. He would seal the walls as he called the *adhan* and the *iqamat* before each prayer he led.

The figurative art on this prayer niche was stunning.

Blue, gold, green, and brown tiles blended intricately and beautifully together like a colorful tapestry. With careful and gentle hands, Hanifa touched the tiles. They felt warm with enchanting energy. The Arabic letters on it weren't hard to decipher in the crafty calligraphy she marveled upon.

Hanifa took her time like she was savoring a delicious meal and touched the tiles, one after another, with respect and awe. Then she finally came upon the middle part of the niche. The *basmala* was inscribed in a rectangle with golden and beautiful designs. She whispered "*bismillah*" and pressed it with the tips of her right four fingers. Almost instantly, the rectangle moved inward and spat out a little matrix.

Hanifa gasped lowly and read the text on it: *Shadow Hunter.* Without considering if it was a trap or not, she grabbed it and uttered, "*Subhanallah!*"

At her cry of amazement, the girls ran to Hanifa to peek at her discovery. Even Dawud left his guard post to come look. When Hanifa explained what it was, they all agreed that it was a huge score for them. Now she could find Ana and she couldn't wait to use it! At the end of the day, with all the events of the day, they left the *masjid* for home, happy and distracted.

The next day came quickly and with a punch to the core of the *masjid* congregation. The school's HD screens displayed a new top score set by Judas—The Secular Tracker and Information Technology guy.

"We're pleased to announce that a site of worship for some Muslim believers has been discovered behind the wall of the library and has been set alight, with containable fire designed by Judas. We will be replacing the site of worship with a Secular party lounge. Hail to the S! The world will never end!"

Hanifa felt sick. They had forgotten to set the alarm and stealth program that protected the mosque the day before. She blamed herself for exciting the congregation while Dawud blamed himself for failing to do his job as the keeper, Imam, and *muezzin* of the mosque. Overall, they were all sad and stricken by the same misfortune. The mosque's cat had died in that fire, and that loss saddened them even more. It was

Dawud's cat and companion more than anything.

"We're truly sorry for your loss," each member had told Dawud with teary eyes and a fallen face.

Dawud nodded, sniffing to all the words of support. His blue eyes had become red. Hanifa gave him a hug and kissed him on his pink cheeks.

"Thanks," Dawud replied, appreciative of the warm and friendly embrace.

Later Hanifa remembered Knights Inn and, with a quick touch of a remote, called them all for a group meeting with the meet-up coordinates. The remote was the system designed by Dawud in case of emergency. The last time the mosque was almost raided, he'd decided to come up with a better plan to warn the rest of the community if something disastrous happened, such as the one they were contemplating at the moment.

This was also the turning point for Hanifa.

In the past, Dawud had insisted that they anonymously share their plans in *The Muezzin* and rally support from other crypto Muslims around the world who read the e-zine.

Hanifa had vehemently opposed Dawud's idea. "Absolutely not. This is a great way to get uncovered fast. I mean really fast. You know the Seculars read it too. Security will increase and more believers will pay the price."

"Hanee, there is no revolution without blood spilled. I know I'm too young to say that but it's true. Okay, let's say you take over the school with about two hundred recruits, based on the crypto list we've put together. What after that? There are millions of Secular officers everywhere. You need the numbers to stand a chance of winning the school!"

She had stayed quiet for a minute and pondered his words. She agreed and then she disagreed. She went back and forth with it.

Now with the mosque burned and taken away from them, Dawud's words were vivid in her mind. He was right; even though she believed that God would be there to protect them, she needed to tie her camel by increasing soldier numbers. She needed to help herself first before God would help her.

"Okay, let's do it," Hanifa said, once the few members of the Castle 5 *ummah,* comprised of the elite team, had safely teleported to Knights Inn.

"Let's do what?" Dawud asked, puzzled.

"Let's broadcast to scavenge more help and speed up the recruiting process."

"Yes! I told you we need to put all the chances on our side." Dawud jumped in glee, almost knocking his computer from the legless, clear counter.

"But we still need an interrogation room at school behind the wall," Hanifa insisted. "We can't risk them following us here."

So with the alias of *Lady H*, her back turned to the recording device and her yellow *khimar* down her back like a superhero cape, Hanifa broadcasted her plans to the world. Dawud and the rest of the elite team worked to disguise her voice so she could safely deliver her message to the listeners and readers of *The Muezzin* all over the world, and *Al Bayanne* on the radio, which was only in Africa. Dawud, face hidden, decked out in a red and white *keffiyeh* and using the alias of Brother D, broadcasted a message, too, encouraging people to stand against the Seculars that oppressed them.

In retaliation to this drastic move, the Seculars launched a raid, targeting anybody whose name started with H and D. If anyone was caught rocking anything in yellow, they were arrested. Students' belongings were searched; if a student was found sporting or hiding a *keffiyeh*, he was in deep trouble.

Lady H, or "Sister H" as others called her, was a hot bug amongst many defiers. She was a new sensation in a world where people loved trendy things. *The Irreligious* dubbed her "The Contumacious Girl." Of course the Zulmists based in Africa and the Fundamentalists based in America despised her and made anyone who read e-zines aware that a woman's place was at home and not fighting wars.

"Fighting a good fight is a man's job," they'd said to the world. Hanifa imagined them spitting as they dropped the words "man's job." *Haters*, she had dismissed them.

CHAPTER TWENTY-TWO : THE SAHABAS X.O & THE (CO)2

Hanifa

Timeline: About mid-school year in Brazil

HANIFA STOOD IN FRONT of the male recruits in the warehouse. "We have a motto for you guys that we found in old books, and we loved it!" she said. "Have:

The faith of Ibrahim-*aleihi salam*

The glory of Yusuf-*aleihi salam*

The life of Mussa-*aleihi salam*

The victory of Issa-*aleihi salam*

The courage of Dawud-*aleihi salam*

The riches of Suleymane-*aleihi salam*

And the wisdom and fidelity of Muhammad-*aleihi*

salam."

Her male officers cheered.

"That's what I'm talking about!"

"*Masha'Allah!*"

"*Takbir!*"

Multiple simultaneous responses of "*Allahu akbar!*" followed.

Hanifa beamed with pure joy. It was a dream come true. Getting a group of determined young men to help take over the school and lead an expedition was an arduous task she had finally almost conquered. She remembered how they'd challenged her in the first days. Winning over Hamza, in particular, had been a huge victory for the birth of the *Sahabas X.0*. He'd since helped her recruit and convince more to join the ranks of the *Sahabas X.0*.

"Read," Hanifa had ordered Hamza when she first started vetting him.

"I don't know how to read," Hamza had replied, strapped to a new kind of lie detector test Hanifa, Dawud, and her grandfather Mustapha had designed to interrogate potential recruits.

Dawud, reading the results, shook his head at Hanifa.

"You know how to read Arabic letters," she said, pointing to the screen displaying the beautiful, curvy letters. Other lie detectors were easy to trick, but not this latest state-of-the-art one. "I told you to read as your superior," Hanifa ordered again.

Hamz, as his friends called him, exploded. "This is bullshit! I didn't even apply to be on the elite team! Sylas is giving you too much power."

"Do you know what your name means, historically, for Islam?"

"I don't know what you're talking about."

Dawud signaled Hanifa with a thumb down.

"I hear that you're a valiant soldier for the Seculars. Do they know your past, like Dawud and I dug up?" She had felt bad about her tactics, especially taking into consideration *she* also had a past hidden from the Seculars. But it worked every time they wanted the applicant to reveal themselves as a crypto Muslim.

"Who told you about that?" Hamza raised his voice, angered. "These records have been sealed! You have no right to snoop in my affairs." His lower lip trembled. "Do you plan on hurting me?"

"Let's not get ahead of ourselves," Hanifa replied.

Hamza's chest had moved up and down as he started sweating profusely. It had been summer in Paraty outside and inside, even in that air-conditioned room. Then his gaze had gone to Dawud, in a pleading manner as if asking, *Help me man. From brother to brother.*

Hanifa grinned. "Let's just say that nothing is a hundred percent secure. The security barriers slow the hacks down, but eventually we break in."

Hanifa didn't even recognize herself anymore. Recruiting Muslims and other believers had changed something in her core. It had made her a bit darker, edgier, and a bit irrational too. Ana would have dubbed her "Gaga." Hanifa would admonish her *nafs*—ego—when her power trips and thirsts that were taking over her, Hanifa's rational-self faded.

"Don't be alarmed," she had finally said to Hamza. "We're with the rebellion."

"*Alhamdulillah*," he praised under his breath as his head hit the desk. His curly brown afro touched the table. She felt like touching it to feel the texture. It wasn't too different from her own.

"I knew it!" She jumped, excitedly.

He eyed her curiously. "So that you know, I never look that weak. I was prepared to meet my maker, but I was willing to put up a fight for myself still."

"Yeah, yeah," she joked, then added, "I'm just kidding. Your file is impressive. It says that you had a digital-sword duel with Sylas that left him seriously wounded. Is that true?"

"It is. To be honest, I don't know how the guy is still alive. He was in some kind of experiment and asked for no mercy. So…I gave none. But you have to give it to him—he's very talented. He was a good match."

"Well, a brother skilled with a sword these days, that's a plus. Welcome to the submitters," Hanifa said, handing him a new uniform with a small 's' to replace the one with the big 'S' he was sporting.

Then Dawud joined the conversation, smiling at them from his spot behind the lie-detector test. "Welcome, Hamza."

"Call me Hamz like my friends, classmates, and fellow officers do," Hamza said, walking to Dawud to shake his small hand.

Next, she had talked to Ridwan, an African American boy who had named himself "Rick" to blend in with the Secular Army. Hanifa had been mesmerized by his calming aura. She almost didn't want his interview to end because of the pleasing vibe that emanated from his calm, beautiful smile.

Bashir and Nadhir were two other recruits, and friends

of Hamza. Bashir was of Saudi descent and the announcer when it came to warning all crypto Muslims that real Seculars were on the move. This helped crypto Muslims be on the lookout and avoid being picked on.

Nadhir was Lebanese and worked well with Bashir. He was also the backup to warn the crypto Muslim students and officers of an imminent threat. Hanifa was delighted to have them on her team.

Recruiting the girls for her elite team had been a slightly different story.

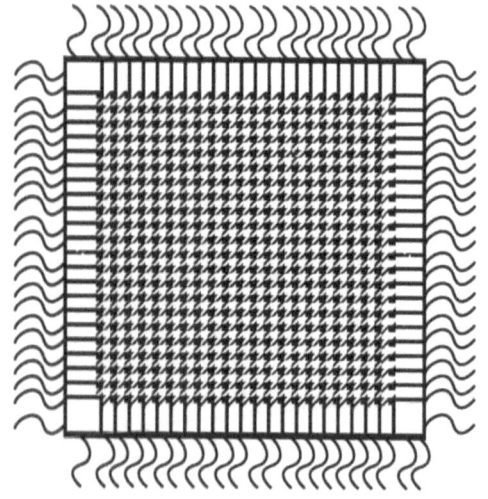

The symbol of the Sahabas X.0 is the black-and-white *Keffiyeh depicted above*.

***

Hanifa couldn't believe her eyes. There before her sat the raven-haired girl, looking sassy and as intimidating as ever.

"Want to tell me why I have to take this test and why I was picked?" The girl scanned the interrogation room, obviously looking unimpressed by the plain white walls of the hidden school room that was different from the *masjid* and Knights Inn.

After six months of undercover operation, they had recruited a good amount of followers. They had slowly etched the team out, one recruit at a time, to remain undetected. Hanifa had Sylas, Judas, Ana, her family, and school to worry about, so she only trusted Dawud with her plans and didn't bring anyone else up to speed on recruiter status.

"Well, get going. I have a quota to meet today," the girl barked.

"Hind? Is that your name?" Hanifa asked.

"Correct," Hind replied.

"Okay, Hind, I know what you are," Hanifa said, finally losing her patience. "I know what your parents were, and why you hide behind this tough exterior."

"So? Tell Sylas about it. Have him wash himself in my blood, have him feast upon my carcass. I really don't care."

Wow, this girl is kamikaze. Straight-out crazy.

"I think you do care—because you joined the Secular Army. Why join if you didn't want vengeance? Why join if you didn't have any self-preservation?"

Hind seemed to mull over Hanifa's arguments. "What are you really selling here?"

"Islam," Hanifa said, and the coin dropped for Hind.

"I knew there was something about you back when you were making noise for us by asking how long the test was during that Secular test we took. Anyway, I'm in," she said hands in the air, with a gangster vibe.

Hanifa couldn't put a finger on it, but she liked the girl

already. She recruited other girls after Hind, too. Coraline, an Island French recruit, was next and Hanifa told her she would nickname her "Marjane." Coral, like she asked to be called, didn't see any problem with only Hanifa calling her Marjane. "I love the Arabic version of my name!" she admitted.

"Me too," Hanifa said and let the tree-nut complexion girl out of the interrogation room after they hugged. Then she recruited Najma, Nadirah, Ya-Sin, and Luluwa. Ya-Sin was so into her own Secular character that she wanted to be called "Sin-D." Hanifa didn't object; the girl was somewhat dark-mannered with her black gothic lipstick, but still an excellent asset to the COurageous COreishy or the $(CO)_2$ team.

Days passed before she uncovered another set of girls. Of the lucky ones was Maknani, a meek Asian Secular officer. Hanifa wondered how Maknani could be authoritative, the way she was so shy. *I'm sure she has strength*s, Hanifa silently reckoned.

"Do you know what they do to people who believe in 'Legends of the former people'?" Hanifa asked, making scare quotes with her fingers.

"I do. They get killed."

Maknani warmed up to Hanifa when she realized she didn't have to end innocent lives.

Yakuta was also a delight to interact with. Of Japanese descent, she was the complete opposite of Maknani. She was very outgoing. At the end of the day, Hanifa thought she had met true keepers, subtle and exemplary gems.

The last recruits of the Courageous Coreishys were Sarah, Nasreen, and Binnur.

When Hanifa was satisfied with the plan's progress, she told her grandpa what she was up to and eventually planned on telling Malik and Shafiya when the time was right.

"Your parents would disapprove and be mad at me for encouraging you, Hanee. Besides, I'm retired now," he had argued.

"Grandpa, you can't retire. You still have it in you. You could be my mentor, our consultant." Hanifa begged him until he had succumbed and changed his mind.

"Oh Hanee, I know how it feels to be a strong-willed Kreedor or a Ducktrinor. How can I refuse to help in fulfilling your dreams? I just can't bring myself to be a hypocrite."

Mustapha became their mentor and sponsor and assisted Hanifa in financially getting her plans off the ground. He also had to pull a few strings so that his granddaughter could recruit more crypto Muslims, some of whom had travelled to Paraty for the sake of the cause.

Not long after, Hanifa told Malik and Shafiya when she felt confident enough they wouldn't betray her by telling their parents. They had recruited enough people to start training at the warehouse. The mosque had also been relocated there. There was also no need to use the hidden interrogation room behind the school walls. Together, the Sahabas and the Coreishys arranged and decorated a corner of the big warehouse to make it a prayer area. And between teleporting for classes, patrolling, prayers, and training, they would sit in *halaqa* formation at Knights Inn, educate each other, and discuss religion. These days, they all realized that there were enough hours in a day to get all the needed work done if they kept to a rigid and diligent plan on daily to-do tasks.

The non-Muslims of the elite team took guard or did other things to entertain themselves when praying and *halaqa* were in session at the Knights Inn warehouse. Mustapha was always there as a mentor and chaperone.

"*Assalamu aleikum*, good morning, *shalom*, greeting of peace, etc. We have finally brought The Supplies today, *alhamdullilah*. You will practice with them and if you have any questions, please don't hesitate to ask me, Dawud, or my grandfather. We will resume working on armed and unarmed combat, archery, and sword fighting tomorrow," Hanifa said and finished with her daily reminder, "remember, 'focus is the point between rage and serenity' and you should take that phrase to heart to help perfect your strengths to defeat the enemy. Also on the schedule are martial arts, wrestling, and long-distance range shooting."

Everybody—especially some of Mustapha's old acquaintances—pitched in to help ready the group so they could fight their best when the time came to use The Supplies.

$$O=C=C=O \quad O=C=C=O$$

$$O=C=C=O$$

1

Since Ridwan knew his way around Morocco like the back of his hand, Mustapha sent him to recruit the Righteous Murabitun. But his luck was about to be tested as he finished his business.

"Hey you, halt!" a senior Secular officer called out to Ridwan when he suddenly appeared from underground to the streets of Marrakesh.

Ridwan immediately stopped and voice commanded his papers to come out of his pockets without reaching for them himself; an invention of the ever-so-thoughtful Mustapha Kreedor. *Wahidun*, he whispered.

"This way, no one can shoot you for reaching in your pockets under the pretense that they feared for their lives and that you had 'a gun'," the old man had pointed out.

So Ridwan's papers came out and levitated in front of him and the Secular guards. At the sight of what was happening, the officers took a step back. Ridwan inferred it was out of this world for them.

"It's harmless. These are my travel papers and I'm a Secular deputy at the reputable school of Sir Landry Big in Brazil. I'm just here to visit relatives since I'm originally from here," he said as he studied the reluctance in their faces.

Eventually, one of them ended the stand-off and took the ID from the air to examine it. He scratched his head and then he handed them back. They apologized and let him go.

"Whew! That was close," Ridwan said and added, "Kreedor is a genius!"

2

"Elder Kreedor is here," Nadhir announced to the elite team at Knights Inn and then went out to chat with the old man.

"Welcome! I would love to use your teleportation device one day. Ours are good but yours is out of this world!" Nadhir said with a cool voice. He admired the gadget again and smiled appreciatively at the Duktrinors' grandfather.

"Ah don't worry. I have a mission for you. You can use it to announce our goals to the Brave Moriscoes in Spain and the Deli Sultans, God willing."

"It will be my pleasure, Sir."

"I know. Come, I need to tell you how to travel covert in these parts," Mustapha Senior said and they entered their headquarters.

3

Bashir El-Amin from Saudi Arabia was also another messenger used by Mustapha Kreedor.

"So I'm also going to Morocco for another business and then Egypt. Right?" Bashir had asked the old man again just to confirm.

"That's right son. You've got to be careful now, ok?"

Bashir nodded and scratched his head full of luscious short black hair complementing his almond-toned skin.

4

"Tariq!" someone had called at Knights Inn. Both former Tim who was just visiting briefly and Tariq Timité, who was an Ivorian with an ebony skin tone, replied "YES."

"No, African Tariq," Malik said, with more precision.

"Is it true that Sir Landry is venerated in your country like a God?"

"Oh yeah, the college students will do his bidding for

him without blinking an eye," Tariq replied wide-eyed. "You've got to see it to believe it. I mean they even go pre-historic and will pull a machete on you if you don't agree with them and their methods. It's like dungeon masters, full of archaic tools."

"Well, that conversation sidetracked in a dark corner," Malik joked, puffing.

"Anything about him and his Seculars is twisted, dark, and supernatural, Bro. Best believe it," African Tariq advised.

"True," was Malik's answer as he wondered about the doppelganger he'd met in school and the cause behind his sudden questions about Sir Landry Big. If he didn't know better, he would say that secrets were finding him.

5

Cliché or not, Nasreen went for "The Princess of Persia" as her war name.

"I mean, it only makes sense that I chose that. I'm

from there anyways," she had said while the team members were picking and/or ruling out safety names. Her teammates, towering over five foot two, nodded.

"A tiny bulldog princess for real," Tahany, the Egyptian, said giggling.

Nasreen was a feisty one and they all knew not to mess with her because she would make you pay with a swift punch to the face.

One day, as the Secular officers of their school were patrolling, Nate, the cocky douchebag officer who caused Hanifa to kill Latife, slapped Nasreen's butt. She turned around and asked, "Who did that?" squinting intensely at the group as she stomped toward them. They all pointed to Nate. She removed her helmet, shook her cascading frizzy black hair, and relaxed her facial features and said, "You want some?" Her tone was inviting and charming.

"Oh yeah, lil mama." Nate took the bait and got even closer to her.

"Good!" she said, and flipped the script by slapping

him so hard on the cheeks that he stumbled for a little, eyes wide open.

"Damn!" the group cried in cue.

"Next time, I'll fucking bury you!" she menaced, and marched ahead to distance herself from the rest of the team. She was going to patrol on her own! Rumors of the incident spread like wild fire and people were wary about her from that day on.

Nasreen was an only child and sometimes she came off entitled and 'princessy.' Thus, no one could argue her choice of name. Even if they wanted to, the final decision always relied upon her choice. And it wasn't Hanifa's style to impose names on her followers.

6

"Chica, I'm going to head out," Najma said, addressing Hanifa after one of their secret meetings at the warehouse. She peered at her hi-tech wrist watch that allowed video calls and recordings and said, "I have one minute before I'm late for class."

"No problem. Enjoy your class and don't forget to remove your *hijab* dear. Your input was on point as usual," Hanifa complimented, smiling.

"Gracias, señorita. Peace out!" she held two fingers out, kissed them and waved them in the air before disappearing with her teleportation device in the blink of an eye.

When it came for Najma to pick a name, it wasn't hard at all. The Perales hailed from Mexico City. Proud of her heritage, as everyone should be and like her parents had taught her, Najma loved to utter, "Vamos" when it was Secular time to patrol. A very vocal person, Najma had the gift of exhorting a crowd. She was a natural born leader. She conducted many learning circles at Knights Inn. When she wasn't doing that she was either inviting to Islam by *dawah* or working on interfaith dialogue. "Vive Islam," Najma always said after the last *Fatiha* of their *halaqa* sessions.

Very tall, Najma was an empowering plus-size young woman who was comfortable in her skin. She was fit and had an imposing figure no one in a room with her could deny.

This bonus came in handy in her covert interfaith dialogue operations. Najma was rarely interrupted when she spoke during these meetings because of the vibe she emanated; respect.

To conceal her identity while still staying true to herself, she went for 'Vive' as her war name.

7

Cindy L'Heureux was born to a French father and a Brazilian mother. A gothic Muslim, she always wore black lipstick and had several piercings. From the ones visible, she had a captive bead ring on her right ear and one on her nose. She also had a horseshoe piercing on her left ear and a straight barbell going from the tip of her left ear diagonally to the other end.

Sin-D was her Secular officer name. To her close friends, she was Ya-Sin.

8

Binnur and her family went in exile, away from Turkey, when the power shifted to Secular Turkish leaders *again*. These leaders called themselves The Young Turks Junior and weren't tolerant of Islam or of Turkey as a leading Muslim country. Secularism in Turkey had a way of being reinvented over and over again since the fall of the Ottoman Empire in the early 1900s.

9

Sarah was a redhead. A non-theist, she supported the

cause of the Coreishys and was a proud member. Her parents came from Alabama, United States. They were Cajun and had sought refuge in Paraty by lying low-key up until Sarah decided to become an activist and Ducktrinor follower.

"But Mom! This is what I want to do."

"Sarah, your mother is right, you know. This is dangerous honey. We left America because the oppression of our race has become standard procedure. Things are reversed now."

"I know what I'm risking but things will not change or go away as long as Sir Landry Big is playing payback with his powers. Brazil is not any better; it's becoming very obvious that the movement is catching on here too rather quickly. As long as you work for him, you're kinda spared but still not safe."

10

Romeehna Torales was Brazilian and a member of The

Bold Malê. Her help was very valuable in approaching this resistance group, as was Malik's first encounter with them. She was the ambassador of the movement at Castle 5 and especially the elite Team of Hanifa.

11

Tahany, the Egyptian, had another name; it was Miss Mystic to those who believed in rare, supernatural occurrences. She was a joy to be around to the point that you could feel her concealed absence or her literal presence. At a very young age, she memorized *"And We gave them clear proofs of the matter [of religion]. And they did not differ except after knowledge had come to them - out of jealous animosity between themselves. Indeed, your Lord will judge between them on the Day of Resurrection concerning that over which they used to differ."* (Quran 45:17) Without a doubt, it was her favorite verse of the Quran.

Upon her request, her favorite verse was framed and

hung inside Knights Inn, the safe house the elite Secular team used to regroup. "They will never find us here," Tahany had declared sure of herself when the whole team agreed to hang the verse. They didn't think anything much of it. In their minds, it wouldn't hurt to have a holy verse adorning the place. That said, Tahany had her reasons why she wanted that particular verse hung in the warehouse. At a young age, her father told her the story of the female *sufi* Rabiya al 'Adawiyya. Tahany immediately found this woman inspiring and strove to be like her.

"Agent 4517 is the name I want to go by," she said sure of herself. "And let me tell you guys, it's not random that we meet here in this school. This was written and we'll bring about a change," she often said with a wink; her green eyes glistening with certainty.

CHAPTER TWENTY-THREE : OLD FRIENDS

Hanifa

Timeline: Toward the end of the school year in Brazil

HANIFA PLAYED WITH the Shadow Hunter until she was able to operate it. There were a bunch of riddles and questions programmed into it about religions, and she had to pass them before she could search for Ana. What she had thought would be an easy affair took her a few months to decode. This inventor/architect seriously didn't want anyone to access it so easily.

Once in, she located Ana moving fast and appearing at different locations at the same time. At first, she thought the device was bugged, taking into consideration the unknown period of time it had stayed undetected behind the prayer niche, indicating the direction of the *salat*.

But when Hanifa searched for herself, it found her without any issue. Next, she put in Dawud's name. It also found him without any issue. She searched for anyone she could think of at Knights Inn and it found them right where they were, sitting right under her nose. Suddenly the lightbulb lit and her face froze, horrified. Had Ana become a clone, a robot, or a vampire? *Subhanallah, this is bad*, she thought.

When Hanifa was finally able to pin Ana down and talk to her, Ana was distant.

"I missed you, girl. Why did you disappear on me? I thought you liked to hang out with me better than your other materialistic friends. Or was that a lie?" She offered her old friend a weak smile. "So much has happened I wanted to share with you."

Ana stayed quiet in a dark recess of the library, a hoodie almost covering her facial features. She wasn't dressed in her stylish Barbie attires anymore. She was now the epitome of BAMF hotness, dressed in black with thigh-high boots and leaning on an obscured bookshelf a few feet away from Hanifa. A few minutes passed before she stepped into the light of the library's aisles.

"Oh, I know what you've been up to. You're a rebel, *Lady H.*"

Hanifa took a step back.

"Don't worry, your secret is safe with me. I had my own reasons for keeping quiet," Ana added.

"Why? What happened to you? You seem so different." Hanifa was crushed that her friend was so distant and cold. She suddenly became nervous to see and know why Ana had disappeared on her so unpredictably.

Finally, Ana opened up. She told Hanifa about how Sylas had been manipulating and blackmailing her because of their stupid moment—something she had regretted ever since. "And you joined the Seculars on your own anyway; I was glad I didn't have any part in it. Also, because I valued our budding friendship, I stayed away."

She then explained what she had gone through at the hands of Judas and Sylas. Hanifa felt truly compassionate for her. They had fed over her, drinking her blood, and they had taken advantage of her. She was just waiting for the perfect time to strike back, and knowing Hanifa's plans made her feel better—she couldn't wait for what was coming to these bastards.

"I felt guilty because I spied on you and many people for months," Ana admitted. "That's all I allowed myself to do in the shadows; spy to stay up to date. Sylas killed me and turned me into a vampire. I was his rat lab. So I thought, '*I'm a freak now. Hanifa won't want to be friends with me.*' "

"You're still Ana to me."

"Thanks, it means a lot. By the way, I learned a few tricks with my brother—and my program Eyes has a lot of data you could find useful. Here's a copy." Ana gave Hanifa a thin cylinder rod. "It's a portable drive. Easy to hide and carry around. Good luck leading your quest. I'm sure you'll do well; you already seem more patient and careful. The old Hanifa would have told anyone she met her plans." Ana winked as she handed over the drive to Hanifa.

"Thanks a bunch. Yes, I figured I had to be more patient to think of all the scenarios that could go wrong with my plans. Also, trusting only Dawud for a while was a great move."

"But my Eyes saw everything," Ana said.

"Thanks for keeping quiet," Hanifa let out, blushing. Then she told Ana that because she had a slight attraction to Sylas, she thought Ana had deserted her and pegged her as a boyfriend stealer. They laughed because Hanifa didn't even date but she was still human and had feelings toward guys. And Ana didn't even like the guy. She was just pretending in the hopes that her brother would be released.

When they had reminisced on their first days and fun

lunch dates, Ana said, "You know who else I like from Gaga's time?"

"No."

"Katy Perry. She has this song that goes 'I kissed a girl and I liked it...Don't mean I'm in love tonight,'" Ana sang. "Anyway, this is goodbye and...I would love to kiss you. It would be a secret memory and a piece of you I'll take and keep with me."

Hanifa brewed on the request. *What the heck?! But it's just a kiss...would I be breaking any religious rules?* But before she could make up her mind, Ana was upon her and kissed her softly on the lips. No tongue, just a sensual lip lock for a quick moment before they suddenly broke the embrace, both feeling giddy and embarrassed that they had crossed that line. Then, reluctantly, they said goodbye and this time they shared a warm hug that radiated through their bodies.

"Friends for life?" Hanifa asked.

"Friends for life. 'See you on the other side,' like my brother usually says. Take good care of you, *Lady H.*"

"You too, *habibti*," Hanifa said with a weak smile.

Ana wiggled her thin fingers affectionately at Hanifa before disappearing again, like a lightning bolt. She was off to find her brother, wherever he was.

CHAPTER TWENTY-FOUR : JUDAS

Judas

Timeline: About nine months or so after the beginning of the school year in Brazil

"WHAT'S SO SPECIAL about her list of two-hundred recruits?" Sylas asked Judas.

"I'm not sure," said Judas, "but I know she has about a hundred males and a hundred females. Nothing special about them except that they seemed to have performed well in a particular section of the Secular admission test."

"Which section is that?" Sylas asked, raising an eyebrow.

"Ancient religions."

Bull's eye, Ana said to no one in particular as she spied on Sylas with the Eyes robot.

"I feel this strong sensation that I didn't peg this girl Hanifa right for some reason," Sylas said. "She didn't want to join and suddenly she decided to join and wants her own army. Now, she picks my officers who are well-versed in ancient religions to make that army. I thought we recommended some officers to her?"

"She dismissed their applications. I guess she thought they could be moles," Judas hazarded a guess. *The bitch is always trying to make me feel jealous by sucking up to Sylas. I'll find what she's up to*, he thought. *I know she likes me even if she pretends I'm invisible.*

You wish! Ana mocked. She continued spying on Sylas and Judas.

"Either she wants to take my spot," said Sylas, "or

she's a believer who is playing low key by hiding behind my ranks to fulfill her own hidden agenda. Only one way to find out. Please get Ana over here, she hasn't reported on that tracker she put on the girl ages ago."

"You know why," Judas remarked with a scoff.

Yes, you do… Ana silently watched them argue in Sylas's office via Eyes. *I'll help bring you two down even if it's the last thing I do.*

"I know. She despises us—and you let me down, man. Her renegade brother is no longer in our custody! How did he escape again?" Sylas stared at Judas, who quickly looked away. There were no signs of a scoff or of a laugh on his suddenly troubled face. "How about the tracker you put on her?"

"It wasn't able to do the job properly; it seems that she can teleport somehow. This is new technology I haven't had a breakthrough with, Sir," Judas finished, swallowing hard.

"New technology? You should be on top of new technology around here! Do I have to do everything myself?"

"No, Sir."

Sylas ousted him with a disdainful wave of a hand. And to avoid more lines of questioning, Judas promptly left the room to try to find Ana, holding his palm to his shoulder where Ali's arrow had grazed it. The memory felt like a shower of cold ice.

On another screen of her program, Ana grinned widely as a slide of a shower of ice danced on her visual feed from Judas's mind. *I bet it's still sore. Jerk! You deserve that!* She cackled eerily to herself.

***

When Judas returned to his office, he slumped all his weight in his enormous green chair. A small picture of a smiling red-headed family was projected on the right corner of his pristine legless table. The projected picture featuring an older man and woman in a tight and friendly embrace emanated from a round lens between the picture that was hanging in the air and the table, a later generation of holographic pictures.

A picture of a woman with beautiful wild curls and a

lively smile stood next to the family picture. His expression softened when his eyes landed on her and then quickly went back to somber. *Rosalba, you will come back to me again after I'm known and recognized as the best engineer of this age.*

Then, he absentmindedly accessed his portable engineering lab out of habit by pressing a little gray triangle which was nested in the middle of his table closer toward the edge and where he was sitting. Within seconds, an inverse room appeared at the ceiling of the room. It was wide and seemed to cross dimensions and exist within dimensions of another dimension. Gravity held it above the ground.

Judas's lab was a standard scientist lab with the usual all-in-one engineering lab stations; from chemicalware, medicalware, software, hardware, and obviously courseware, his office was on campus to help wiz engineering Secular recruits get the experience they needed to face the rebellion and other insurgents.

An expert in mechatronics, Judas had not always been a heavy set person. He used to be very fit and he helped design on-field training programs. But because he was always behind a computer, he started eating unhealthy meals and exercise less because he could never spare time to properly care for himself. His obsession with gaining knowledge or cracking a code or just making a breakthrough had become a bit too much just because his ultimate goal was to regain the love of his life.

There is indeed such a thing as too much of a good thing causing harm. He knew he needed balance but he could never live up to it. That and his girlfriend dumping him for a hot native Brazilian like her made him eat all his sorrows.

As he checked his projects in progress, he checked a camera feed on a computer; a beautiful woman was having dinner with a muscular hunk who was feeding a tanned skin baby. *That baby could have been mine!* Judas snarled bitterly. Full of rage he switched the stalking feed to some students taking military techniques simulations that he was monitoring. Hanifa was one of them. He had been watching her and the agile way she moved around gave him the envy to try to be fit once again. *Hmm, perhaps I can rival with Rosalba's husband and win her back!* He mused.

On another screen, the voyeur had another program running that was trying to get into the firewall around Hanifa's home.

"Bummer, no luck again today. Hmm, whoever designed their security system is a true pro!" he said to himself and launched into a combative training simulation to pass time and clear his mind. He chose four hologram companions to help him in his test and pass-time mission. Then, Judas produced with a summoning wave of a hand from its original spot on the lab counter, a pre-loaded fancy military shooting gun ready to simulate the heck out of his test.

Judas and his helpers faced an army of hologram

dummies that started shooting blanks at them. He gave directive to his robots and from squad line formation, they went into squad file, and then squad column before ducking behind hills of greens. It felt like they were playing a 3-dimensional war video-game.

While Judas himself was a good shot with his weapon, he was terrible at moving deftly and ducking to avoid being touched by fake bullets.

What a pig, Ana exclaimed as she grew tired of Judas's antics. She cliqued off her feed and felt dirty by watching others via Eyes. Having a family again was what she yearned for most so she hatched a plan.

Judas checked out of the simulation after a few minutes.

"Perhaps, I should start with basic training first. But that boot camp will be the death of me," he said to himself as reality dawned on him. It was easy to put the weight on but tough to shed it off.

CHAPTER TWENTY-FIVE : LAST MINUTES ARRANGEMENTS

Hanifa

Timeline: About eleven months or so after the beginning of the school year in Brazil

HANIFA AND HER ELITE TEAM had been training for weeks. Now they were ready for the next move—taking over the school.

They had been communicating about their rising rebellion in *The Muezzin* and support letters had been coming in from all over the world. It was time for Hanifa to face reality: This was bigger than her, and she needed to tell her secret plans to her parents once and for all. Maybe knowing about the support she had amassed from around the world would change their minds.

She entered her house and greeted her parents, who were seated on the living room couches.

"*Assalamu aleikum*, Father and Mother." She found herself being so formal while addressing them, and she wondered if they had picked up on that. Normally, she would say Mom or Dad or even Baba.

"*Wa aleikum salam*, Hanifa," they replied.

"You're home early. Is everything okay?" her mom asked, and her dad followed, "Did the library close early today?"

"There's something I need to tell you." Hanifa started fiddling with her fingers as she slowly approached them.

Both her parents sat up. This was another déjà vu.

"This doesn't sound good," her father said.

"It depends." Hanifa winced and her head volleyed from left to right. "Remember when you said we should stay away from *The Muezzin* because we were done bringing attention to ourselves?"

"Okay…" they said on cue.

"Alright, just out of curiosity, have you been reading it lately?"

They looked at each other with wide eyes and then looked away before dropping their gaze. Hanifa searched their eyes. *Oh no, the shunned look. They think I did it again. They're judging me.*

Finally her father harrumphed, stopping her racing thoughts. "We have been reading it and hiding it from you children."

"How? I never saw the tablet even once since we moved up here!" Hanifa said.

Her mom sighed and took over the floor. "Every night,

after dinner, we told you children we were going for a walk. Instead, we would sneak into the Bordinis' basement to read the e-zine."

Hanifa gasped; were her parents really that sneaky? *Gurl, they knew the world before you*, her conscience sassily snapped.

"Well, this is going to be a shock then. I'm Sister H and I'm the new face of the rebellion."

"What?!" They jumped out of their seats.

"It can't be. How did you accomplish all this without us finding out?" Her father's voice deepened as he continued questioning her nonstop. "Are your siblings in on this too? Young girl, even though we're proud of you, you're in trouble!"

"Serious trouble!" her mom added by Adama's side, nodding.

"Mom and Dad, please! I'm a big girl now. What's done is done. There is no turning back. I love you and I respect you. But…you have to leave tonight. There is a great danger coming for you."

Malik and Shafiya entered the room. "Come in when you start to hear shouts," Hanifa had told them before she opened the front door a few minutes earlier. They walked into the room and stood by her side. Malik on her right, and Shafiya on her left.

"Let me guess, Brother M and Sister S?" their dad quipped sarcastically.

The pair nodded and Hanifa could see the light bulb moment on her parents' faces.

"We aren't going to lie; we enjoyed reading *The Muezzin* every night at the neighbors' houses," said their mother. "Your courage and your better rebellion against the Seculars amazed us—but you're still grounded!"

"Code *fitnah* has been activated despite all our efforts to live a stable life and keep our family safe," her father said.

"Dad, we're tired of running," said Malik. "We're proud to do something and to stop running for the rest of our lives. We'd rather die heroes and martyrs than die afraid of an oppressing regime."

Their father shook his head. "This is suicide. What do you young folks know about war? You can't survive against these infidels. Just like that, I could be legacy-less. Because you're of age, I can't tell you Malik and Hanifa what to do. But you, Shafiya, we won't allow that. Neither will we allow your sister Pristine to join. When you're mature and eighteen, Shafiya, you and Pristine can join if you want—and that's if this nonsense affair is still going on."

"That's not fair! Tomorrow is not guaranteed. I can fight. We've been training!" Shafiya defended her case.

"Let them be."

They all turned to see Grandpa Mustapha a few feet away, sitting in his wheelchair.

"Baba!" roared their father. He vehemently pointed his

finger at his father. "I know you have everything to do with our children rebelling against us and playing heroes."

"Son, war is upon us. You have to get with the program. What you need to do is tell them the year that we're in and pray for them. You can't shield them for life. They're ready and I've seen it. Weren't you both amazed at the accomplishments of the anonymous challengers until you found out they were your own children?"

Their parents couldn't answer as the light shone on their hypocrisy.

***

"The great scholar Imam Rabbani, *rahmatullahi ta'ala alaihi*, estimated the end of times during his lifetime. According to him, we had about five hundred years left then. But only *Allahu alim* for sure."

"Okay," Hanifa prodded him and he continued.

After their dad taught them everything they needed to

know about the *hijri* and Gregorian calendar, their grandfather, parents, and Pristine followed Malik, Hanifa, and Shafiya outside to the front yard. This was goodbye.

Hanifa carried her backpack, which looked like nothing special, but would surprise anyone who peeked into it. "May Allah protect you, Mom, Dad, Grandpa, and Pristine. We will keep you in our prayers, God willing."

"*Ameen.*"

Hanifa, Malik, and Shafiya group-hugged the rest of the family.

"May He protect you all as well. We will keep you in our prayers, too." Their parents and Pristine replied with teary eyes.

"*Ameen,*" Malik, Hanifa, and Shafiya replied.

Then, Hanifa turned to her mother. "Mom, I want you to know that I'm a big girl now. If I'm meant to survive this, I will *insha'Allah.* If not, I will see you in the *akhiret, insha'Allah.*"

"I hope we see each other again, God willing, and this time with a candidate to marry you."

Tears gliding down her cheeks, Hanifa kissed her mom's cheeks. Her mom kissed her back on the forehead and gave her another warm embrace.

Then, Hanifa approached her grandfather's wheelchair and she squatted down to meet his eyes face-to-face. "Baba, I'm grateful for all the knowledge and tricks you taught me. They surely will come in handy."

He smiled. "*Masha'Allah*. Here is another gadget. It is called *DjahayreePro-SpyPro*. When the time is right, it will reveal our location to you *insha'Allah*."

"*Jazak'Allah khair* Baba!" She was elated by his thoughtfulness. She loved the gift; it looked like a horseshoe with seven star tips in the middle, adorned with a small screen and coordinates on the starfish look alike.

Her father was the last person Hanifa said goodbye to. He gave her a chip that had "*M4*" etched on it and said,

"This has all you need to know about the four Sunni *madhahib*. It'll help you solve issues you encounter as you lead the soldiers in your quests. Wear it as an earring. Now, we have to go, after we warn the Bordinis. You three have our blessings and take good care of yourselves. Be careful, and join us soon *insha'Allah*."

"*Insha'Allah*," Hanifa, Malik, and Shafiya replied.

"And, if we never meet again and you have children, teach them the protection supplications in all the languages you speak and especially Arabic. Do not forget," their mom said.

"*Tamam*," the trio had replied and said their goodbyes.

After they warned their friendly neighbors, the house transformed into an airship and took off. Their house was an advanced kind of trailer, another of Adama's inventions. When the house/ship disappeared, a poplar tree flipped up from the hole left and there was green grass all around the place where the house used to stand.

***

Through *The Muezzin*, the elite team declared war on Sylas and the Seculars of Castle 5. They replied with an invitation for Hanifa, the leader, to come meet them. She thought it might be a trap, but her advisers in the elite team thought she would look cowardly if she didn't go.

"You're right. No one will take me seriously if I refuse to meet the tyrant." She would go and disappear by teleportation if things went sour.

So she dressed in a knee-length navy-blue *abaya* with slits on the sides and matching pants underneath. It looked even better than the picture in the history books that it was modeled after. The tips of the sleeves and pants had gold embroidery. The cherry on top was her trademark golden headscarf. The software she had used to design this piece of art was one of a kind.

Today, this is it. I'm going full-blown Muslimah. No more hiding. She knew she would make an entrance at that party with her latest inventions.

Standing at the entrance of the coliseum, she grabbed her black, crescent-shaped device from her backpack. Then she pressed the white star button on it to activate it. It always amazed her how real the horse looked. Ecstatically, she hopped onto the stallion and finally made her entrance.

As soon as the crowd of infidels noticed her, whispers started growing.

"Sylas will have her head for this after she kneels before him," she made out from someone in the crowd. But she only knelt before Allah. She wasn't scared to stand before Sylas.

Perched on top of her mechanical black stallion Buraqa, power and grandiose feelings took over her emotions.

So, she made a quick *dua* to come back down to earth and asked Allah to save her from this *kabir*. She immediately felt better after the quick prayer. The attention wasn't her main focus anymore, but spotting the villain of Sylas was.

It wasn't hard to find him. He displayed his opulent self on all the screens around the stadium. Half-naked girls surrounded him, catering to his needs like he was a king.

What a perv!

He addressed Hanifa as she was standing in the middle of the stadium with all the lights on her. "So you came. I should have known it was you all along. I thought we would have to find your family and relatives and kill them all if you were a no show. Either way, someone is dying tonight." A grin spread across his face and the crowd cheered like it was normal to wish for the death of a human being.

Wow…These people need help.

"Give her a voice enhancer," he ordered. And in the blink of an eye, a servant boy ran to her to give her the device:

their modern-day microphone. She felt sad for the boy.

"I did come, but not to be the toy of the night." Her voice was clear and sure. She was pumped by an invisible certainty that things would turn out in her favor. Whether or not she was right was still to be uncovered, but she was a true believer in her Master and in the fact that right always wins over wrong when you're ready to make a stand.

"Is that so? What makes you think so?"

"I know so," she replied with her head high as ever. Malik was right; she was cocky, and it scared her sometimes.

"Why are you on a fake horse? You remind me of one of my favorite villains." He caressed his chin.

"Which one? I never pictured you as much of a learner." Her dare triggered a few giggles in the audience. *Bingo!* Clearly he had followers who didn't like him. She promised herself to capitalize on that when she got a chance.

"Silence! Or I will have you disobedient rats

slaughtered." Not a single fly made a noise after that. He continued, "I read to know what people like you are up to and I come across interesting things every now and then. You remind me of the ancient character Tywin Lannister."

"Classic!" she snarled and a loud laugh escaped her lips.

"Enough, young lady! I didn't ask you to come here so that you can humiliate me in front of my servants."

Who does he think he is? His servants? This guy is hilarious and so narcissistic.

But he only kept talking. "Tywin Lannister made such an entrance, on horseback, because he didn't want to kneel before his grandson, Joffrey Baratheon, the new King. I am very inclined to think that this is also your intent. But because I like to play with my food, I will give you the chance to explain."

"Well, you're right on the kneeling part. I am not kneeling in front you because of my ego; I only kneel before my Creator and you aren't a deity!"

"Seize her! The first person to do so won't have to hunt for her daring kind for a month."

CHAPTER TWENTY-SIX : RUN FOR LIFE

Hanifa

Timeline: About twelve months or so after the beginning of the school year in Brazil

THAT WAS IT! THERE was a price on her head. The crowd zeroed on her and she threw another device in the air, escaping them by an inch. *These people have to be dealing with djinns to travel that fast to me,* she thought.

Her little device transformed into a sort of stairs, and she took rapid steps toward the person who put a price on her head. A new step automatically appeared in front of her every time she made the motion to take a step. With the commotion and the crowd around her horse—which vanished as soon as she jumped into the air—Sylas didn't see her coming. Before he knew it, she had a knife on his throat.

Hanifa's left arm was around his neck while her right hand held the sharp knife to his throat. "Tell them to stop their bounty hunting or I will slaughter you before their eyes."

"You smell very good, and your body pressed to mine is a welcomed change. Who knew you could look so tempting in such an outdated outfit."

"Keep your insincere and cloaked compliments to yourself." She was in no mood for distractions and especially not from someone like him.

"You can't kill me. You don't have it in you. Your religion forbids you to kill." He continued his laugh as his mob of followers was closing in on her.

"Don't push me. Tell them to back up or I will cut

your throat right now. I'm not joking. Besides, you tried to kill me first and you will again if you have another chance and for that reason, so long!" But before she moved to slay him, his body slumped in her hands—shot by an arrow.

Hanifa turned her head around to spot the person who had shot the arrow and stolen her moment.

"You're welcome. Don't feel bad; he had it coming. Everyone, fall back!" A few rows below her, a brown-skinned man with big eyes and thick eyebrows roared. He was imposing and very easy on the eyes.

The crowd fell back, as he'd instructed.

Who is this guy? "I had it under control." She finally found her voice to speak.

"I don't doubt it," he replied condescendingly.

Jerk! she thought to herself. *What a showoff.* "Whatever, I need to address the crowd. We can have a talk in a little bit. Brother…?"

"Ali."

"Thank you, Ali." Then, she turned to the bemused, greatly mixed crowd. Some had tears, some had frowns, many had arched brows and arms crossed on their chests. Some had their teeth revealed as they smiled and looked relieved and hopeful, and some had no emotions on their faces at all. Hanifa took a deep breath to stop being intimidated by the glares in her direction and started her prose.

"My name is Hanifa Ducktrinor. I'm going on a quest to find the cave mentioned in the Quran *sherif,* the holy book for Muslims. The cave, as we know it, houses some *ashabi kiram*—companions—who will come in handy in helping Issa, Jesus as you may know him, *aleiyi salam* fight Yajud and Majud, the alien creatures that will eat everything in their way. I know many of you are Muslims but are hiding your religion because of the *fitnah* upon us today. I need some volunteers to come with me. If you oppose me and come after me, Sylas's fate will be your fate. Kneeling before a creature of Allah *subhanahu wa ta ala* is a grave sin and you should know better. I'm also here to spread the message of Islam by teaching the four Sunni *madhabs* because that's my area of expertise and my religious invitation to you."

She had her *niqabaya*, her invisible cloak, close by in her backpack in case anything went wrong while she was addressing the crowd.

"The offer is very tempting, but before we go, some of us need to talk to our families," a male voice in the crowd said.

"I've heard this statement before," Ali said, squinting his eyes.

"Shush!" Hanifa yelled at him and turned her attention to the crowd. "That's fine. If anyone needs to put some order in his or her affairs before we leave, please do so now. We will leave by dawn. Those who don't have to go anywhere, we will set up camp here. I have everything we need in my backpack here. We can't stay longer than dawn because the Seculars will be after us soon. We can outnumber them but zero to fewer casualties is my goal in this *hijra*."

"She is right, people. Get on with it now," Ali added.

"Excuse me? Did I ask you for anything, Ali?"

"I was wrapping things up because, like you promised earlier, we still need to talk."

"Okay, talk. What's your story?"

Ali began to explain to her that he'd had an epiphany at the beginning of the school year. When he finished telling her about the premonitory vision, he added more details about himself. "I'm an orphan and I'm on a rampage. I might as well join your cause, whatever that might be, like *hijra* to a lost place. I'm usually not the talkative type, but you make me act different. And you look familiar. Do you have a sister?"

"Look here, handsome," the words flew out of her mouth before she could take them back.

"So you find me handsome? That's a plus. I thought I would have to do more impressive things to get your attention." He smirked.

"Whatever! Pay attention! Your move is cliché. I do have a sister and I doubt you've met her."

"What if I have?" he asked.

"Don't we have more important things to talk about?"

"So your sister isn't important. Wow!" he said.

"Look, I guarantee you've never met Safi or Priss. Okay? We share everything."

"I know Safi. I helped her when she faced a bully just like I just helped you. Maybe if you weren't so engrossed in yourself, Safi would have told you," he added.

Then it hit her. She *had* been engrossed in her own dreams and goals and drilling them into everybody's brains around her. She couldn't remember the last time she'd had a girls' night in with her sisters.

"I need to go!" she quickly uttered. "My cause has nothing to do with your rampage. You got that?"

Ali yelled up as she was trying to leave the stadium to fix her relationship with her sisters. "Calm down. Our causes aren't that different. Sylas's type slaughtered people I loved dearly, and I've been returning the favor when the occasion presents itself."

"Vengeance, I see." She eyed him while her eyebrows made V-shaped forms. "I'm sorry to hear that, but don't kill anyone of his kind unless they come at us first. And don't go purposely looking for them while you are associated with my cause."

"By the way, where is your orphan butler at?" Ali asked.

"For your information, he is my protégé, not a butler. And how do you even know Dawud? Don't answer that. Do you have to know everyone I know?" Hanifa shot questions at him, irritated.

"We met a while back when I came to free the prisoner."

"Ugh! You were that guy from the rebellion?! You never reported back to Dawud so we never met. We didn't know what happened to you."

"It wasn't safe. The guy's sister, a blonde, had just been beheaded and the SOs attacked us so we had to leave promptly. I think her name was Ana."

"Did you say Ana? Ana Undeapsided? If we're talking about the same person, she's sort of alive and also looking for him," Hanifa added.

"She is? *Subh*—" he ate the rest of word and quickly glanced around out of habit even though there was no need to hide anymore since they had gone public with their faith declaration in the broadcasts. Saying God is glorious was still very risky but in reality there was nothing left to risk. Then he continued, "That's great. Maybe Tariq will snap out of it when he finally sees her. He went through a major mental breakdown. He kept saying that because he didn't disclose the location of the Shadow Hunter they brutally killed her."

"Don't worry. Ana is resourceful; she'll find him," Hanifa forecasted, sure of herself.

Before she left the stadium, Hanifa wanted to take another look at Sylas's corpse but realized it was missing. He'd disappeared. *Dang it! I'm now certain that he has a clone and many more lives to waste.* She alerted Dawud and Hamza, and they hatched a plan.

She looked up Sylas on the wildly accepted invasive internet and effortlessly found his home address. She asked Ali, Dawud, Hamza, Hind, and Hazera to meet her there. "This is a covert home invasion, be discreet. Don't tell my siblings. If anything happens to all of us at once, my parents would be devastated," she had told them.

Little did she know, Sylas had also done some research on the real Hanifa Ducktrinor.

***

Hanifa had urged Sahabas X.0 and $(CO)_2$ to get their families to safety or sever all ties with them so that their relative could have a chance to live.

After the elite team settled things with their families, they threw a potluck party before setting off to war. Even though the possibility of death was a very plausible outcome, they'd made their peace with that. They were true believers and knew that going to *jannah* was more rewarding and eternal. So instead of rushing to get married like many would do in those situations, they accepted the high stakes and enjoyed each other's company while indulging in high calorie food and sweet minty tea.

During the slumber party, Hanifa reconnected with Safi and the other sisters as they enjoyed singing *nasheeds* and other religious acappellas. They braided each other's hair and confessed which boys they thought were hot and husband material amongst the boys and men of the elite team. And if they made it out alive, they would get married. In their time, marriage wasn't frowned upon but people were more liberal and preferred open marriages and, often, no sacred unions.

The girls enjoyed their slumber party on one side of the

warehouse while the boys enjoyed themselves on the other side. Some of the boys creeped to the girls' side, but they were quickly yelled at by little Dawud who played the *haram* police—he himself was free to roam between the two sides because of his young age. He was the youngest Shiite Imam they had ever seen and accepted. The girls giggled and laughed at his "manly" authority, and Dawud enjoyed their cajoleries.

***

Hanifa had allowed Ali to join the elite team, but she still had mixed feelings about him. Since Shafiya vouched for him as a good guy, Hanifa's hands were tied. She accepted his help and voluntarism. Besides, he had offered to help during Sylas's home invasion, which turned out rewarding yet almost deadly for the home trespassers.

The next day, Dawud spoke to Hanifa while packing his belongings. "When you're done eating, Ali wants to talk to you. He's standing right after the divider wall."

"Ugh, not him again," she replied. Her eyes rolled

towards the ceiling.

"You like him!" Dawud remarked.

"No, I don't!" she refuted.

"I lived alone in the streets and know how to analyze and read people," Dawud countered. "You would be surprised to know what you see when you sit far from a real-life mosaic."

***

As Hanifa inched closer to talk to Ali, another person at the main entrance got her attention: Sylas! The "Seculars" surrounding him at the door didn't fight him or try to stop him. *What now?!*

"The ever-popping-Sylas, to what do we owe a visit from you?" she asked.

"Don't play me, bitch! I know you're planning a mutiny against me and I can tell you right now that you've signed your own death sentence!"

"Ouch! Watch your words and tone, Sylas. We

outnumber you."

"This is high treason and you know it. All of you! You won't be able to touch me, I can tell you that, and I'm not that easy to kill. Know that each of you here has been uncovered and will be charged with spying," Sylas said to the group of people who had started to move closer to him one by one. The pseudo-Secular officers had circled him.

"Plus, I can summon real Seculars officers in the blink of an eye for back-up," he added as his voice trembled.

"Well then, why don't you?" asked Hanifa, face to face with Sylas.

"I haven't yet because I want to know what motivated you in wanting your own team. I followed you for months before I could find this place. One of your members let his guard down in the last few days as he rushed here, so I followed him. I could have had this place destroyed in the matter of seconds, but I wanted to hear your version of the story."

"I don't have to tell you anything. Do what you have to do. Besides, we will meet soon enough for you to see the big picture," Hanifa replied.

"Fine, but don't say I didn't warn you. *Ciao!*" Sylas said and disappeared before her eyes.

"Well, someone knows how to teleport now," Hanifa said, unimpressed, and prepared to carry on with her day. The rest of the group dispersed too after she said, "There is nothing to see here, guys! Let's go fry him!"

CHAPTER TWENTY-SEVEN : THE BATTLE OF THE STADIUM

Hanifa

IT HAD BEEN A YEAR since Hanifa had started going to this school. Temperatures were getting less warm. The Courageous Coreishys and the Sahabas X.0 took their positions at the end of the autumn season and the school year. The leaves of the fake trees, which were remote-controlled by the city, had mostly turned the color of flamboyant trees with some specks of light lime green in them. The air was a mixture of fresh and little moisture.

With the touch of a remote, Dawud suspended the flag of the resistance, a golden minaret on a deep green fabric, between the two groups. Hanifa, perched on her horse, led the girls while Ali stood on his horse in front of the boys. They all faced Sylas, Judas, Ata, and the Secular Army. The walls of the stadium had been pushed up at the base and opened wide, like French windows, allowing more room for the future fighters to enter.

The $(CO)_2$, also perched on top of their mechanical horses, wore white *abayas* on top of their white pants. They used black-and-white *keffiyehs* as their headscarves. Brown steel armor protected their chests.

The Sahabas X.0, on the other hand, wore red-and-white *keffiyehs* as turbans on top of their white tunic and pants. Their chests were also protected by armor while they sat on their mechanical camels.

The day had finally arrived to see what the mechanical horses and camels, also known as The Supplies, were made of.

Between the ranks of the Sahabas X.0, Hanifa saw Malik cock his head in all directions. She inferred he was looking for someone. *Probably Safi.* She thought. Her intuitions were spot on; she saw two pairs of hazel eyes smiling at each other. They brought their right palms to their hearts, whispered words that only both of them knew, and looked away as if accomplished.

"We outnumber you two to one, Hanifa," Sylas ridiculed.

That prompted Hanifa to focus and gather her thoughts.

"Swords and fake animals? Is that all you think you need to beat us? Why don't you surrender? It'll be better for you."

"And God. We have God on our side," Hanifa replied. "Our numbers don't mean anything. You should worry about something else. Let's start this thing, shall we?"

"I'm already *scared*. Sure, why don't you ladies go first and attack. Then we can save the best for last and finish off your men in a proper and fair fight."

She ignored his misogynist comments. "If we win, we take over the school. If we lose, you let us go. Deal?"

"Deal. I'm a man of my word even though you don't think much of me."

"Alright," she said, and pressed a finger on her ear to whisper into the cordless device covered by her white headscarf. "Dawud, make sure to block any frequency transmissions or SOS from their side to the outside world. And make sure we have secured lines of communication, okay?"

"*Sim*, Hanifa," Dawud agreed.

"*Bismillah*," she whispered and switched the channel to Ali's. "Start with the archers." Then to Hamza's channel, "Have the sword fighters follow up the archers like we planned. I'm going for Sylas himself but he won't see me coming. I'll make him think that I'm going in another direction." She activated her Maverick Horse's wings and rose up, flying.

As she rose in the air, she thought of the night of *miraj*, which she and all the other crypto Muslims she knew had just observed a few days ago. In that moment, she wondered how it must have felt when the beloved Prophet *sallallahu aleihi wassalam* felt as he ascended into the galaxies. She tried to fathom the feeling to the best of her capabilities and decided to snap out of it and go on with her *jihad* mission: un-oppress all the believers and the non-Secular masses.

"Good luck, may God be with you, sister," they all prayed for her.

"*Wa iyyakum*, and with you too. See you on the other side *insha'Allah*."

"Malik and Shafiya, when you hear this message, know that I love you," she recorded onto the family channel, hoping they listened to it sometime before, during, or after the fight.

After the words of love, she zeroed in on Sylas like an arrow. A few Secular officers shot at her and she activated her shield to protect herself. She dodged and shot back at them, proving herself to be as good a shot.

The archers followed their orders and quickly dismounted their camels at the touch of a button. In harmony, the fifty archers dropped to one of their knees like they'd rehearsed in the old abandoned warehouse. It was Ali's showoff move he wanted all the archers to adopt. They pressed the side of their right boots, and once they grabbed the levitating matchboxes that emerged from their shoes, their quivers full of arrows and bow were quickly activated. They did all this in less than sixty seconds with precision and deftness. Before the Secular officers knew what was coming, the fifty archers bombarded them with arrows. They hadn't had time to react yet, still under the trance of the perfect performance of Ali's signature move. They also had no idea that the believers had more than one trick up their sleeves.

**

"Damn it! Where did all these ammunitions come from?" Sylas cursed loudly at the sight of the multitude of his officers taken out by the high-tech arrows. The androids were either shut down or malfunctioning while the human officers who were hit were either dead or bruised, moaning with pain. The arrows had a substance called anti-hydrocodone coated on their tips. While hydrocodone relieved pain, this component was a pain-inducing substance.

"Get extra help now!" he hissed at Judas.

"Sir, the lines are down. Plus, you told Sir Landry not to send any help and that we would be able to handle such a *small defect* within our ranks."

"I know what I said!" Sylas snapped and turned to Ata. "Do you have any ideas to offer before they crush all my men and robots?"

"Sir, how about fighting *her*? She's coming straight for us," Ata pointed out. "Or am I the only one seeing the determined look on her face?"

"She won't make it here alive," Sylas promised. "A follower will kill her before she gets here. The bitch deserves that much for trying to recruit my followers at my party. The nerve she has! Ugh! In fact, if you kill her I'll give you Judas's position."

Judas's jaw dropped.

"I will, Sir! You won't regret this, Sir," Ata promised excitedly. He grinned and shot up in the air like a jet pack powered by his boots. "Your job is mine, Judas!"

"You aren't serious?" Judas asked.

"Watch me. First you let Tim escape, then you fail to capture this brat, and the lines go down. Should I continue? You were competent at some point. What happened to you, man?"

Judas stayed silent. Yes, he had failed some important missions. Nonetheless, he had captured many believers—he'd even discovered their site of worship and destroyed it with pleasure. "You will regret this, Sylas. I have been nothing but loyal to you!"

Ata was making his way to Hanifa when Ali shot him in the air with an arrow. Like a hit bird, Ata cursed, "Oh no! Not again!" and dropped to the stadium's floor with a heavy thump.

"Take that, woman beater!" called out Ali, dusting off his right shoulder in a cool fashion. "That's called an Abutalha defense mechanism," he added, gloating.

***

"*Jazak'Allah khair,* Ali," Hanifa said into her earpiece. "I didn't see Ata coming." She activated her wings and ditched her flying horse. She had plenty of star-shaped devices to turn into flying horses or camels when the time came. Right now, though, she didn't have time to retrieve the horse, let alone let him get back to his normal shape.

"No problem, sis. I'll cover you. Hamza and Hind are leading the archers, swordsmen and women like we planned," Ali said.

"*Masha'Allah, subhanallah.* Awesome." She peeked down to see the $(CO)_2$ and the Sahabas X.0 going head to head to head with the Secular officers. A few of her bodies were down.

A ping of sadness and fury lit in her heart, fueling her to fly even faster toward Sylas.

When she reached him, on the other side of the stadium, she pulled both her swords from her side sheaths, at the ready.

Sylas clapped his hands. "Well done, I must admit." Judas stood next to him with a calculating look. "You can't kill me. You can try but I'll be reborn again."

"So that's it, you aren't going to fight a fair fight? Why? Because I'm a girl? Admit it, you're afraid I'm going to kick your ass."

"Just try—but know that the new me will come for you, harshly."

"Hamza told me you're a brilliant fighter," she said and threw one of her swords at him. He instantly grabbed it in the air. "Just humor me and fight with me like you did with him."

He caved in and accepted her duel.

"You're a fool. You should know that a woman that bargains is very dangerous," Judas advised.

"I didn't ask you for counseling," Sylas snapped. He danced an invisible circle around Hanifa. They stared at each other for a while and then the *cling* of the swords started resonating in the air.

He lunged his weapon at her chest a few times and she ducked. Then he lunged at her neck but she moved fast and the weapon only brushed her chin, cutting her at the shoulder. Focused on the fight, she ignored the bleeding, prickling pain.

In a swift movement, she grazed his shoulder and poked him in the thigh before burying the sword into his foot.

"Not bad," Sylas admitted. "But I've had enough of playing with a girl. Go ahead and give me your best sword lunge. I'm ready to be born again and I love to push the limits of the pain that I can endure. I was starting to get tired of this body anyway,"

Hamza was right. This guy is a loony with the pain stuff, Hanifa thought. "You don't have to tell me twice. As you wish!" She dug her sharp sword into his heart.

He seemed to welcome the painful feeling with pleasure as he smiled and spread his arms wide open, like a bird spreading its wings.

"You won't be born again, Sylas," Judas spat behind him. "Not if I get rid of your original carcass, DNA, and stem cells first."

"What?" Sylas stumbled, shocked.

"That's right! What makes you think you can treat me the way you do without any consequences?" Judas yelled before punching Sylas in the gut, inciting a painful grunt.

"Gentlemen, no need for this drama to take place," Hanifa purred. "We've already caught up with your scientist Hamani, and as we speak right now, it's being taking care of." She pulled up a video of Sylas's original body submerged in a cylinder-shaped aquarium filled with a light blue solution.

"What's that around it?" Sylas asked, hunching. He was starting to become weak and heavy on his legs.

"Explosives!" Hanifa excitedly replied. "I have the remote right here." She held it up high.

"You believers and your affinity for explosives," he snarled bitterly.

"Hey! That's offensive! Didn't you and Judas use the same containable explosives to destroy our mosque?"

"Don't remind me! I've had inexplicable guilt and bad dreams since!" Judas said and madly launched at her to get the remote for himself.

They struggled. Equipped with unarmed combat techniques, Hanifa defended herself against Judas. The remote fell as they fought, and Sylas, who was now on the floor, crawled towards it.

"Hey, you two!" he said to the fighters as he waved the remote in the air.

Hanifa elbowed Judas and kicked him in the groin, then got up to go snatch it from Sylas. He wasn't going anywhere; he was fatally wounded. But as she rose on her two feet, Judas tripped her and she fell on her face. "Ow!" she screamed.

Then he got up as fast as he could to acquire the remote.

"Ah! I have it!" he beamed and gloated. He started happily jumping around.

Hanifa dropped her head and said, "Shit!" Then an idea hit her and she pressed a finger to her ear. "Dawud, are you there?"

"Yes, H. What do you need?"

"How's it going over there?"

"Alright, we lost Yakuta and Hazera, and many other strong fighters. But we took down a landslide of them. Your siblings are also okay. They are fighting a good fight *masha'Allah*."

Bittersweet, she closed her eyes and said, "*Inna lilahi wa inna illayi rajiun*. Look, Dawud, do you still have the other remote for Sylas's carcass?"

"Yes, why?"

"I just lost mine in a stupid fight and gloating contest. Just light it up right now! I repeat, light it up!"

"**R**eceived **O**rder **G**iven, **E**xpect **R**esults! Oh I meant RAHMAN (**R**eceived **A**rray **H**ope **M**ajor, **A**waiting **N**ew)! Aaaaand done," Dawud finished. Hanifa had come up with a clever Arabic-English version to say ROGER THAT, which somehow would tie into the *deen*. Dawud thought it was cool but still had issues remembering it since ROGER THAT was more common in the rebellion and in the military world.

"You're a savior D! I love you. See you soon *insha'Allah*."

"Love you too. And it's in a different way. Anyway, see you soon *insha'Allah*," he agreed.

"I'm too old for you," Hanifa laughed and switched off the radio. "And now, to get rid of Sylas's clone and vampire self once and for all." She had learned that finding and burning the real human body would get rid of the starter the recipe needs. Destroy the starter, and the batch is ruined. She turned to Judas. "So are you going to frame that remote, dude?"

"Yeah, something like that—after I'm done with it."

She wheeled around to find the video she had shown them earlier. Upon seeing what she had done to Sylas's clone, Judas's face turned somber.

He dropped the prized remote, defeated. "That was supposed to be my moment!"

"It's over," Hanifa announced. "The leader of this school will not be resuscitated."

Victory was palpable. The support of about 3,500 more soldiers flooded into the stadium from around the world. Because the fight was broadcast around the world, Sylas's lifeless body was visible to many of his followers and they then either surrendered, fled, or died. The walls of the stadium had been opened in a French window fashion to make room for the imminent possibility that supporters might come, and if Sylas and his followers hadn't been so sure of themselves, they would have paid attention to these details instead of belittling and underestimating the enemy. The walls hung high in the air, vertically to the ground and provided lots of shade like parasols do.

"You're a good tracker, Judas," Hanifa admitted. "We could use you even though you hurt my friend Ana. Forgiving is divine. It goes without saying that Islam is also about forgiving, and I forgive you. What do you say?"

He stayed quiet and nodded to accept the new alliance. Then he spoke. "I've wanted to leave the Seculars ever since I burned the mosque and the awful things I did to Ana, but I couldn't. It could be the reason why I let my own subconscious sabotage all the missions given to me by Sylas."

"It's all right, we all make mistakes," Hanifa said.

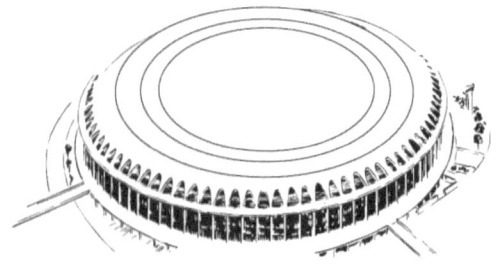

CHAPTER TWENTY-EIGHT : LEAVING SCHOOL

Hanifa

AFTER THEY WON the Battle of the Stadium, and Sylas's troops had retreated or were taken prisoners, Hanifa and her team collected their dead and performed their *janazzah* services. The supporting troops from around the world helped.

Afterwards, Hanifa decided to take a nap to rest, as did most of the others. And she dreamt a mind-boggling dream.

"Mom, there is somebody I want you to meet!" she screamed as soon as she stepped foot in her parents' house. The smell of her mom's delicious cooking permeated the air.

Mmm, yum!

"You have?" her mother replied from upstairs and gracefully made her way downstairs to meet Hanifa and her guest. When she reached them, she added, "Wow! Such big beautiful eyes for a man." She gave him a motherly look and silently approved of the first man Hanifa had ever brought home. But a distant voice in the background distracted Hanifa and rudely yanked her out of her family moment.

"Hanifa, Hanifa, Hanifa! Wake up!" Dawud was shaking her hard.

The eyes she saw were still vivid in her memory. She had seen them before but couldn't remember where. *And what was that about? I rarely remember my dreams,* she silently pondered upon waking up.

"What's up?" she asked, rubbing her eyes and groaning at the early wake-up call. It felt like she had been asleep for only thirty minutes.

"It's four o'clock. You slept three hours. Get ready—

we need to leave after the *fajr* prayer. Most people have returned from their homes. We will be packing all the tents soon and set to travel with the fleets you brought. You've got to be scared of a woman's bag. *More Supplies.*" Then he *tsked.* Her backpack was full of small matchbox-looking rectangles that, once activated, transformed into fleets.

"Oh, and Ali wants to talk to you," Dawud continued.

As soon as he said that, it hit her. Those eyes! *Damn it! How did Ali manage to end up in my fantasies and dreams?*

***

"As you know, we are in the Americas," Hanifa announced. "We need to go to Tarsus, Turkey. And that's in Eastern Europe if some of you didn't know. Dawud, are the fleets ready?"

He nodded.

"Alright people, go toward Dawud, he will take you to your traveling devices. Make good lines. There is enough space for everyone. No Titanic drama will occur *insha'Allah.* I hope you prayed and put your fate in His hands. Whether or not we will find the cave is in the Almighty's hands now. *Yalla!*"

As they left to sail on the South Atlantic Ocean, Secular forces closed in on them with flying military and patrol cars and descended upon the victors. Then a voice enhancer resonated through the air, "Hanifa Ducktrinor, this is Sir Landry Big speaking. Let me show you what we do to moles in the Secular system."

A projector displayed the picture of her uncle Abe brutally tortured and hanged.

She gasped loudly, along with the rest of the crowd.

Sir Landry continued into the speaker, "If you want something done right, you've got to do it yourself. I don't care about any arrangements you've made with the late Sylas, who tried his best and had a major breakthrough by finding your previous name, Kreedor, and a few other interesting details that had escaped our organization. No one is going anywhere. Secular officers, get them!"

"Hail to the S! The world will never end!" the officers chanted before going after Hanifa and the victors of the Battle of the Stadium. Still under the shock of her uncle's death, with whom Hanifa was looking forward to sharing her success and the meaning of her cryptic questions, she froze, bewildered. She hadn't thought of or designed a plan B for this outcome.

Malik Ducktrinor gave Hanifa that intimate fraternal lock of eyes he was so good at, and Hanifa instantly understood. She stepped aside as the rest of the elite team let him take the lead.

Sandwiched between the ocean facing them and the Seculars behind them, panic set off like wildfire among the ranks.

CHAPTER TWENTY-NINE : FORSAKEN?

Hanifa

INNA LILAHI WA INNA ileihi rajiun uncle Abe. You weren't the most religious person but if I don't see you in Jannah, I'll ask for you insha'Allah. Hanifa sighed before her mind continued to race. *I didn't make all the right calculations. The Seculars catching to us wasn't supposed to happen now. I hope Imam Malik saves the day as usual. I should have known that at least other Seculars would try to cross us,*

Hanifa thought with a heavy heart. *Maybe Ali is right. I might be over my head with this whole rebellion thing. Imam Hanifa declined offers to be a judge for questionable people, maybe I should have declined the Seculars' offer to become a deputy.* She paused, contemplating. *It's too late for regrets now, you might die a martyr like him,* her conscience pointed out.

Ugh! Maybe, who knows? Not that I don't like the rewards but I want to be married and live a little before I die. Her thoughts continued to ramble. *Besides, I want to keep my intentions pure and try not to die a martyr so that people can praise me as a shahid or heroine.* And the voices in her head continued to prattle on when she laid eyes on the *Mujahideen.* It was out of this world. *Aliens and Cowboys is a definite remake if these guys make it with us to Tarsus.*

These Cowboys definitely know how to abduct the enemies, Hanifa thought as she saw the Seculars disappearing as the lassos engulfed them left and right or the high-tech riffles took turns obliterating them.

Hanifa snapped out of it when she heard an interesting comment Dawud made in her earplug which was still turned on. Her childhood memories came rushing to her like a flood of adrenaline. *The Science Fair!* She tuned in just in time as Malik gave further instructions. Sometimes Dawud reminded her of Pristine with the sass mouthing. She decided not to dwell too much on the youngsters because time was of the essence and she was once again hopeful and her faith in Malik restored. *I hope they don't think a man had to finish the job. Who cares what they think? He is my older brother, and I will welcome his help. Nobody can do everything by themselves. Only Allah can, and there is nothing wrong with seeking help. In all, it's about team work.* She retorted at the voices in her head.

Malik had always had her back, since they were children. He helped her deal with bullies when they were kids, and she knew he would do it anytime in a heartbeat but she thought this situation was different and he was perhaps out of his league with Sir Landry himself.

Malik's contribution at Sylas's mansion was essential to the success of their covert operation. If it weren't for him, the mission would have been a disaster. She pondered as she started reminiscing how it came about for her older brother to find her whereabouts that day after he had joined the ranks of the elite team, the Sahabas X.0. Hanifa didn't dwell too much on these events due to the support she was perusing at the same time.

The crowd that showed at the stadium reminded Hanifa that the *Taif* period she had read about and seen in time travels was over and that Muslims and other believers were once again united to stand against oppression. Hanifa and Dawud had met several resistance groups through their broadcasts on *The Muezzin*. The *Mujahideen* were only a fraction of the resistance movement. There was another strong faction called The 4Cs, short for the Four Caliphs. All the members of the group were men that were divided into groups of four when they went into missions against the Seculars. They operated like a SWAT team and were very efficient in rescue missions to retrieve hostages.

She could distinguish The Hui-Han Descendants of their time with their distinctive renovated Chinese banner. The

Righteous Murabitun, those who hold fast. The ones of the Futuristic Muwahhidun, the Brave Moriscos of Spain, the Last Mamlucks, the Deli Sultans, Team Muhammad, and The Bold Malê from Brazil where the Battle of the Stadium was taking place.

Warfare rules of Abu Bakr (May God be pleased with him) had been extended to all of these groups during the broadcast and recruitment period. And they were all ready and fighting according to the real *sharia* law; not the perverted laws the extremists went by. All these groups had made an alliance with the Resistance, which was somewhat the governing body under which all the different resistance movements around the world stood under.

1

The Hui-Han Descendants were part of the 3500 support number that came to the elite Secular team assembled by Hanifa. Their banner was a red flag with a gold star right in the middle of it. The elite Secular team had asked for 350-500 bodies to support them at the Battle of the Stadium against Sylas.

"We will help with 500 bodies, *insha'Allah*," General Kai had replied through an encrypted message via broadcast.

"*Jazakh'Allah khair* General Kai. See you on the battle field *insha'Allah*," Dawud had replied and then informed Hanifa that the Chineses were on board.

2

The Righteous Murabitun hailed from Morocco. Their contact with the elite was Ridwan, a.k.a. Rick. Ridwan was African American but he grew up in Morocco so he knew the place very well.

"Hamza, there is an underground movement I know in Morocco who might agree to help us during the Battle of the

Stadium," Ridwan had said soon after he had been recruited by Ali and Hanifa.

Hamza informed Hanifa, one thing led to another and contact was made with the group. The Righteous Murabitun provided 700 boots or 350 soldiers. Their banner was a gold flag.

3

The Futuristic Muwahhidun were another faction which developed in Morocco. While Ridwan knew some of their members, he wasn't the one who recruited them. The Righteous Murabitun sought their support by praising a new movement of believers (the elite team) with hope in the far lands of Brazil. That was all it took for The Futuristic Muwahhidun to agree to lend their help.

4

Upon his arrival in Spain, thanks to Mustapha Kreedor's inventions, Nadhir first noticed the white flags over the city waving as he read their golden inscriptions: *Wa la ghalib illallah* (There is no Victor except Allah). He smiled and said, "Indeed, no matter the religion, His victory can't be denied." Nadhir looked at his mission's instructions and found the place he needed to be at. Several minutes later he was seated awaiting the person he was there to meet.

"*Assalamu aleikum,* my Andals brothers. I bring exciting news *masha'Allah,*" Nadhir announced as he settled down in the compound of The Brave Moriscos he was visiting upon order of his superiors back in Brazil.

"*Wa aleikum salam,* brother Nadhir. Welcome to our city Granada," the leader by the name of Abdul Rahman said.

Nadhir admired the Andalusian décor for a moment,

smiled, and continued talking. When he finished, a young woman in the room with an intimidating posture from the entourage of Abdul Rahman spoke.

"We will send a message to the leaders in Seville and Cordoba so they can help too. Have a safe trip back," Rashida promised.

Then, the Brave Moriscos said farewell to Nadhir, the messenger sent from Brazil. Spain didn't have a strong Secular force but it was still risky travelling especially with the kind of business and news he was bringing to parties that didn't support the Seculars. It was grounds for treason.

5

From Egypt, The Last Mamlucks were a group of students just like the majority of small resistance movements lending their help to the Ducktrinors in Brazil. Knowledge was power and students having been educated had started to realize the state of affairs the global world was facing.

"We will pick The Last Mamlucks because we all come from underprivileged parts of Egypt, but the knowledge we sought paid for our tuitions in top rated schools. The last hours are upon us, and we will go out in style *insha'Allah*. The Last Mamlucks it is!" their leader had yelled and his followers did the same in return and agreement. Their coat of arms was a pink banner with an open brown book at the top right corner.

6

In India, there was the Deli Sultans. In Turkish, *deli* means mad. During a conversation, an Indian girl from Delhi and an exiled Turkish boy decided that their social activism group would be called the Deli Sultans. Oh, it was befitting, inclusive, and reflective of both the Turkish and Indian heritage of the sultanate.

"For six hundred years, the Ottoman empire ruled the

world and was tolerant of other nations and religions. Why do we have to put up with less than par with this Sir Landry Big ruling the world and oppressing us?" Emre had asked the group of students who were following him and Pilar.

It didn't take much for Pilar and Emre to convince their followers that Brazil is where it was at.

"They even have Mustapha Kreedor, the former genius of the fallen Resistance, sponsoring and mentoring them. This is the support we need to get our cause heard and flip the table!" Pilar said, encouraging the rest of the group.

The group nodded and "class" was dismissed in the unmarked room of their Indian school's basement. Pilar and Emre also recruited their South Asian compatriots in South Africa. Hanifa enjoyed them singing "Nkosi Sikelel" meaning God Bless Africa, the South African national anthem.

7

Team Muhammad was on the extremist list of the Secular government for one reason only; activism on social justice. Minorities were no longer being picked on anymore *alhamdullilah* compared to the early years of Malik's life. However, another racial group was being targeted: Whites. This was all the doing of Sir Landry Big. Many White families had escaped the United States to seek asylum in other countries that were lax on the way they enforced the laws designed by the leader of the Seculars. Many countries turned a blind eye and that helped humanity to some extent.

Their team name was inspired first and foremost by Prophet Muhammad *sallallahu aleihi wassalam*. Then, on other inspiring black African Muslims in America. These other inspirations were Bilali Muhammad, Dalila Muhammad, Ibtihaj Muhammad, Warith Deen Muhammed, etc. Before another civil war in the history of the United States erupted, many justice seekers left the country and took refuge in several of Central and South America countries until they settled in Brazil.

8

The Bold Malê from Brazil were already a constant thorn in the hands of the Seculars, much like the first Yorubas in these parts during the transatlantic slave trade. Malik sought their help after he had been recruited by Hanifa. He knew about them because he had met them one day while taking a long walk in the slums of Brazil. It was an interesting meeting for sure because he almost got robbed and killed.

"*Allahu Akbar!*" he had exclaimed when he was rapidly accosted out of nowhere by black males who looked like thugs based on their weaponry and covered faces. Upon hearing his unintended supplication, they relaxed and asked him if he was Muslim.

"Yes, I was born Muslim, and I was just trekking to clear my mind. I didn't realize I had crossed to the wrong side of town."

"*Masha'Allah*, for you it will never be the wrong side of town because you are protected by Him. Welcome brother," a man that looked like the leader of the small group said, lowering his face cloth revealing a full beard. As he relaxed, Malik finally noticed their flowing white garments which were covered by leather jackets. It was winter time and a new friendship was born.

9

Hindus For Peace, an interfaith Hindu group had made an alliance with the Deli Sultans to protect each other in the highly oppressive era of the Seculars in India. Indhira, the leader, was a good friend of Pilar. Both girls knew their religious boundaries and never preached to the other. They just respected their respective beliefs and bonded as friends.

10

Peaceful Christians United was an interfaith Christian group who had ties with Dawn, the bakery shop owner of Greenwuhud, America. Hanifa reached out to the old woman to see if she had connections that wouldn't mind lending a hand for her cause. Part of Dawn's family was non-Muslim and she had kept civil ties with them. They didn't live in a safe haven anymore but they still kept contact.

"*Insha'Allah*, they will come to your help in Paraty. Peaceful Christians United were one of my best customers, *masha'Allah*. I'll talk to them. Don't worry, child."

At her words, Hanifa was appeased and they said their goodbyes.

And she was right, they came in numbers and praised singing in acapella "When the Saints Go Marching In." It was befitting, as all Hanifa, the creator of the movement, and her followers had always wanted was to be in the number of the Saints when they came marching in, God willing.

11

Coraline, a Jewish $(CO)_2$, was a member of the Shalom Keepers, an interfaith Jewish group. She helped recruit their help because social equality was a must. Freedom of religion was needed and all the oppressed parties and those who believed that oppression was inhumane joined forces.

She loved to say, "The one who goes to the end of his religion will meet the others—Anonymous."

12

Agnostics and Atheists United didn't need to believe in a religion to disagree with the Seculars. They had strong ethics and good moral values so they landed their help. Sarah, a White American $(CO)_2$, was their ambassador at the elite Secular team.

CHAPTER THIRTY : OF BRAVE AND DAUNTING

The $(CO)_2$

1

HIND WAS THE FIRST to react amongst the girls. "Courageous Coreishys! What are we going to do about the current situation? We're tired and extremely exhausted but we need to fight these Seculars once and for all. Who is with me?" she had said to the girls around her reach. Many nodded while others, from the looks on their faces, were trying to decide if they should accept Malik's offer to board his safe device and hope to live another day war-free.

Her gray eyes were challenging the girls to be brave. As she waited for their answers, she removed her headscarf revealing sweat soaked raven curls. It wasn't hot, it was almost winter actually and the cold wind whistled in her ears, drying the sweat beads on her face rather quickly. She reattached her headscarf and said, "If you think you can handle another battle and still have some fight left in you, follow me. Let's finish so I can enjoy a good cup of tea mates. " She mounted her mechanical horse and went bravely into the mayhem.

Hind Clark had always been a brave and bold person. As a British Muslim, her country had a long history of Muslims starting from before the famous Victorian Muslims she had read about. However, Muslims in Great Britain were still persecuted. Her family escaped persecution in England and took refuge in Brazil. There, they hid their religion because no one knew them and they didn't want the attention and become singlehanded. She had asked her family and young brother to leave in case she was arrested and the link to them became obvious. They declined her wish and told her that they were tired of running. They added, "If our time is here, it is here. Besides, you guys should all have war names. We accept what will happen as the *qadr* of Allah but having a war name can help the members of your resistance."

Hind agreed and ran the idea to Hanifa who loved it. The fallen ones would be listed in *The Muezzin* and their relatives would know the fate of their family members. Thus, the Resistance of Castle 5 had alternative identification documents which displayed *nom de guèrre* on them out of safety. They were supposed to keep these on them at all times. Thus her *nom de guerre* was Damme de Fer.

As she slayed Seculars one after the other, all Hind wanted to do was finish this second battle at the stadium and retreat on an Island around Turkey not too far from the rest of the crew with a cat and a wide range of herbal teas to savor daily. This was the motivation that was keeping her valiantly strong. She had a weakness though: Malik. She found him uncontestably good looking, but the fact that another Coreishy was also drooling on him made Hind give up on that foolish desire to be with him. She was a lone person with no penchant for cat fights or romance drama, especially love triangles.

2

"Hey Jackass! Come this way," Yakuta had yelled to the Secular officer who was about to stab one of the Coreishys with his digital sword. The guard turned around to assess her and accepted her invitation. As bullets and swords flew left and right, she effortlessly dodged the intended attacks along with the unintended attacks of the warriors around her. She took long and graceful strides toward her opponent while euphoria washed over her. She had long lost her real horse and her backup transportation, a mechanical horse and a mechanical camel. Now, she had to fare by foot, and she had no problems with that. Several times she hopped over dead bodies in her short walk to meet her adversary. And when they finally met, their weapons clung in the air. When the Secular officer overpowered her and removed her weapon from her hand, she deftly unsheathed a real Samurai's sword from her side. Her white robes billowed in the breezy autumn season for a moment.

"You are a lucky guy. I've only used this sword on one very rare occasion," she said, smiling as she wiped the blood from her lips. He had punched her in the face and pushed her on the ground when he overpowered her.

"When was that, doll?" the officer said, indulging her words.

"When I killed the people who forced my parents to perform *seppuku*—suicide—before I escaped with my uncle and aunt from Secular Japan."

"Well, I will kill you with it so you can join them too," he had mocked with a hint of surety in his voice.

So they fought and fought. They cut and stubbed each other until the duo fell to the ground exhausted and fatally wounded.

"Told you I would kill you," the Secular officer had found the strength to say.

"Sure." Yakuta had rolled her eyes as the pain of her own inflicted sword was spreading through her body. She winced and then smiled at the beautiful sky before closing her eyes.

She knew she couldn't defeat her opponent and had met her match, so as he was strangling her with a lock of his arm and elbow, she plunged her sword into her left side with all the strength she had left. The pain of the sharp sword spread through her like tiny needles and blades. Then it entered her opponent, who was leaning on her back. Blood had stained her uniform and that was the least of her worries. As her last moments drew faster by the minute, she quickly attested that there was no God but God and that Muhammad was His last messenger. Then, she imagined herself laughing at old funny newspaper clippings.

Yakuta had always enjoyed good jokes and lived her life

fully. Her war name was The Last Samurai Girl. Yakuta Yao died a valiant warrior in the eyes of her teammates who saw her die but were engrossed in their own fights as well.

Her round facial features, her well drawn eyebrows, and her pink lips tugged in a closed smile made it look like she was peacefully sleeping when her Coreishy sisters finally liberated themselves from their opponents and approached her body to pray and say their good byes.

3

Hazera fought until her last breath too. She was a Secular Muslim up until she met Hanifa and Ali at the mosque. Her Bosnian relatives stayed Secular. She always thought of this verse, "Perhaps Allah will put, between you and those to whom you have been enemies among them, affection. And Allah is competent, and Allah is Forgiving and Merciful" (Quran 60:7) when it came to her family. She loved them dearly.

They weren't non-Muslims but to her it felt like it because they were only Muslim in name as they didn't pray or even fast. All they did was celebrate on the *Eid*.

Her war name was The Balkan. She chose the name because she believed that arbitrary mapping rules divided her people and that they were one instead. Therefore, she didn't pledge allegiance to Bosnia only but to all the Balkan countries as they were her true roots in essence. In her mind, she was their Muslim representative. A poet, she loved anything from pre-Islam to current day. She followed e-Poets and was one herself. With complete bias, her all-time favorites were the *Mu'allaqat* or The Seven Golden Odes.

Unlike Yakuta, who couldn't be helped to say her last rites as in rituals when she was dying, this Balkan received helped from her Coreishy sister Nadirah. Nadirah held her hand dearly and helped her recite the words. Back lying flat on the sand, her sky blue eyes stared in her helper's hazel ones. Her thin lips cracked a smile at Nadirah as her soul slowly departed her body.

4

Coraline washed her hands and studied her face in the mirror. "It looks like I'm losing weight," she said to herself. Her round face had become a bit thin thanks to the intensive training sessions of Hanifa. She left the ladies room on the heel on that thought. It was on the night of the slumber party before the Battle of the Stadium. As Coraline was coming from the ladies room, she saw Malik standing in front of the men's room waiting his turn. *Oooh, it's hot stuff. Strike a conversation with him but don't be stupid.* "So I read that my ancestors the Jews fasted on a day similar to yours," Coraline said, addressing Malik.

"Yes, it's the tenth day of *Muharram* for us. History has it that it's the day Allah saved the children of Israel from Pharaoh," he added.

"That's what I heard too," she said, smiling coyly at him.

"We aren't that different uh?"

"I guess."

"Are you the one my sister likes to call Marjane?"

"Yea, sorry. I'm Coraline Hanifin. Nice to meet you," she said mock-formal like and saluted with a quick wave of her right hand.

Malik laughed and added, "I guess proper presentations are in order. Malik Ducktrinor, pleased to make your acquaintance."

She lowered her head and brushed invisible dust from the native and traditional clothes she was sporting because she had just performed a play for the girls. She couldn't wait to change into pajamas.

"Lovely colors by the way. Martinique?" Malik asked.

"Correct. Ever been to that part of the French Islands?" she asked, her short brown curls peeking under her Creole head wrap. She had cut her hair during the summer season and now it was finally growing as winter downed upon Brazil.

"Yea, in my family we time travel a lot."

"Nice. Lucky you! Wait a minute. Time travel? Teleportation yes, time travel is a bit far-fetched," Coraline said.

"Oh, if you think about it, it's time travel. I'll give you a simple example. New York and Dallas are one hour apart based on the time zones. If I take a plane in Dallas, which is on central time at 9 a.m., I'll land in New York in a little over three hours, say 12 p.m. It will be 11 a.m. in Dallas at this hour in New York. That my friend is what I call time travel. I went to the future. If I do it the other way, it's the past."

"Damn! You're good, even though I want to say that these times are sometimes so arbitrary. But I have a feeling I won't win since the sun plays a role in these hours. Anyways, I think we can also call that space travel."

"You know it! I can be very convincing. But you're right, depending on how you look at it, it could also be called space travel." Malik winked at her.

Coraline laughed deeply. "I want to go to Palestine one day to see the Promised Land with my two eyes. When all this quiets down, God willing," she said absentmindedly and leaned her back on the wall.

"Me too," Malik confessed.

They smiled and Malik ended the conversation by hinting that he needed to use the leak room.

She understood and made apologetic movements followed by, "Oh sure! See you around. *Shalom!*"

He is hot, Coraline thought on her way back to the girl's section of the warehouse, Knights Inn.

5

Makhnani Uzumakee was originally from Japan like Yakuta. Contrarily to her compatriot Yakuta, who was outgoing and bubbly, Makhnani was a very meek person. She was probably more taciturn than Malik. Very skilled in the arts of fighting, she couldn't untie herself from the attacks of the Seculars to finish off that monster that caused the death of her bestie Yakuta. Parentless, the two had bonded over their common ancestral background.

When she finally got rid of her opponent, Makhnani made a bee line to her dear friend, closed her eyes, marked the spot where the body was, and pocketed her sister-in-Islam's heirloom samurai sword.

You're only gone in this life and I'll miss you. There is no doubt about that. I will make sure you get the Islamic burial rituals you deserve insha'Allah. May we be neighbors in Jannah, dear beloved friend. Ameen, Makhnani whispered. And like a lightning bolt, she was back on the battle field fighting the bad guys. "Take this suckers!" You could hear screams as she launched herself toward the Seculars brandishing her weapons in the air with renewed vigor.

6

Nadirah Beauregard had well-taken care of natural hair. The night before the Battle of the Stadium, her Coreishys had played in her soft hair. She didn't let anybody touch her hair but she made an exception just for her sisters in Islam. They had managed to braid her full head of hair in twisty box braids without extensions. During the battle she had covered her hair with a headscarf but left a space at the front where we could see the root of her hair from the fringe. After fighting and kicking around, one twist came out and danced in her face. She didn't get a chance to put it back when she saw Hazera being shot in the neck. Her bulletproof vest was dented from multiple attacks. She still had her teleportation device with her so she ran to Hazera's help. *Should I teleport to a quiet place*, she pondered rather quickly. *What if she dies in the process? There is no time, we will have to do it here and be vigilant.* So she helped Hazera say, "*Laa ilaaha ill-Allaah…*"

She bitterly concluded that their rebellion database would be updated immediately because the tracker embedded in Hazera should automatically shut down as her heart gave its last beat and she took her last breath. Tears filled Nadirah's almond-shaped eyes as she tried to keep her composure. They rolled on her skin without permeating her coated skin. Nadirah inhaled with her thin Nubian nose and exhaled. *I can get through this*, she said to herself, and continued fighting.

Her skin was the color of glistening ebony. Her white robes accentuated her skin color matching her pearly whites. Nadirah was resplendent indeed, like her name. Her parents hailed from Africa; Guinea to be exact. The Coreishys called her Beauregard because she had piercing brown eyes. Thus she chose Agent Beauregard as a war name.

7

Miss Mystic had recited her favorite verse for the billionth time in her lifetime and during the fight at the battle of the Stadium, it was like she was invisible to her opponents as she came out unscathed and unruffled. "I woke up like this," she teased later to her teammates who were sweaty and ruffled up from the battle. Did she perform a *keeramat*? Perhaps.

CHAPTER THIRTY-ONE : DAWUD'S STORY

Dawud

AT THE LOUD NOISE provoked by Malik, with his gimmicks, Dawud said, "Mobi Dick?" and finished the rest of his thoughts mentally. *You've got to be kidding me. This guy is going to save the day with a mere fish look alike. He better have a good plan and it better be a super fish for all I care because waking up old memories with loud noises like this better be worth it! These Seculars will pulverize us into oblivion with their state-of-the-art military technologies. They steal ideas at science fairs and make them their own, but I could have rigged his tool better.*

Very loud noises had the effect of stirring Dawud's demons to the surface and he didn't like when the past visited him because he wanted to forget it.

A couple years earlier, Dawud had heard a boom in the house and then screams from the other tenants. Their house had been bombed. *Oh no! The Seculars have found us.* His parents, the Broussards, had been American religion activists and went from country to country to rally support to fight the oppressors. They stayed in safe houses and never dallied too long in one area. But on this day in Alepo, they had been cornered. The door to Dawud's room was on fire and smoke had started to seep in. "Ya Allah please help my parents," he had said, staring at the door, hopeless, before fleeing through the window as he coughed and covered his nose. Small, agile, and flexible at eight winters, he didn't look back. He ran and ran until he couldn't. He found himself in the markets of Syria with abandoned stalls and cats, dogs, and other rodents roaming the starry night. He found some discarded boxes lying on the dirt and an idea struck him. Tired, thirsty, and sleepy, he grabbed a few and covered himself with them under one of the wooden tables. He made a prayer to Allah to protect him during the night from the shadows and anything else lurking in the dark that wasn't good for him.

Later, Dawud woke up to the sound of the *adhan* from a nearby mosque. *It's probably a mosque that the Muslim merchants use during the day when it's time to pray,* he said to himself. On the day before, Dawud had become homeless and an orphan to his knowledge. "If we get separated one day, don't look back! Save yourself!" his parents had warned once they went into politics. "Always have your papers on you in this plastic pouch and never take it out. Understood?" his father Imran had said.

Dawud had nodded and taken the papers and secured them safely under his clothes.

"If we are to disappear one day, make sure you get into contact with the rebellion as soon as possible. You know how to do that because you're a computer genius. They will help you get out of the country and support you."

As Dawud roamed the streets before trying to establish

contact later that day, he witnessed the spirit of Zaltun controlling the markets. His flag was colonizing almost every other market stall. Merchants were shamelessly scheming their clients. People were arguing and screaming at each other about prices and product quality. It was a loud and overwhelming experience. He was disheveled and had little money in his pockets. He didn't know how it would stretch it because he had no idea how long it would take for the rebellion to come to his help with the whole country so torn apart.

So during the days, he looked for easy errands and jobs to perform— such as delivering teas or carrying women's bags of groceries— and during the nights, he slept hidden under market tables. He always prayed at the mosque and helped the Imam when he needed.

"Good boy, *insha'Allah*, one day you will lead your own *djamat* as well," the old man had told him once when Dawud fixed his voice enhancer for the *jumah* sermon.

"*Insha'Allah*," Dawud had answered, smiling.

His friendship with Imam Samee grew. He let Dawud

sleep at the mosque sometimes. In better times, the mosque's doors would have been open at all times of the day, but with thieves, thugs, and ill-intentioned people running around these days, the doors of the holy site were closed when the five daily prayers weren't in session. Food and a shower came easy after that for Dawud when the Imam noticed him because the mosque was never short of donations from the believers who gave anything that could be of use to the other believers and the needy of the area in those dire times.

In the meantime, Dawud continued to try to establish contact with the rebellion, but it seemed liked they had moved, with the Seculars unto them. He still continued to frequent the market when it wasn't time to pray or he didn't have to execute a job for some pocket change. He learned to read people, to study them, and watch out for their tricky ways as he continued to pray daily for Allah to protect him and help his parents whether they were in this life or the next. He missed the comforting smile of his mother Asiiya and the strategic mind of his Cajun father Jaysun.

In those dark moments he faced, Imam Samee and his wife Souzane took him under their wings and taught him many things such as Islamic History, the *deen*, Islamic calligraphy, and many important secular subjects. Anse Souzane was a retired nurse who was very gentle with Dawud. She helped him memorize the Quran. Dawud was the son they never had and they became the parents he yearned for. They had taken him in and raised him as their biological child. Dawud felt blessed and was immensely grateful to them second and to Allah first.

His new parents always loved to launch discussions of how Syria used to be. It gave them comfort and peace of mind.

"Syria was once a thriving country, son," Imam Samee always pointed out, lost in his thoughts with a distant smile on his bony face covered with white hair from one cheek to the other and also encircling his mouth. Dawud could see the reminiscence hitting the old man hard who shook his head in disbelief in a long sigh.

Dawud listened attentively to the tales of the slender old man about Syria, which were short of being called paradise on earth. From the accounts of the Imam, Syria was once beautiful, green with tall palm trees and other strong bushes lining the country. The architecture was old, magnificent, and attracted tourists and other visitors. Stylish fountains of water with intricate designs built by engineers several centuries before and beautiful holy sites were a sight to see, a sign of wealth and prosperity. "Sometimes I think it could also be a city of *djinns*, like Delhi in India. I mean, it has been destroyed and rebuilt so many times, *Allahu Akbar*," Iman Samee often speculated.

And every now and then, Anse Souzane would pitch in and say, "It's a romantic land for sure." She had met Imam Samee there one day when she was lost in the market trying to make her way back to her tour group.

"*Subhanallah*, I didn't know what to do. I didn't have a phone and I had strayed from the group because I saw something so beautiful on one market stall that I wanted, a beautiful necklace," she would say pressing her fingers at the silver double heart pendant hidden beneath her long blue flowing dress, nested just under her neckline. Then she would give an accomplice smile to her husband before continuing.

"Then I heard the *adhan* for the first time in my life in a moment of confusion. It awakened something in me. I wanted to get close and meet the person behind the lovely voice. So I asked around. Some people could understand me but wondered why I would want to go there because I looked conspicuously like a non-Muslim," she would pause there, dip her head forward to stare at her lap and stop the emotions pouring out of her as her eyes would start to glisten with small tears. Dawud knew that she was still struggling with some of the locals even though she had converted to Islam a while ago and was very knowledgeable in the religion. She had *deen* on the brain but her white skin color and feminine gender weren't always playing in her favor in that land.

"Determined, I set off to find the mosque letting my sense of hearing guide me and sometimes I followed people that looked like they were Muslims and going to pray. You know the rest. We've told you that story too many times," she said, smiling like a shy person.

"One thing led to another and we fell in love and I taught her about the *deen* even though at first I opposed her conversion. I felt like she was doing it for me but then I realized that the *adhan* had awakened some kind of spirituality in her and that I was just the means that Allah chose to guide her to Islam. *Masha'Allah*," Imam said, smiling fondly at his wife as they locked fingers sitting on the floor side by side on the *musalla* of the small but elegant mosque of the neighborhood.

The Imam and his wife were never shy to discuss taboo subjects with Dawud. They took it upon themselves to teach him about sex education, love, and romance. They loved to say, "One day, they will be useful to you. Our love story is the best example of how a married couple should be, son. May Allah always bless and protect you long after we are gone from this world. *Ameen*."

"*Ameen*."

When Dawud finally made contact, his new parents decided to stay behind. Last he heard, the mosque and Aleppo where he had stayed were unrecognizable. They had been blown to oblivion. Dawud had no idea if Baba Samee and Umm Dawud were still alive. A vision of a blast always flashed in his memory when he thought of them. "Syria, you will rise again and be rebuilt again, God willing. Natural disasters destroyed the third Muslim holiest site, al-Aqsa, and it was rebuilt again. So you will rise from the ashes *bi'ithnillah*," Dawud always promised under his breath as he glanced at his adopted city when he looked at the latest online posts of Syria. He always hoped to see his two pair of parents alive again one day in breaking news.

Dawud pulled himself together to carry on his job as the flag carrier after these thoughts. *I doubt Abu Ayyub al-Ansari, the flag carrier, was day dreaming on duty. I better stay alert!* He scolded himself.

CHAPTER THIRTY-TWO : ALI'S STORY

Ali

"ALI, THIS IS WHERE your vengeance can be warranted. Go after Seculars and target as many as you can with your skills to allow the troops and the elite team to make a safe escape. This goes as well to anybody who is willing to sacrifice himself for the cause," Malik ordered.

"R.A.H.M.A.N! Challenge gladly accepted!" Ali yelled back.

Like a lightning bolt, Ali appeared like a magician to

strike the Seculars and annihilate them and disappeared before he got hit with their gun that had the power to turn anything into nothingness, wind, dust; something unseeable by the human eye. Many dodged with their own state-of-the-art techniques, but not as fast Ali. He was driven by a force that gave him ecstasy. The feeling that he was an invisible warrior had drastically taken over his senses.

He wasn't the only one fighting back. Other members from the elite team and the supporting troops came to join him fight as many ran to safety. As they fought back the Seculars, Sir Landry Big from the air with other Secular troops shot at them. Some of the bravest were hit and were gone instantly. Ali had a shield that blocked their attacks as soon as they were too close to him, protecting himself thus far. His blind spot hadn't been detected until he saw danger approaching her: one of Malik's sisters. His past came rushing to him.

Not again. Not another woman I admire. I won't let this happen.

***

When Ali was a few years younger, he lived in a safe

haven with his family. His father was a retired military personnel. They lived on a peaceful prairie in Jerusalem. One day, Seculars came and dropped bombs on them because his father didn't want to join them. Abu Ali had been declared enemy of the state. Aaliyah, the maid, hid Ali the teenager in a well and told him to stay there and not make a noise. He was infatuated with that maid because she was a motherly figure and he secretly admired her. In fact, Hanifa's bossiness reminded him of Aaliyah at times.

He didn't come out of the well until he thought it was safe to climb out. The Seculars had searched the whole place for any survivors to make sure no one was alive. They peeked in the well but it was too dark to see anything so they closed it back and left. That was before they shot bullets into it that Ali tried to dodge as he prayed to Allah to let him live another day if he was meant to. And he did see many days after that. Young, starving, and angry, he swore revenge that day. He wept as he held the maid's body riddled with bullets and covered with dried blood a few feet away from the well.

"I couldn't save her or any of them. I will get strong and I will avenge my family," he continued saying that day as he dug holes to burry whatever remains he could find in the remnants of the burned prairie. Jaded and desensitized, he covered his nose with a cloth and retrieved for burial the scattered and burned parts of his father, mother, two sisters, and one brother who were ready to eat when the bomb landed on them. He had been to a *janazzah* before and his father had taught them how to perform one because in their time, believers died like flies so it was in the best interest of all Muslims— young or old— to know how to perform the death rituals. He saw his lost relatives as *shahid* so he didn't cleanse them. He buried them as they were, decapitated and burnt.

Aaliyah had gone out to look for him in the stables where he loved to practice archery and talk to the horses. They should have both run to safety but Aaliyah had insisted that he was smaller and faster than her. They wouldn't make it far so she would make a distraction while he escaped. "No!" Ali had replied. "I want to stay with you. I'm a man!" he had argued.

She gave him a nervous smile and said, "I know you are. But don't play heroes today. What has been ordained for me is here. Stay in the well until things get quiet. Don't get out. I mean it!"

It was reluctantly that he agreed to her pleas.

Now a former member of the 4Cs, he looked forward to seeing his brothers at the stadium. They had promised to come through for him. He had missed his buddies and couldn't wait to reunite with them again.

***

Before they shot their missile-like high tech arrows that could calibrate for any angle or trajectory, Ali and his brothers always uttered, "Ya Haq!" They had their own communication devices and teleported in and out of the battlefield like Ali had done when he had been cornered by Ata and Judas while he was rescuing Tariq. It was mayhem at the stadium as soon as the battle started after the green light of Hanifa and Sylas. Ali had dodged attacks left and right while shooting arrows with agility and speed all around him to keep himself safe from

Seculars and other extremists; Fundamentalists, Zulmists, Almourabitoun, Crew Sadders, Radical Zionists, and last but not least, Bloody Mongols.

CHAPTER THIRTY-THREE : SAFI.D

Shafiya

WOW, THIS GUY GOT moves and he is so Muslim cool. Too bad he only has eyes for Hanifa these days, Shafiya thought as she watched Ali run toward the Seculars when everybody else was running away from them. She was oblivious to the fact that Ali was very protective of her. Swiftly, Ali decimated their numbers with tact, speed, and his teleportation device. The Seculars also had their own technology and while many dodged him, others couldn't. As she watched Ali go to work, three young men also joined and helped him. They moved just like him and had similar gadgets like him. Safi was grateful that the newcomers were helping him.

However, not even an hour after the second fight at the stadium had started and Malik was trying to get as many as he could to safety, many of the Seculars retreated and the crowd started to cheer, "Malik! Malik! Malik!"

Sure her brother had the technology to match the Seculars, but her intuition told her otherwise. This was confirmed when she saw Sir Landry hovering over her older brother with a person by his side: Marcel!

She had first spotted her brother's look alike during the past year when Hanifa had joined them for the first time at Castle 5 after her year off outside schooling.

***

"Yo Malik, you're going to pass in front of me and act like you didn't see me. Not cool Bro! Who you trying to impress? Let me remind you that I'm fly," she had said to the young man with her head high. She noticed that the clothes she remembered him wearing that morning weren't the same he was wearing now.

"I don't know…" the young adult had replied sultrily, in the midst of his colorful entourage who had started whistling and cackling at the daring Safi.

"Who is this girl? Your baby Mama, M?" one member of his crew had pointed out.

"Ew!" Safi had let out shocked by the comments. *Normal people don't sleep with their siblings. Gross!*

"Make your friends behave or I'll tell Mom and Dad tonight. You'll be very sorry for acting this way toward me as well," Safi added and a line formed on her forehead. She was dead serious. "Plus, what are you wearing?" she asked, pointing at his colorful, see-through clothes. He was also wearing pink shades with three lenses on each eye. The lenses closest to his eyes were square with some animal prints on them. The one in the middle were round, green, with some star patterns to them, and the most obvious lenses were yellow rectangles with parallels stripes going through them; shutter shades in a way.

The boy she was threatening got closer to her and said in a whisper, "Joke time's over. Look Ma, I think you got me confused with someone else. And word of advice, don't ever threaten me that way." He stared deeply into her glistening eyes. "Do you know who I am?" he asked raising his voice this time while glancing back at his friends. It was a cue for them to answer but he prodded them anyway. "Yo fellas, tell this young fine mama here who am I?"

"Sis you don't want to mess with our boy here. He's Sir Landry's son," one of Marcel's goons advised.

At the words, Safi backed down and ran in the other direction as fast as she could while the boys went into a fit of laughter. Yes, Safi was scared shitless but it wasn't why she ran away so fast. She was afraid her family would be in danger again. They would have all been scared shitless in her opinion. Shafiya first notified Malik by phone so that they could assess the situation before alerting their parents of the imminent threat.

Malik thought the resemblance was bizarre and didn't deserve any attention. Her parents on the other hand became nervous. Her mom and her dad exchanged worried looks and told her not to worry, but the expressions on their faces told her otherwise.

"Are you sure this is nothing?" Safi had asked again.

"Yes, everyone has a look alike. Don't worry, he can't hurt us," her mom said with a forced air of certainty.

"How do you know that?" Safi insisted, not convinced. So she continued to drill them with questions in their bedroom until they spilled the beans. At the knowledge of the secret, Safi was floored. It was a big secret to keep from Malik.

"We have to tell him. You can't keep that a secret, Mom and Dad!"

"No!" They had both yelled. "Absolutely not! He can't know."

"He can't know or it's not the right time to tell him yet?"

Her parents stayed quiet as if they were carefully weighing their next words. Her eyes volleyed between them as they fidgeted in their seats, paced in the room at some point, and finally sat down on the plush king-sized bed adorned by soft beige duvets.

"He will be mad if he knows that I knew and helped you cover it up! You will drive a wedge between us. It's very simple. Just tell him the same way you just told me," Safi tried to tell them.

But nope! Her parents would not hear any words of wisdom their daughter was shedding and telling them. They had made up their minds. The secret would stay buried until further notice.

Safi had hit a wall. She became sad and depressed. Every time she saw Malik, she tried not to give him a pity look that would give her away because Malik could sometimes read into her soul. She always tried to avoid his gaze so that he couldn't read her thoughts. One time her behavior almost gave her away.

"You okay sis?"

"Yes. What makes you think I'm not okay," she replied, stirring the honey into her coffee. They were having breakfast before heading out to school as usual.

"It just seems like you have been acting weird since you saw that guy who looks like me at school. Don't worry, I stay clear of his path. We aren't in danger. Having said that, it makes sense why people are sometimes acting skittish around me. They think I'm Marcel, son of the most feared man on earth. Not that I want the company anyway but they always have that look of fear in their eyes when they accidently bump into me or lock eyes with me. He must have done a number on them to think that I'm the bully behind the terror they are experiencing."

"That must be it," she had said, glad of his interpretation of things. Her heart twisted and she felt awful for colluding with their parents to keep a huge secret from him; a secret that could change everything, including the dynamics of the Ducktrinor family going forward.

CHAPTER THIRTY-FOUR : AWESTRUCK TOO

Hamza

SAFI. I LIKE THE sound of that name. She is very beautiful and brave, masha'Allah. When this is over, I want to get to know her. I wonder if her cock-blocking sister is going to oppose, Hamza thought as he watched Shafiya fight off Secular officers along with Ali.

Hamza was Brazilian and he was the first Sahaba X.0 recruited by Hanifa and Ali. When he was at Knights Inn, he donned his *kufi* proudly on top of his afro hair, and many of the girls gushed over him whenever he walked around. He and Malik had bonded rather quickly because of their shared interest over swords. Malik also introduced him to the Far East Muvemant who welcomed Hamza with opened arms.

"You can join our group whenever you want," they had told him once they came to support the elite team at Knights Inn.

"Sure, thank you. I'll think about it," Hamza had replied feeling ambivalent about the offer. He didn't think it was a best fit for him and he already had a clique he hung out with. Nonetheless, he decided to be just friends with them and introduced them to one of his buddies who went by the name of Salah Ad-Din. Ad-Din was quickly welcomed between the ranks of the Far East Muvemant, a.k.a. FEM.

"We're feminists. Is that why you don't want to join? Ar-Rasool *sallallahu aleihi wassalam* was a staunch feminist too," Umm Manee, who wasn't the talkative type, said jokingly. She always tried to chatter with him. Perhaps he sensed that she was too friendly toward him while she ignored other boys that tried to get her attention.

Typical, she likes me while I have my eyes set on another girl who barely notices me, Hamza had remarked gingerly to himself.

Hamza was very focused and the only thing that could distract him was Safi. Being in her proximity always had that pull on him and he tried as much as he could not to stare at her. *She wouldn't appreciate a freak like me gawking at her shamelessly,* he told himself every time he locked eyes with her in the room or while on Secular patrol duty. Safi always smiled politely and carried on. "And Ali is so protective of her!" he always said out loud to no one in particular when he was alone.

When *Muallim,* a light-skinned man of a slender demeanor, came to show his support to the elite team at Knights Inn and revisit his pupil Malik, Hamza found the man intriguing so he approached *Muallim.* The aura around the teacher was so powerful that he had drawn one of shyest persons in the group.

"*Assalamu aleikum, Muallim.* I'm Hamza."

Standing in the corner of the room by himself, *Muallim's* face lit up and he returned the greetings of peace. "Hamza, huh? *Masha'Allah,* that is a beautiful name. May Allah bless you with the strength and faith of the uncle of the Prophet *sallallahu aleihi wassalam, ameen.*"

"*Ameen,*" Hamza hummed.

Hamza learned that *Muallim* was originally from Mali and *Muallim* in return learned that Hamza was Brazilian. The two men talked of religion and secular subjects until Hamza asked him the difference between a *sufi* and a learned man of the Quran, like *Muallim* himself.

"They are a bit similar but they are not the same thing. The sufism of this age is a bit corrupted and diluted compared to the first days of sufism. Today there are too many travesties claiming to be *sufi*. Our Prophet, peace be upon him, was a *sufi* in my opinion, *masha'Allah.*

"Anyway, let me tell you a story. A long time ago lived a rich man who had two sons. When he died, one of his sons decided to give up the desires of the world and focus only on worshipping Allah. So he went into the wilderness. The other son stayed and took over the father's possessions, which were composed of many things amongst animals and land.

"The son who went into the wilderness was such a devout worshipper that he received powers from Allah. He was thus able to see Allah clearly because his heart was free of this life's wants. Allah provided him daily with food and anything he wanted. See, a *sufi* is a mystic whose first and foremost goal is to forget this *dunya* and solely focus on the love and adoration of the Lord of the Worlds. This *sufi* lacked nothing because whatever he wished for in sustenance simply appeared to him. He could go anywhere he wished in all the galaxies by just sitting in the wilderness. His will would just take him to see all the hidden places of the world because the glory of Allah was with him.

"Several years passed and he was content in the wilderness until one day he thought of the brother he had left behind. His brother was also a *sufi*. He decided he would go see him. So he summoned a lion and mounted it with ease. Then he summoned a snake that he used as reins and put it between the teeth of the lion. Holding the head and the tail of the snake in each hand, he set off on a journey to see his relative.

"When he arrived at his brother's, he parked his lion and snake outside and went up to his brother's place. Food was prepared in his honor and the family ate in happiness. While they were eating or before they began, a female servant came to bring more things. As she was retreating, she sashayed out of the room. At that moment an impure thought crossed the mind of the visiting *sufi*. An idea of what he could do with this girl lodged itself in his mind and heated him, but he quickly dismissed the desire and ate.

"When it was time to leave, he went down to mount his lion and grab the snake as the reins. As he made the motion to mount the lion, the animal became aggressive and showed all his teeth in disapproval. The *sufi* tried again to approach the lion or the snake but one growled and the other hissed angrily at their master.

"The brother who was also a *sufi* had witnessed the scene from up high. So he went down to talk to his brother. He asked his brother if he knew why the animals had turned against him. The travelling *sufi* said no. 'It's because of the thoughts you had when you saw my servant the other night.' The travelling sufi realized that in order for him to gain clarity of mind and be taken seriously by his animals, he had to let go of the desires he had started to harbor in his heart," *Muallim* finished at last.

Hamza nodded, stayed quiet for a moment and said, "So the woman is not a temptress, right? She is just a desire of this world. It could be the same for a woman *sufi* who might remove the love of any man from her heart."

"You, my friend, are very insightful. Many would have concluded that women are evil, but you saw beyond that. The gender is irrelevant. The bigger picture is the ephemeral desires that cloud our hearts and minds and keep us from worshipping Allah. Having said all that, we can also take the example of the brother who was also a *sufi* and had many riches. The key is to not let oneself get blinded with this *dunya*."

"I would like to be your student," Hamza had said impulsively, and *Muallim* had smiled approvingly.

CHAPTER THIRTY-FIVE : IMAM MALIK AND THE MUJAHIDEEN

Malik

AS MALIK STARTED LAUNCHING his noisy devices and putting his plan into motion, the memory of the day Hanifa challenged him to save "fictitious" everybody in play with a sword came back to him. It was the real deal now and by the look he gave her as he stepped in her leading spot, he knew she understood he was going to do just that. As he pulled out his sword, Sayf Ibn Zulfiqar, to brandish it in the air, a very distinct group of warriors from the supporters of Hanifa started to fight off the crowd of Seculars.

They looked like Muslim cowboys. They had colorful clothes covering their noses; half their faces were covered. They were in denim, khaki, cowboy hats, *hijab*, boots, the whole cowboy shebang but with a few tweaks. *Burqa avengers? Hijab avengers?* Malik thought not really sure how to call them. But because they weren't dressed in black he dismissed his first hypothesis. One thing was certain: they were avenging the non-Seculars. He would call them the *Ansars,* Helpers, for now and whispered *alhamdullilah.*

But Malik would get his answer soon enough about these Helpers when he made out the writing on the back of one of them while she rode her horse in her long khaki skirt and her hat bobbing on her head toward the armed Seculars with her high-tech riffle in tow within his reach. It read "The Mujahideen Cowgirls." He bet the men in that group of saviors had "The Mujahideen Cowboys" stitched on their long sleeve shirts. Malik said *alhamdullilah* again and he made out other girls in long denim skirts and jeans being daredevils. While the cowboys of the *Mujahideen* slayed, wrangled, and tangled more Seculars with their high tech lassos while dodging deftly attacks like matadors, Malik admitted to himself that Hanifa— his global citizen sister— had certainly reached many remote places around the world if his instinct about these Texans were on point. *SHOWTIME IMAM MALIK*, he thought and smiled. This had better turn out like in the pool when he practiced. He needed to get the *muhajirun* to safety, like pronto.

History repeats itself. Let's reenacts it once more, Malik thought. *We aren't in Muharram and this is not the day of Ashura but I'll just assume it is. Cheesy? I'm cool with that.* Since Hanifa told him that they would leave by sea he had thought of all of the backup scenarios in case they were attacked by sea and there was a flaw in his sister's plan, who always thought she was so darn perfect at military strategizing. In their engineering home lab, they had created Exodus 1.4, also known as Yunus 1.4. The FEM members preferred Yunus 1.4 while the head of the group, Malik, preferred the former. In the end, they kept both names.

While his mentor, *Muallim,* had helped him master some mysticism, with time Malik had perfected the school project he never had the chance to showcase to his classmates into a masterpiece to save the day, if God willed.

He set Exodus 1.4 to 99 mph and engaged wind blowing and global shield. His classes of Oceanology, Physics, and Mathematics came in very handy then. Science always has a way of explaining miracles so he left nothing to chance. According to his research, scientists hypothesized that Musa *aleihi salam* moved the people of Israel when he knew that the water and wind levels were optimal; strong winds and low water levels that allowed the oppressed to cross the sea without being drowned. Now, he had to be realistic. Pulling a *keeramat* was perhaps out of the question and he didn't trust himself to think that he had the badges necessary from his Lord to save the day that way. Allah created Science. *Today is the day I show my science project to the world! Bismillah. There is nothing wrong with seeking attention every now then in front of a sizeable audience.*

So armed with his super hydrophobic lazered sword, he struck the sea ahead of him and simultaneously threw in Exodus 1.4, a tiny marble look alike cylinder.

The sea split and Exodus 1.4 expanded to become a huge mechanical whale.

"Believers!" Malik said through the radio lines in his ear piece, "I'm Malik Ducktrinor. Don't panic. If you haven't used or opened your fleets yet, forget these Supplies. Make your way as fast as you can to the whale. It's a ship. *Ya Haq, Yallah*, let's go! There is no time to waste. If the Seculars are closing in on you, teleport right away to the coordinates I will give you. We've already lost many comrades. We don't need to waste anymore."

The possibility that Seculars could misappropriate the ear pieces of some of the fallen comrades crossed his mind as he gave out the coordinates. *Ya Mubeen, make our enemies evident to us*, he prayed. *Ameen*.

So the believers made their way to shelter, and the Seculars pulverized the crowd with their latest ammunitions.

If Zul-qarnain used iron and copper to stop Gog and Magog to this day, this will do as well, insha'Allah. His whale was made of high-density iron, copper, steel titanium, and other alloys that he had particularly selected. Once in, the believers were safe from outside attacks, whether from the air or the ground. All they had to do was run to the mouth of the device. It was The Beast at the moment and stronger than any presidential car. Just like acid doesn't erode plastic but eats at soil-based materials, this Beast was immune to Secular bullets, bombs, and other types of attacks.

To ensure that they didn't face any technical issues, Malik made sure to learn how to operate a sextant-and-chronometer. He then equipped the whale with it because you can never go wrong when you go old-school. The whale was also a submarine, but it didn't sink to the bottom of the water right away as we would expect.

Malik had other plans in mind; otherwise it would have been too predictable and textbook historical material for the Seculars to decipher.

"Make sure you're buckled in and prepare for impact!" he warned the crew and passengers. Without any delay, Malik pressed the shapeshifting function of the whale, and it turned into an ave machine which shot high in the sky with such a velocity that we would think that the enormous machine was a weightless rocket. Then, he activated stealth mode and the device became invisible. He knew the Seculars also had impressive technologies and could trace them. For those reasons, Malik's next moves were meant to leave nothing to chance.

So Malik gave the reigns of the machine to Shafiya while he went into a quick meditation. He needed to talk to his friends and especially the members of the Far East Muvemant.

The words of *Muallim* settled in his mind in that moment: *Put your mind to it and you can do anything by the will of Allah.*

Malik breathed in and out slowly, uttered a small prayer and just like that he was conversing with his friends. He had closed his eyes and sat on his knees like he was about to say *tayihat* followed by *tachahood*. He had said the *basmala* and with his mind called the names of his friends in his mind to see if they were available. They had all responded promptly and connected for the conference meeting.

"How was the fight?" his friends all said at once referring to the second Battle of the Stadium. They couldn't physically attend but they had promised support in other metaphysical ways.

"Obviously, it went well since I'm still alive. *Alhamdullilah*," Malik said.

"*Alhamdullilah*," the rest of the group replied sighing deeply from relief.

"Something strange happened as we were fighting the Seculars though. They started to retreat at the order of their leader. 'A favor was called in for you, little pest. I'll spare your lives today but make no mistakes: if any of you cross my path or interfere with my rules, I'll end you all. I don't care if any of you are my blood,' Sir Landry had said and turned around with his aero devices. On his way out, he zeroed in on me to have a quick chat. I will get back to that in a minute.

"But look, I don't have much time. I need your help to conjure a big storm to get rid of the rest of the Seculars for good. They left us alone for now but I doubt they won't follow us. I don't care what it is; sand or rain. I just need a big natural event to take place so that they retreat from where they came from *insha'Allah*."

Since he could multi-task better than the rest, Malik detached his body again to quickly go peek below the clouds to see what was happening. There were still Seculars scavenging and some extremists out for blood. He returned quickly to the group meditation. "We can start."

They prayed to Allah and a strong wind blew wiping all their enemies miles and miles away. The wind was so strong that the large and heavy ave shook slightly. When they were done, Malik thanked his friends for their added supplications that gave more heart to the power they sought from Allah. The Battle of the Stadium was officially dealt with. He took the reins back from Shafiya and piloted the ave to make their descent above the sea. Upon close impact with the water, Malik shifted the machine back to a whale and activated the submarine function which allowed the mechanical whale to sink deeper in the vast water. He went back to meditation again.

"I almost forgot to tell you. Guess who invited me?" Malik said.

"Your sister's hot girlfriends," the boys chimed while the girls rolled their eyes.

Malik laughed out loud. He conceded that his sisters— not just Hanifa— had hot friends but that wasn't what he was thinking about even though some of them had been a bit distracting.

"Shut up guys!" he laughed again. "No, the devil himself; Sir Landry Big. The weird thing is his son keeps calling me Bro. Remember, all of you said he looks like me? And he kinda does."

"Relax, he is not related to you. Maybe you had ties at one point in life but it's different now. Your family and your home is where you grew up. Remember that no matter what happens."

"And so what if they are related to you? It shouldn't surprise you. We are all brothers and sisters from the same parents anyway; Adam and Eve. Therefore, no big deal."

"Y'all talking like the guy said he was my father or something. What if he wants me to join the rebellion?"

The FEM pondered on Malik's words and agreed. "Yeah, maybe. Well best of luck! And you better teleport there so you can escape if things go sour."

"Understood. Alright FEM, a.k.a. family, it was nice talking to you. *Wassalam!*"

"*Wassalam* Imam Malik!"

Malik smiled at their respect and ended his meditation.

CHAPTER THIRTY-SIX: EVA'S SECRET

Eva

Timeline: Flashback to the first Battle of the Stadium

"THINGS HAVE CHANGED. ABE died. *Inna lilahi wa inna ilahi rajiun.* This is unfortunate. Now the children are in over their heads!" Eva said hotly as her eyes went from her father-in-law to her husband. The Battle of the Stadium was all *The Irreligious* was talking about on the news and frankly she had had enough and feared for her children's safety. "You guys can't stay here and let your children fight off the Seculars on their own. Besides Sir Landry Big is more Baba's opponent than anybody else," she added, staring at Mustapha intently.

"The children didn't want us to butt in, especially Hanifa," Adama pointed out with a solemn line on his forehead. "I think I should do anything in my power to retrieve my brother's body at least. And Baba, you have to do everything in your power to get your old friend off the backs of our children. This is getting personal now."

"I agree," Mustapha said, lost in his thoughts. "I knew Abe might meet an unusual death one day because of the kind of risk he took to protect us but even with all that mental preparation, my mind wasn't prepared to see the brutality he went through." He wiped a tear from the corner of his eye and portrayed a brave face.

"Well one of our children might be the key we need to save them all," Eva said, sighing deeply.

It took twenty-three years to perfect the religion. And as an accountant, Eva looked forward to be married for twenty-three years and still have a perfect family and marriage beyond that number. For her, it was a good omen and numbermark. Now, things would rapidly come undone thanks to Hanifa and her stubborn followers. Malik's father wasn't Adama Ducktrinor and the truth had to be told.

***

Eva Ducktrinor was born Mawa Fofana. From Ivorian origin, she took all the savings her folks could gather so that she could have a better education and went to the West to study. When she arrived in Paris, she sought help and sponsorship from her compatriots and she was introduced to Sir Landry Big. He was a "Generous Dean," like the people from her native country called him. He was a bit older than her but she fell for his charm and mannerisms. Being a beauty in his eyes, he told her, "Ask no further. I'll cover your tuition fees and you will attend the best of schools to become the professional you aspire to be. I have connections everywhere and schools too."

So to repay his generosity, she let herself fall in love

with the powerful man. Sir Landry Big had such a way with words. He always recited poetic verses he had freestyled just for her. She always giggled and enjoyed the pampering so she indulged him. He wasn't Muslim and that bothered her. However, she continued having a forbidden relationship with him in the hopes that one day, he would accept her beliefs. It was the only way their marriage could become permissible.

He would often tell her to close her eyes and when she opened her eyes, she would be transported across the world. She saw Paris, Rio de Janerio, Pretoria, Abidjan her beloved city again, and many more remote places around the world in a wink of an eye. They dined and explored those places with delight. Though Eva knew that kind of power was possible, existed; it had been told with the story of Queen Sheba when the *djinn* told the Master of the *djinns* that he could bring her throne right away before he blinked his eyes. However, she told herself that the reasons Sir Landry Big showed her the world with such speed by 'science' was because he was a research philanthropist, amongst the other honorable and intelligent titles he held. She refused to believe— like her heart told her— that Sir Landry Big could be dealing with unseen creatures since he was obviously not a Christian monk or a Jewish Rabbi.

One night as she freshened up in the bathroom, she heard voices in Landry's bedroom. She tried to listen by lifting her head and straining her ears, but she couldn't make out the words. The water for a bath was running and Landry was supposed to join her soon. Against her better judgement to not eavesdrop on other people's conversations, she tiptoed outside the bathroom to find him speaking to a hideous creature with a pungent smell peeking out of a mirror.

She confronted him because she wasn't scared of such a creature. They were made by Allah and Him she feared.

"Fine! They give me the power I need to do everything I want," Sir Landry finally confessed after she went at him like a dog with a bone. She was the kind of person who always had to get to the bottom of things.

"And in return, what do you give him back?" she had asked dreading his words.

Sir Landry stayed silent avoiding her gaze. So she repeated herself, her foot tapping the marble floor; the tie of her peignoir drooping to both sides of her feet.

"I give him children that nobody wants; especially twins," he said, wiping his face with his right palm. "Please understand, I don't enjoy doing this. But it's for the greater good. Nobody misses these poor orphans. They are the sacrifice needed for other children to blossom in life."

Eva was floored. Here she was thinking that she had met a kind soul but it was all a sham!

"The creature knows you're pregnant with twins and he wants them both," Landry said, this time with a shaking voice.

"What?! I'm not even showing yet! It doesn't matter. It will be over my dead body. I'm leaving this place and don't dare try to come after me because I will expose you!"

She grabbed her belongings in a hurry and left. When her anger subsided she realized that Sir Landry Big would always be a part of her life no matter what. He was the father of her unborn children, if the *djinn* was correct. Since these things are known to be untrustworthy, she took a pregnancy test a couple of days after she had missed her period, and wouldn't you know? The deed was solid and she was expecting. She brought her hand slowly to her lower belly and made a prayer. She was ambivalent and scared. *Perhaps I can kill myself,* she thought a few times. Then she remembered it would be hell for her if she attempted that. "I'm up to the challenge," she told herself. She ditched her sinning ways and stopped having unlawful relationships before marriage and sat off on a path of redemption. It was in the Muslim Students Association of her school in Paris that she met Adama Kreedor, born Adama Madhab, from Ethiopia in one of the schools Sir Landry Big owned and that she was also attending. The thought of ditching his help crossed her mind but need and want got the best of her.

Time revealed that her father-in-law Mustapha was an old classmate of Sir Landry Big. They had studied in England together to obtain their PhDs. Mustapha had majored in Engineering and Sir Landry Big majored in Theology and

Engineering. And Adama's father had taken his old friend up on a favor.

"It would be my pleasure to vouch for your son. He has good grades. Any school will be glad to have him with that amount of knowledge, especially mine. Please let me call in some favors and he will have a generous stipend," Sir Landry Big had promised Mustapha Kreedor.

However, when Adama and Eva decided that they were meant for each other and had to tie the knot to avoid transgressing, Eva came clean. She told him about the pregnancy and the source of the wealth of their benefactor.

"I'm sorry I couldn't keep it to myself," she had said, crying and blowing her nose. "If you want to cancel the wedding, I'll understand."

Adama had stayed quiet for a moment trying to process all this. The weight of it all was immense. He breathed in and out, said a little supplication of guidance, relaxed his shoulders, face, and body, and finally replied, "A strong marriage is based on honesty. I appreciate you telling me. The wedding will go on but we have to go to another country. Perhaps South Africa or America."

So they informed Mustapha who was really enraged! "You son of a gun Landry! How could you involve us in something so sinister?!" Like that, an old friendship was dismantled. The Kreedors tried to pretty much disappear from the face of the earth after that.

Her pregnancy was hard. She had to be put on bedrest. Many nights, she had to be sedated because she had awful dreams. Finally, she asked them not to anymore. "I'll fight evil with the Quran and *dua*." Once she made that decision, her nightmares about hideous and indescribable creatures hunting her stopped. Eva felt at ease.

After the birth of the babies, Sir Landry managed to find her with an unnatural way; his genies. They told him where she was and he came to personally serve her with custody battles and court papers. The mediation went on and on until two years passed. Then, the judge reached a decision.

"Honestly, I'm quite tired of this case that keeps

dragging on forever. None of you will get the babies." They both gasped.

"I'll make it simple. Pick one child and go your separate ways."

See, Sir Landry had managed to keep his demons at bay by offering other children to spare his own children's lives. Plus the genie wanted both children and not only one. He had entertained the idea of giving up both children and setting himself free from the powerful demon that was starting to annoy him with his upcharges and caprices. But he knew Eva would never let that happen.

Eva had named the twins Abdoul Malik and Abdoul Moussawwir. How to pick was the next question for Eva, feeling rushed. She loved them both but the verdict had been delivered. Before she could decide, Landry said, "Where is Marcel?" One of the babies cooed and he picked that one. He then renamed the child wanting no Muslim connection with his child.

Crushed, Eva was left with one child, Abdoul Malik.

She had a picture of both of them in her hands; she signed the back and handed it to Sir Landry. "Make sure he gets it. Make sure he knows my real name too."

Landry nodded and left the courtroom, leaving Adama to console an inconsolable mom. She had lost a part of her.

CHAPTER THIRTY-SEVEN : THE EXTREMISTS

Sir Landry

Timeline: Flashback to the first Battle of the Stadium

SIR LANDRY RECEIVED A call as he watched his officers go to work under his command. The bloodbath was taking a toll as the battle had attracted other unsavory extremist groups besides the Seculars. That gave him pride.

"Most Honorable Leader, I have Mustapha Senior *Ducktrinor* on the line. He insists on talking to you," Corayto said with a quivering voice.

Are you afraid to say your half-brother or use his alias Kreedor?
Sir Landry thought snappily. Sir Landry was really reminiscent of Hitler. He declared wars on the non-Blacks but he was discrete about it, something Sylas knew and the reason he wanted to surpass Sir Landry Big.

"Tell him to leave a message. I no longer have time for him."

"He said that your son will die because of miscalculations on his part with his military devices and tactics. He added that his son Adama— my most hated nephew, I might add— married the woman you always wanted. And for her sake, to let her children go," Corayto finished, and then pursed his lips.

Sir Landry grumbled and waved his hands in the air dismissively. He was clearly annoyed that Mustapha was using his weakness, Eva, to make him fall back.

Sir Landry finally took the call when Eva Ducktrinor called him and ask him to let the children go, especially his son Malik, as they had been lovers at one point in their lives.

"Part of me still cares for you Eva. Otherwise, we would have reduced these brats to dust!"

"Thank you Landry. Goodbye. Tell Marcel I love him. He's welcome to look me up when he is ready to talk. I know he still hates me but maybe with time that will pass."

"I'll tell him. Bye."

Sir Landry Big had then ordered his men to retreat. With his son Marcel in tow, he had located his other son, Malik, that he had fathered with Eva in their younger years. He invited Malik over in the attempt to get to know him personally and then convert him to his ideologies. When Malik refused, Landry tried to poison him. Malik switched the glasses and Sir Landry died choking on his words.

"You will pay for this you brat!" Sir Landry had cursed through gritted teeth as foam came out of his mouth. Malik took over Sir Landry Big's regime and his brother Marcel swore revenge.

The Zulmists and the Fundamentalists got wind that Sylas had been killed by Hanifa.

"Our coup failed and this Contumacious Girl is going to pull it off and put us to shame? We told her to stay in her lane but she isn't obeying," the leader of the Fundamentalists had said during their meeting with the Zulmists about the state of the world. They couldn't handle a woman's victory so they made their own plans. As they set their plan in motion, some of their disciples were given a transparent solution to drink. Those who drank the solution were immediately controlled by the spirits. Malik, with his extensive knowledge, would have said they were under Haffaf who controls intoxicants.

"It's another Malala and we just have to deal with her the same." A high-profile member of the Zulmists had said from his location as they were in a video conference call with the Fundamentalists who had settled in one of America's greatest landmark, the Hoover Dam. The Zulmists, on the other hand, had taken a great chunk of West Africa with their radical movement. Each extremist group sat opposite of one another with a projection of the other group displayed in the air.

"Alright, the subject is closed and dealt with. Next order of business is the little boy with her. Hasn't he heard of Iqbal Masih? Let's deal with him the same way. That should send a clear message."

They all agreed.

"*The Muezzin* said that there was a visual of Sir Landry Big at the stadium of Castle 5," an extremist in the conference pointed out.

"He's going to make our job easy," the extremists said to each other and deployed.

They made fun of Hanifa's Islamic state constitution which mirrored one of the greatest in Islamic history. "Her supporters also say that she fashioned her state constition after the one used in Medina in the early years of Islam. What a joke!" they had laughed.

2

"Eyes on the target," the hitman had said.

"You have permission to shoot."

"Roger." He shot and Hanifa fell to the floor. A young boy ran to her and he was shot too.

"Mission completed," the mercenary repeated over his mic and left as he turned up his loud rap music in his cordless earphones.

Almourabitoun was the evil side of the faction The Muwahhidun. They were once one group, but when disagreements plagued the Resistance faction, and the once united group divided. One part of the faction went with the French sounding version as their official name while the good ones decided to be called The Muwahhidun.

The former Almoravides would have turned in their

graves if they found out that their legacy had become and inspired evil blood thirsty mutineers.

Malik suddenly jumped out of his bed, sweating. He believed he had just had a premonitory dream; the *jihadi* rap music of the mercenary was still giving him a headache. *Murra, one of the progeny of shaytan, is behind this kind of corrupt music for sure,* Malik thought absentmindedly. It was an intrinsic habit of Malik to see beyond the sin or action. He always saw the motives and actions of people around him more clearly that way by looking at the bigger picture.

"*Insha'Allah*, she will have a long life," Malik interpreted and added, "Dawud will too, God willing."

Malik told Hanifa and Dawud later in the day.

"We need to take measures so that we can avoid this untimely end," Hanifa had wagered.

"That's a good idea. We can also travel in time to see it and then we can take them out instead," Dawud pointed out.

"You're onto something little man," Malik said, wagging his long, thin index finger in the air. "But remember, we can't wander in time too much, otherwise we will get stuck there and lose ourselves. We can't try to see too much either. The mission is to go in and out. Understood?"

"Understood," said Dawud and Hanifa.

So they did. They sat in a circle and started a meditation session in the basement of the Ducktrinor home by first saying *"Bismillahi ar-rahmani ar-rahimi."* They then had to fight off the Fundamentalists and the Zulmists at sea. Just like that the Battle of the Sea subsequent to the Battle of the Stadium occurred before they even happened.

3

The Crew Sad was an extremist Christian group that came to help the Seculars even though Seculars despised believers. The enemies worked together to fight their common enemies: those who dared to assert their right to freedom of speech and religion. No one had invited them though. Surely not the interfaith supporter Christian groups that had shown up to support the right cause and the elite team of the Ducktrinors. The Crew Sad had no problem killing their brothers and sisters in faith at the Battle of the Stadium because they saw them as sold-out Christians.

4

The Radical Zionists were an extremist Jewish group and the polar opposite of their other Jewish brothers who believed in peace between different faiths and non-denominational creeds. They just came to observe and watch the Battle of the Stadium from far. In addition to being bystanders, they brought the element of intimidation with them by displaying gory flags of racism and faith supremacy. "Death to the heretics and non-Jews" was what their blood red banners read.

Bloody Mongols, a nationalist movement claiming lineage to Ghenghis Khan, came late to the party and they were blown away by the combined efforts of the FEM.

***

The Profane

The Profane, called *The Irreligious* by non-Secular supporters, made a full exclusive on the Ducktrinors and the rebellion. The head of the organization was called Albert Musawwit.

They had displayed Hanifa's school identification picture as one of the main faces of the rebellion. She had always hated that picture. She hadn't been ready for the camera when the flash captured her wide eyes, her mouth slightly open. She definitely looked crazy. She was so not photogenic. The blurb under her picture read: *This is Hanifa Kreedor. Current alias is Hanifa Ducktrinor. She is no longer an enemy of the State. She is in*

fact an enemy of the World! The World ruled by the Seculars.

There was One Ruler of the Worlds and his name was not Sir Landry Big for sure. Hanifa would have certainly pointed that out upon reading her feature in *The Profane*.

Her brother Malik's mug was expressionless. The caption on his picture just said, "Brother of the Contumacious Girl." *If you would like our opinion, there is nothing threatening or interesting about this kiddo who wants to play hero with his younger sister. They are leading many astray. If the lot of them knows what's best for them, they need to give up now.*

Little did they know that after Malik's Exodus, they would be forced to add "Peculiar Kid" to Malik's info card.

***

Word got out that Sylas was still alive and what was the best medium to circulate the news on? *The Profane* of course.

"We have breaking news for you. Sylas is reported to be still alive. And we have a video to prove it," the anchor said, laughing with pure mischief. The laugh was cynical and it gave a chill to the listeners who quickly brought it to Hanifa's attention.

"I saw him die. It can't be," Hanifa kept repeating to herself and the crowd of supporters they had amassed.

"Hanifa Kreedor, stay hidden if you're smart. Why? Because I'm coming for you!" And the transmission was lost, leaving the watchers with an eerie feeling because of the black and white flat screen tablets that screeched unbearable noisy static.

The Profane was known to relay false news but in this case, Hanifa and her supporters didn't know what to believe anymore.

"Dead or alive, what has been ordained for us will follow its course so let's get back to work," Malik advised to everyone on the ship.

He heard people agreeing and other people not so convinced by the looks on their faces. Nevertheless, the crowd dispersed and he turned off the transmitter hung in the main room of the ship like a flat screen TV. Malik stared up at the flat dark board with racing thoughts, and he could see his reflection that he barely recognized. *I have big shoes to fill*, he thought absentmindedly.

***

Hamani

"Wew! These brats would have made me dead meat if I hadn't bargained with them. They think they got rid of his entire DNA. Haha! They are so wrong. I'm the best scientist that there is. Not much of a fighter, but I can survive. How can they be so naïve and think that I was going to go away peacefully? Ah! They are kids," Hamani said aloud with a heavy Middle-Eastern accent to no one in particular in his safe house lab. He was underground and knew no one would come to these parts. He was in a deserted area, in the middle of the desert. No one would find them there. He adjusted his glasses on his pointy nose when his bug eyes smiled at the reanimation of Sylas in front of him. He was jubilating inside and seriously looked like Jafar in Aladdin with only the shape of his eyes. His white and messy curls circled the round bald spot in the middle of his naturally tanned head.

"So I was telling you that I went to Sylas's home to take some samples of the body in the tank when the security breach alarm went off. '*Rookies*,' I snarled as I glanced at the cameras showing young intruders in the mansion. I pleaded for my life because they found me unarmed. I claimed that I had been forced to work for Sylas," Hamani said and stared straight at the empty wall facing him in the lab.

"What did that young man with the bow and arrows say again?" Hamani crazily asked himself. "Oh! I think he said, 'If we let him live, he will tell all our plans to Sylas before the day of the battle'."

"These children have no respect," Hamani continued talking like a mad man while adding, "they left me with only my underwear, no gadgets or money. That was uncalled for." He finished, brooding over the next series of events.

One comment their female leader said had made him ponder and he questioned what he thought he knew. Because he had an excellent memory, he easily recalled it. "I think her name is Hanifa," he told himsef, continuing his animated monologue, 'Well, well, the Quran did say in surah 10 verse 92, [*This day shall We save thee in thy body, that thou mayest be a sign to those who come after thee! But verily, many among mankind are heedless of Our Signs!*] when Allah promised Pharaoh that his body will be preserved for the sake of disbelievers to take heed. Look what we have here. The science of Allah is preserving his real body.' Her team agreed with her in the mansion. Does that mean that religion is a science?" Dr. Hamani finally asked aloud. "Whatever, I don't care," he said and continued to narrate his plight to his other invisible personalities.

"If you breathe one word of this to Sylas, I'll personally hunt you down and flay you," the young man with the archery gear added this time as he dangled his pocket knife in my face. Me, one of the best scientists in the world, if not The Best! Then, Sylas came home because the alarm had alerted him. He saw Marcel waiting at the door and he was about to let him when he got clubbed on the head by the so-called Marcel! When Sylas woke up, upon inquiring he realized that Marcel has a doppelganger. Can you believe that?" he paused for an answer which he was likely to receive none and proceeded to answer himself, "me neither. Anway, we're unto them."

"The body is not safe here," Sylas said when he recovered consciousness and scolded me for being mediocre help. "Where did you leave your bodyguards?" he asked haughtily and I let it slide."

"I didn't think I needed them here. Your security sucks! You're getting cocky and careless in my opinion," I replied wickedly. "These brats apparently scanned the underground. How else could they have found the body so easily?" I even retorted.

"After our heated argument, we carefully removed the explosives from the tank and moved the real body of Sylas. Then we replaced the inside with a cloned body, we put less than stellar explosives on the tank to decrease loss of property, and we let Hanifa and her team at the Battle of the Stadium think that they killed Sylas for real. Sylas and I have a much bigger plan we need to put in place against Sir Landry Big and

the insurgents. They better watch out."

CHAPTER THIRTY-EIGHT : HOUSE DIVIDED

Corayto

CORAYTO HAD ALWAYS DESPISED his family, the Kreedors. They were also known as the Ducktrinors. The original family name of his relatives was Madhab but because of political unrest, the Madhabs had to flee Ethiopia to live in England. The journey proved itself treacherous in the hot desert and then the stormy waters they had to cross under the radar of search crews. But praise to God, they made it safely to their intended destination: England.

There, the family changed their name to Kreedor, a

close Latinized version of the meaning of their real family name to protect themselves from persecution while maintaining the meaning of their real surname through time.

They were hiding in plain sight; something their enemies wouldn't think of because it would seem too simple to use the same name in another language. The enemies would expect a more challenging and obscure name from the Madhabs to avoid persecution, his family had thought. In England, like in Ethiopia, no matter how much Corayto's family tried, he never liked their ways. He called them self-righteous people. When Abe died, he thought, *They received love so easily! Now, Abe is dead. Power to me and thanks to the tip from Sylas—that deputy Brat.*

Abe was your nephew, for heaven's sake, a voice in him scolded. *I wouldn't care even if he was my whore of a mother!* he replied, indifferent. His mother had him after Mustapha's father had passed away. Because Mustapha looked like his late father, their mother always had a special soft spot for Mustapha Kreedor.

"I love you both, sons," Mrs. Kreedor had told him numerous times when Corayto went on huge fits of jealousy and anger.

"No you don't! You only love him because he reminds you of your first husband!"

"Watch your mouth, young man!" his mother would say gasping.

"Whatever!" Corayto would reply again disobediently, and storm out of the room, breaking things around the house.

For his anger bursts and lack of respect, his real father often gave him a serious beating. So Corayto grew to despise both his father and mother. When he was old enough to be on his own, he left home and swore never to come back again. He changed his name from Cheekoo to Corayto because he always enjoyed a good villain in the stories his family had told him, like Coré. When his parents passed away, he exclaimed, "Good riddance!"

Mustapha reached out to him but Corayto never wanted any support from his older half-brother.

"Are you coming to the funeral?" Mustapha had asked when he was finally able to get a hold of his little hermit of a brother.

"You know the answer to that," Corayto had replied, puffing and humphing into the phone.

"Come on brother, you need to pay your respects and gain their blessings."

"I don't need their blessings," Corayto had spat. "My own father beat me to a pulp every time he got a chance and she never stopped him."

Mustapha stayed quiet, perhaps thinking. "Okay brother, nobody is perfect. Yes, they wronged you but you have a mouth on you too. Only cursed children mouth their parents. You need to take responsibility for your actions as well." The elder brother had tried to speak slowly and tactfully with a tone that called for calmness. Corayto didn't go for it.

"Now you're blaming me? Unbelievable! Adieu Brother. Don't call me again to convince me to attend their burial. Save your energy. I'M NOT GOING!" And click! Corayto had hung up the phone. He changed his phone numbers numerous times, but each time his brother Mustapha found him to check on him no matter how much the call was not welcomed.

"You don't give up do you?" Corayto always asked when he accidently picked up a phone call he thought he knew the interlocutor. Months would pass at times before Mustapha would be able to reach his younger brother. Corayto was left to himself in the rough neighborhoods of England. He gave himself to gangs, drugs, and other questionable things that come with the territory.

When Mustapha and Sir Landry Big fell apart, the powerful Sir Landry sought out the disgruntled half-brother of the Kreedors to make of him an ally.

"It would be my honor, Sir, to be your right-hand man!" Corayto had sung. The ghetto life was below him now. Sir Landry promised him riches and status he couldn't refuse. He went from wearing sneakers and hip hop attires to wearing very expensive suits overnight! He had a collection of tailor-made suits, designer watches, and whatnot. He was on top of the world and ready to bring down his despised family at all costs for the emotional damage he thought they had subjected him to!

However things changed when he announced the lynching of Abe to Sir Landry Big.

"What?! Who ordered his death?" Sir Landry's voice had boomed in the room to the point that Corayto trembled. He knew his Master was evil bonified who still had soft spots for only a few people in life: Eva and his children.

"I'm not sure, Sir. All I know is that Sylas, the little brat from that school in Brazil, intercepted a call from Mustapha since he was following Hanifa. From there, he told the region leaders who then told the national Secular leaders, and before we knew it, they had attacked him. In their eyes, he was a clear spy," Corayto finished.

Sir Landry sighed deeply. "This is bad."

"Why? This is what we wanted all along: take this family down once and for good for stealing the love of your life and taking one of your sons!" Corayto was puzzled by the reaction of Sir Landry. The man was so confusing at times. One minute Corayto thinks he understands his benefactor, the next it's complete confusion.

"Don't you see it? Abe has a connection to both of us. Our followers can become skeptical and think that we're double agents. This can turn against us if people think we're related somehow. We have to beat the masses to the punch by flipping the story. Whatever happens, make sure we save face. We will retrieve his body and show it to the world so that they don't think we are spies. We have to show that we are greatly disappointed by this treason and make an example of him. I hate to do this to my old friend's son, but my hands are tied and it has to be done. I'm not going to lose followers over this rush of action! They should have waited for my order before sentencing Abe to death! Tell them not to do that again and to consult me before they execute any high-profile spy or insurgent. I have the right to know and make a decision in the matter. After all, I'm the leader of the world!" Landry slammed the desk and Corayto jumped. The noise had startled him.

"Yes Sir! But with all due respect, Sir, they might take it as micromanagement and turn on you," Corayto tried to explain.

"I don't care. They can try. The forces that protect me are stronger than all of them combined!" The words of Sir Landry had an eerie and cynical effect on Corayto, who decided it was time to leave the office of the leader.

As soon as he put one foot out of the office, a fiery orange portal opened below his marching feet and engulfed him in a single gulp.

"Until you learn some family manners, you will be stuck in oblivion forever," a familiar voice said to him as he descended into nothingness. The voice reminded him of Mustapha.

"Don't do this! Please get me out of here! Please! I beg you!"

"Too late Bro. You will get enough time to reflect upon ALL your actions in here. In peace!" Mustapha said, then silence, heat, and strong chemical fumes surrounded Corayto in oblivion.

CHAPTER THIRTY-NINE : THE MUEZZIN

Malik

Timeline: Flashback to the first Battle of the Stadium

Bismilahi ar-rahmani ar-rahimi,

This is The Muezzin's correspondence. As we expected The Irreligious has done some serious damage with their false reports. May Allah protect us from all the Al Musawwit satans. We've just confirmed that Sir Landry has just arrived at the stadium of Castle 5 to join the battle. Sylas is presumed to be dead but we can never know for sure with a clone lover. We also have to report the fallen ones. May Allah grant Jannat al Firdaus to the fallen ones. Ameen. Fi Amani Allah. Wassalam readers.

THE SAME MESSAGE WAS translated in other languages by the different writers of the e-zine and sent all over the world with mechanical birds. The *Muezzin* headquarters was located in an unlikely place: The warehouse was under vast water.

The writers were scribes from all over the world. They rolled the small and very thin e-zine tablets like yoga mats and attached them at the feet of the mechanical birds before sending them away. Because the distribution mechanism was an ave and aves are known to migrate, this made it harder for the Seculars to detect the source. The messages were encrypted using *Aljamiados* from the Muslim civilization in Spain, which is a Latinized Arabic alphabet and Arabic numeric numbers. The messages were also in a do-not-reply fashion and the birds were made in a way that they couldn't be traced back to the manufacturer or the source. The Seculars had intercepted several birds but that was all they had accomplished chasing the ghost that was *The Muezzin*.

The most recurring symbols in the messages were ⟨and

∧ which are 1 and 8 respectively. It was befitting because of its

infinite meanings. It could be about decoding a hidden message

using *surah* 18 or it could be about *surah* 81. And it could be

about both, thus $18+81 = 99$ names of Allah. It could also be

$1+8$ and $8+1$ which gives 99 names of Allah as well. In all, the

possibilities and probabilities of the messages were just

immense. Only in the right hands, they made sense; submission

to the One by the meaning of 9 and 0 in numerology. That is

why the Seculars needed people well versed in religions to stop

the believers of all faiths.

***

Malik and the Far East Muvmant had visited the first

believers of Islam once and this is how it went.

"Welcome, you must be the Far East Muvemant, we

have a name for you here: Al Goraba," the Prophet of Islam

(peace upon him) had told them and out of amazement the

group was speechless. Their eyes scintillated with enchantment, and they just nodded to follow him to his quarters.

Once they were refreshed and properly fed, Malik spoke, "O beloved Prophet, we thank you for you kind hospitality." He paused and looked at his peers who echoed the same feeling before he continued, "We're here to see if you can ask Allah to let us borrow your angels after the battle of Badr. We've seen the battle many times in our time travels *alhamdullilah*."

"You're very welcome, children. I would love to help you but I believe you won't need it. Allah promised help and glad tidings for the believers like surah 61 verse 13 says in the Quran. *Insha'Allah* you will do well in the task you need them for. And remember, Islam began as something strange. So it will go as something strange. Therefore, don't worry too much about the legacy of your movement," the Prophet *sallalahu aleihi wassalam* said to them with a smile.

The children nodded approvingly, consulted each other, and the siblings in the group took the lead this time. "We see but it doesn't hurt to go out in style, right?" Khalid, the brother said with a sly smile.

"What my brother is trying to say, dear Rasoollulah, is that if we knew the last members of our group were being recalled by Allah let's say tomorrow, we'd want to make sure that these last callers went out as exceptional devoted members," Nusaybah, the sister, clarified this time.

"*Insha'Allah*," the Messenger replied with a knowing smile.

"*Insha'Allah*," the Far East Muvemant replied before finishing their teas and then giving their farewells. The call of the *adhan* melodiously being uttered by the *muezzin* as they disappeared and travelled back to the future made Malik and the rest of the group wonder if it was Bilal *radihallahu anhu*'s voice they had heard.

***

When the crowd started chanting 'Malik! Malik! Malik!' victory was palpable for the second time at the Brazilian stadium. So Dawud notified *The Muezzin* and victory was officially announced around the world. But as Malik tried to figure out the meaning of his unscheduled victory, Sir Landry had hovered in front of him with his doppelganger.

"Come to our home. Here is the address. We have a lot of things to discuss: your victory and the future of our *family* business," the doppelganger said.

"And Son, you better come alone or someone will pay," Sir Landry warned.

Malik didn't want to look weak so he agreed.

This time, Marcel gave him a brotherly nod and fist-pumped his heart, and smiled before he and his dad left. Marcel had done this before but this time it seemed strange to Malik. It seemed that the act was more heartfelt. He wasn't sure, it was just an intuition and only his parents could answer that question they always dreaded. He didn't look like his father or like his mother. In looks at least. Something sordid was at play here but he couldn't place his finger on it. As the crowd cheered for him, he became lost in his thoughts.

In fact, no matter the convincing words of his parents, Malik could never understand why he seemed thinner and taller than the rest of the family with a long neck even though they shared the same caramel skin tone. The neck wasn't the only thing Malik had noticed that was different from the other Ducktrinor children. His hair seemed to be coarser compared to his siblings. Not that he hated his hair but it was very obvious that something was amiss in his bloodline and that his parents were not telling him everything.

***

Malik went to the invite when he assured himself that everyone on the machine was safe. He saw pictures of two babies all around the house of his host. He wanted to ask but he wasn't sure he was ready for the answer. *It would be very insensitive if you asked and his brother died,* his conscience piped in several times.

"You keep looking at all these pictures of me and my brother. Do you have a question in mind?" Marcel asked.

Malik hesitated at first and then asked, "Where is he?" Then he took one of the old picture frames in his hands and the glass side dropped and crashed to the floor. Malik was horrified.

He apologized incessantly and took the picture, which was facing back on the floor. There was a note on the back.

I'll always love you boys,

Love,

Mom (Mawa Fofana)

Malik couldn't believe his eyes. He knew that name so he flipped the picture. The resemblance was stricking and there was no doubt to him that this woman on the picture was his real mother.

"Don't feel bad: I caused it to break with my mind. I have a gift and I don't need a holy book like yours to do so. At least now you know the secret: we're family."

Malik's chest tightened and he became dizzy all of a sudden. He gasped for clean air for a moment. The people who raised him, his supposed parents, were liars. They had been lying to him all his life to protect this awful secret. Even though he wanted to throw a fit, he quickly composed himself and kept his cool out of respect for the home of his host, his biological father. While confusion flooded his mind, one thing distracted him greatly: the power of his twin brother. So they were gifted. While he wanted to tell his brother that the Quran is the greatest book of spells that there is, he kept that to himself. *Certain things are better left unsaid. I don't want to come off like I'm trying to convert anyone. My parents have a lot of explaining to do. And I will make this intervention very painful and uncomfortable for them!* Malik had sworn.

***

As he made to leave, a horrible-looking creature arrived to try to claim both Marcel and Malik since they were both under the same roof. He arrived in a strong, whistling wind to the point that the father and sons had to cover their eyes.

"You can't have my children! A deal is a deal! I already gave you many others to try to pay for their lives back," Sir Landry Big argued.

"You and I know well that it's not enough. The power of these two, good and evil, is far greater than the worthless orphans you tried to feed me," the voice of the thing bellowed in the room.

"I don't care! Besides, you can't just barge in like this!" Sir Landry Big said, incensed by the lack of respect the *djinn* showed.

"I can do what I want!" the creature snapped.

The trio composed of father and sons put themselves in a fighting stance, at the ready. The demon launched attacks at them which made things fly off the living room aiming and targeting them intently. The battle lasted five long minutes. The whole living room was upside down. They were broken glasses everywhere. Malik had some cuts and bruises while his twin brother was bleeding from the nose. Sir Landry Big had a cut on the side of forehead.

Malik used verses from the Quran to protect himself while his brother and father used spells from their repertoire of dealing with unseen creatures to fend off the attacks. Finally, the *djinn* stopped fighting them.

"My brothers will hear of this!" A'wan the genie swore and then he added, "Especially, Al Musawwit! *The Profane* will be all over tips of your affair which gave birth to twins; one of which plays a lead role in rebellions! I swear you third born, you will be ruined! And fyi, the young Sylas will make a better dictator than you will ever be! HAHAHAHA." Then A'wan vanished the same way he came; in a cloud of wind and strong blowing dust.

The trio regrouped and formed a plan that they knew couldn't be heard by the spirits. With their combined forces, they had forged a soundless bubble which was pitched black.

"This is what's going to happen sons. You will tell the world that Malik poisoned me and he took over. You Marcel will tell the tabloids especially *The Profane* that you have declared war TO Malik and his followers."

"But why? We are stronger against them Dad?" Marcel said.

"No son, it's time for me to retire and pay with my life. The bill is due and I have to settle it," the father said embracing his sons tightly to bid them farewell.

"How about Corayto, he will never agree to this one,"

Malik pointed out this time. "He is power hungry."

"Don't worry about Corayto, I'll deal with him with the help of Mustapha, my old friend." Sir Landry Big said and turned to Marcel. "Please forgive your Mom. I made it hard for her to raise you with your brother. I was mad at her for leaving. She has always loved you and wrote you many letters. Once you're ready, you can find them in my safe. The password is your birthday."

With tears in his eyes, Marcel nodded, pouting.

"Marcel for the love of this old man, please let Malik be the leader of the world and let's be a united family for once even if doesn't last after my death because it is certain that they will claim my life in exchange for you. Just stall the followers if they want to retaliate."

So it was a deal. They came out of the bubble acting like they were fighting and then Marcel suggested that they cool it off and have a drink. Marcel would then proceed to serve drinks to the three while Malik would switch his with his father's. The father in turn will pretend to be choking and dying while Malik escapes and Marcel would be crying over his father's body. They hoped the spirits watching them fell for the trick. If they believed that Sir Landry Big was dead, they wouldn't see him come with a punch before going out like a hero.

And it worked for the most part. Malik's statement had been recorded by his twin brother and approved by the dad he never knew. Marcel had a correspondence at *The Profane* and she was delighted to have a major scoop. It didn't take long for her to relay the info to her bosses who played the tape right away for the whole world to see.

The heir to the Seculars' Empire goes to Sir Landry's son Marcel. But since I defeated his father fair and square when he tried to kill me first, I'm the winner. Marcel and I had a peaceful discussion and he agreed to start on a fresh page. We should be more tolerant of our differences. From this day forward, there are no more restrictions on calendars and there will be no persecutions of the minority groups in the world. I'm Malik Ducktrinor, your new ruler. Peace.

For the viewers it was surreal. The balance of power had shifted overnight much like a coup.

Malik took over the world when *The Profane* released false breaking news which indicated that Sir Landry Big had been killed. Then, that is all it took for the Seculars to give up their arms and cease fire.

CHAPTER FORTY: THE BATTLE OF THE SEA

Malik

Somewhere in the North Atlantic Ocean several hours after victory in Brazil

EXODUS 1.4 WAS MOVING at a steady pace under the North Atlantic Ocean when Malik noticed trouble ahead. He tore his gaze away from the magnificent, colorful, and lively ecosystem to see the giant octopus that was blocking the way and making a lot of waves that made their ship shake and start to get off track. Malik made a silent prayer over and over, "In the Name of Allah with Whose Name there is protection against every kind of harm on the earth or in the heavens, and He is the All-Hearing and All-Knowing." He then called Dawud and Hanifa to join him in the cockpit. Safi took the reins of the ship once again. "*Jazakh'Allah khair*, sis," Malik said to her.

"*Wa iyyak*," she replied, and started maneuvering the whale with ease just like he had shown her in the first three versions of his science project years ago.

"The time is almost here guys," Malik said as soon as Dawud and Hanifa showed up. "But in the meantime, we need to get ready for the upcoming challenges. Are you ready?"

"I was born ready," Dawud said, hyper.

"Sure, let's get some fresh air," Hanifa replied.

"We also have a case of sea monsters," Malik said, pointing behind Dawud to the transparent windshield that was in lieu of the blowhole and melon of the mechanical whale.

"Do you think it will charge at us?" Dawud asked.

"Maybe, maybe not. We will see. I've been reciting an

authentic *dua* and from what I gathered in my marine biology class, they are smart so perhaps if I try to reason with it, it will leave us alone," Malik reasoned.

"I think so too," Hanifa replied and said words that seemed like a silent invocation to Malik.

Suddenly, the sea monster charged toward them and landed on the transparent shield with a loud thump, which shook the whole convoy.

Malik remained calm and continued saying the prayer he had first recited when he saw the creature. Not too long after that, he could hear the octopus speak.

"What are you doing on my turf, young man?"

"We're just passing through. We have a mission to complete for the Creator of the Worlds."

"Ah you're believers. There was something strange about you and your crew. There is a fluorescent shield around you and it has a weird energy about it. Alright, I'll let you pass through, dear friend. Any believer is a friend of mine. Call my name *Aktaboot* if you face danger in these parts, I'll come to your help. May God protect you on your journey. So be it."

"*Ameen*," Malik replied and the octopus retreated.

"Dude! Where are you?! We've been screaming your name for like five minutes," Dawud and Hanifa said simultaneously.

"I was in a conference," Malik said. But before he could add more, Hanifa and Dawud spoke with utter amazement. The voice of Dawud was louder.

"Look! The giant octopus left us alone," Dawud exclaimed as his eyes bulged out of his sockets.

"I know. I was just talking with him. That's why I was momentarily unconscious when you called my name. I learned this with *Muallim*."

Hanifa and Dawud gave Malik a look of surprise and awe while Hanifa said, "Okay…I knew you could talk to the original Buraqa but not to all animals. *Masha'Allah*. Now, let's go to work before you no longer have a sister called Hanifa in this life." They all laughed despite the seriousness of the moment.

"Alright Safi, make the ship emerge from the waters and let us out on the deck," Malik said, and Safi nodded and did as she was told.

When the trio was above water, the frigid breeze whipped their faces and their garments billowed in the air.

Hanifa took position. Dawud too. Malik closed his eyes and tried to locate their assailants then he disappeared from sight.

Not too long after, Hanifa fell to the ground. She had been shot in the back. Dawud ran to her.

When Malik reappeared, Dawud was in a panic mode.

"Are you sure you switched the bullets? She's not waking up!" Dawud asked.

"Yeah I did." Malik's response was certain. "Just give it a few more seconds." And he started a countdown. "3-2-1—"

Right then Hanifa moaned with pain, "Dang... this stuff hurts. It feels like I have been hit by a train." She was twisting with pain.

"Stop lying, you wouldn't know because you would be

dead," Dawud joked and the trio let out a loud laugh.

Before they could rejoice and head back down, more trouble came their way than they had expected. However, they had thought they could hide before these unsavory threats showed up.

CHAOS

The waves became stronger and the wind blew with more vigor. As the strong winter wind whistled in their ears, Malik split his mind from his body again and conferenced call the FEM to come to their help.

They were surrounded by their so-called brothers in Islam: the Fundamentalists and the Zulmists.

Strangely enough, they extended *salams* greeting to the

children which the children replied to reluctantly.

"Turn your ships around and everybody lives happily ever after," a high official of the Muslim extremists said.

"Why?" Hanifa asked.

"We don't deal with children and women," he added haughtily.

"Well, my brother will not say a word and I'm in charge around here," Hanifa said confidently, glancing quickly at her brother's frozen expression. She knew Malik was not mentally present even though it seemed that he was standing right there and staring right at the sea and the rebels. The trio was standing in a circle with each of their backs facing each other in a fighting stance, the right foot in front and the left foot behind.

This time, it was Hanifa who said the prayer her brother had uttered at the first sight of *Aktaboot*. "*Bismillahil-ladhi la yadurru ma'as-mihi shai'un fil-ardi wa la fis-sama'i, wa Huwas-Sami'ul-'Alim - In the Name of Allah with Whose Name there is protection against every kind of harm in the earth or in the heaven, and*

He is the All-Hearing and All-Knowing." They had learned this powerful supplication from *Muallim*. She repeated it several times between backtalk pissing contests with the rebels.

They went at it for a while until the rebels gave in and said, "We aren't going to deal with you because you're a band of heretics who believe they will find the cave in Tarsus."

"Well, we can say the same of you guys with your loud and offending rap music," Dawud spoke with more courage than ever.

Hanifa cracked a smile and whispered, "Way to go."

"We aren't going to say it again. Turn around and you will live another day."

"You aren't Allah to make such promises," Dawud added, highly irritated.

Just then the rebels started shooting around them and Malik cried out loud, "Duck or take cover!"

"Welcome back bro!" Hanifa cheered.

"I'm not back yet. The FEM will help me take care of them. Just call the name *Aktaboot*."

Before Hanifa or Dawud could ask more questions, his body completely disappeared this time. "Well, that was straightforward." She laughed as she and Dawud were hidden from the line of shootings.

Suddenly the winds grew angrier and more violent. It became even harder for the rebels to land accurate attacks at the whale and the duo hidden somewhere on the deck. Hanifa took the time to repeat her supplications and asked Dawud to join with her.

"Oh I remember that. Imam Samee taught me that. *Ya Latif* please answer our prayers and save us from those who seek to hurt us," Dawud said wholeheartedly.

Then Dawud and Hanifa saw the hologram versions of Malik and the FEM zipping to and fro at an unimaginable speed between the ships and air devices the rebels had brought. They pushed them in the water, pulled their ears, and tickled them. The bottom line was that Malik and the FEM messed with their opponents. The extremists had no idea what was happening to them because before they realized it, the hologram had moved on to another victim. There were screams of rebels fearing the current below where they were headed, people slapping themselves frantically because of an invisible mosquito— or should we say the tip of a very thin sword Umm Manee used—, and laughs coming from the deck where Hanifa and Dawud watched in awe the circus they had front seats to.

"Malik could always pull off a show," she said, impressed.

The children defeated the Fundamentalists and the Zulmists who had decided to team up against the children. These rebels weren't good Muslims and had struck a deal with evil spirits to win. The proof? The group of children saw an indescribable creature spring from the vast waters with a lot of ruckus and say, "You will pay with your lives for failing this mission. You knew the risk. These children were never going to back down and you promised their lives in return for immensurable power." And then it swallowed all their ships— both flying and sailing— with its might.

"Well, that must have been Wathan; the shaytan that controls unnatural waves and catastrophes," Dawud remarked.

"Ditto," Malik acquiesced.

"*Alhamdullilah*, our combined power was stronger against them and we didn't have to call the octopus," said Hanifa.

"*Alhamdullilah*," Malik and Dawud echoed.

Our heroes had saved the day again and bagged another win the Battle of the Sea.

CHAPTER FORTY-ONE: OF CLOSURE AND TARSUS

EXODUS 1.4 ARRIVED SAFELY on the shores of Turkey and the mechanical whale disassembled in several small compartments that were also whales like the small fishes in Malik's dream several years earlier. The passengers were thankful for such an invention as they disembarked. While some argued that Malik was the savior, many argued that it was a team effort by the siblings and their following. Neither Hanifa nor Malik could have pulled it off without the contribution of the other. A small number of people, on the other hand, were rooting for Team Hind because she was very pivotal in their overall success.

When Malik caught fragments of such conversations, he told the *muhajirun*, "Hanifa is the leader of our cause. I'm just the supporting leader. I'm not a savior, and she can handle herself without anybody's help. It's just that team work always wins, and it is a better option for survival."

The *muhajirun* agreed with Malik and they settled in Tarsus waiting in the tents (The Supplies) that Hanifa had provided them while they would wait for the cave to open. Others brought their own gear or built their own dwellings. Soon, the community thrived on the skills of each of the members; there were seamstresses, hunters, and fishers to name a few in the mist of the new community that had decided to start a new life in Tarsus.

DjahayreePro-SpyPro found the Ducktrinors children for Mustapha, Eva, Adama, and Pristine. Hanifa had lost copy her copy during the battles so she couldn't initiate the search party as planned.

And it was time for Malik to finally have a talk with his

parents. "You're a bunch of liars! I hate you! You ruined my life!"

"I'm sorry Malik for the pain we've caused you," Eva said, tears quickly starting to streak down her face.

"I don't want to hear it! Many times throughout my life, I pointed out that I didn't look like my sisters or this man I called 'Dad'! But you said I was just imagining it," Malik spat and continued talking over them as they tried to place words. Since they weren't successful in trying to calm him down, they let him give it to them. He unloaded his rage and hurt on them, uncharacteristically of him.

"I don't ever want to see you. I'm done with you. You're the worse Muslim parents ever!" Malik added, seething. His fit chest heaved up and down. *They have crossed a line.*

At Malik's last audible words, Eva's sobs grew louder. She wailed and commenced supplications to Allah to intervene. The room was thick with tension and Malik's eyes sent daggers and unspoken threats. They couldn't even look him in the eyes. Their heads were cast down.

"Ya Naseer, Ya Musawwir, Ya…," she started to implore Him using the 99 attributes. Every now and then, she would pause the recital of the names and add, "Please give our son a change of heart." She chanted as she wailed on her husband's snot-and tear-soaked shoulder in a span of minutes.

"Please go easy on your mom, son," Adama wagered with a careful tone, lifting his head for the first time since the showdown started.

"Shut it! You're nothing to me! You aren't even my real Dad!" Malik raged further with bloodshot eyes. Then, he got up and thrashed everything in the tent. His 'disowned' parents had to duck a few times to avoid impact with the objects that went flying across the small space. They stayed quiet murmuring inaudible supplications while holding one another and crying. After a while, Malik calmed down, drained of emotion. He was sweating profusely, and his respiration was erratic, like he had performed a sprint. Malik had thrown a perfect fit he was secretly proud of. He picked up an old-fashioned chair that had managed to stay intact from the mess he had created in the tent, and sat facing his parents. At that moment, they took it as a cue to further explain themselves.

"One night, I found him over your crib conversing with you and it scared me because it was a hologram version of him. It scared me because I knew him personally. Landry had dabbed in the occult when we were together; another reason why I left him. Your father Adama tried to convince me that Landry's apparition was technology based but I wasn't buying it. I was positive he used dark magic to conjure something like that. Therefore, I wanted you to have the Quran in your corner. So I hired *Muallim* to teach you all his secrets after I had taught you the basics. I knew that if you memorized it, you would use His verses to help you in distress," Eva Ducktrinor finished as she dabbed the corners of her eyes with a tissue. Her husband just kept rubbing her back to soothe her nerves. The family talked more and Malik came around after many angry and jaded stares, eye rolls, and huff and puffs. He knew he had to forgive them and give them the respect they deserve as his parents.

"I'm sorry I disrespected you earlier," Malik confessed and his parents forgave him.

***

Hanifa's relationship with Ali flourished and she introduced him to her mother. Her mom gave her a valuable message after they had done a small *nikah* ceremony so that the couple could be *halal* for each other. The *walima* would come later. Mrs. Ducktrinor had told the pair, "Dasim controls houses. A man that doesn't greet his family falls prey to this *shaytan* and dissent befalls the marriage. So beware and be courteous to one another."

"Thank you for the advice," the pair had responded, all smiles.

"Malik, *Jazakh'Allah khair* for pulling it off at the stadium and thank you for being my witness at the *nikah*," Hanifa said, turning to face her brother, tears glistening in her eyes. "At last, we're here and it's all about teamwork. I couldn't have done it without Allah, you, and the rest of the people who believed in me and in us."

"Ah don't mention it. At last we're here. I got your back," he said in return before hugging her and then congratulating his sister on the wedding bells.

***

"Yo Malik, your blade was sick but I could have rigged it better. If it were me, I would have made a double-edged one like Hazrat Ali *radihallahu anhu*," Dawud quipped as he made a cool handshake with him once they had arrived at their destination safely. Their enemies had either been blown away by a sand storm or drawn at sea with the help of the Far East Muvmant and perhaps the angels of Allah.

"I can see that. You're *shiite*," Malik pointed out and winked.

"Don't forget Brother, I'm a Ducktrinor now. Your Grandfather adopted me."

"Welcome to the family, lil bro. I always wanted a little brother. These girls are hysterics and drive me nuts even though I don't show it."

"I'm not your little brother. I'm your uncle now. Haha!"

"Stop it! Don't be like Pris now. The brat is always saying similar things."

"I'm just kidding. I see you as a big brother anyway," Dawud said and they broke into a fit of laughter.

Later Malik gathered people and told them, "I always wanted to be a teacher. And the opportunity just presented itself. We're out of school, yes, but we can continue to learn while we train daily. I have every syllabus you need for any major you can think of on the hard drive I brought with me. If I don't know, I will tell you I don't know and we can work together to find the solution."

"*Masha'Allah*, that's awesome," he heard many in the crowd say while others said, "Really? I'm done with school." There was a mix of reactions because some people thought they had accomplished what they needed out of education already and chosen their career: the military.

"How would you call your school?" a person asked in the crowd.

"Good question. I don't know yet but *insha'Allah*, I'll

come up with a good name that is reflective of all of us like C.O.R.A.N." As Malik said that, it came to him. They would call their school, **C**ommunity **R**eligiously **O**bjective **A**nd **N**ot. *It's important that the "A" in C.O.R.A.N be capital because it means we'll emphasize eclectic sources and contributions*, Malik mused to himself and he continued fine-tuning his education plans in his mind. *A New Muslim Golden Age, insha'Allah!* he thought excitedly. *Pray that they don't see your skin color as an issue even though you're knowledgeable!* A voice said to Malik. He quickly dismissed that thought as *waswas* but he recognized that the voice made a valid point. As a black Muslim, he had to expect this pervasive outcome even if he had *deen* on the wit.

***

The night the whale arrived on the shores of Turkey, Shafiya was walking about when she spotted Ali and Hanifa sitting next to a fire having a good laugh while Malik listened to Coraline, half-distracted. She could tell it was hard for him to take his eyes off Ali and his younger sister.

She wondered if Malik had sent Ali to fight the

Seculars with the intention of getting rid of him because like everyone else he had noticed that Ali had a soft spot for Hanifa who had finally relaxed around the guy. A twinge of sadness and jealousy seeped in her heart. *He saw me first but I guess it wasn't meant to be or he liked her more. I need to stay focused. Obviously, they can relax after such a praiseworthy performance. Hanifa and Malik have played a huge role and part this far. I'll lead the next mission, insha'Allah,* Shafiya thought. Malik had always told her that the reason they could meet important Muslim scholars in their time travels is because these people who helped shape the world as they knew it were visionaries. They had a *vision.* She certainly hoped she could make the trips on her own now to bring to C.O.R.A.N's students the contributions of other unsung heroes. Shafiya smiled to herself, hopeful. Right then, Hamza greeted her with a charming smile, *"Merhaban* Safi." Safi replied with a smile and the two trekked in silence toward the inviting bonfire.

To be continued ...

EPILOGUE

Muslims were united at last. Malik ruled the world very shortly because he didn't like the spotlight. When things went back to order, he became an adviser to the next voted leader. The *ummah* was united as they waited for the last days in Tarsus with a governing body composed of five subgroups: the Hanafis, The Malikis, the Shafis, the Hanbalis, and the Shiites. Naturally, the Ducktrinor children ran for the Mufti title of the respective *madhahib* they were named after. Did they win the elections? That's an answer for the next tome (book) with Shafiya, *insha'Allah.*

A C K N O W L E D G M E N T S

Alhamdullilah for the completion of this book. Special thanks to those who have made this possible with their books, insights, designing, feedback, support and editing services. You know yourselves. *Jazak'Allah khair* to y'all!

Papatia Feauxzar

8th Dhul Hijjah, 1437
(September 9th, 2016)
Revised Jumada Al-Awwal 29, 1439
(February 14th, 2018)

INDEX OF SOME FUTURISTIC TECHNOLOGIES

CLONES

Inventor: The Secular Scientists

Uses: Weapons, Extend life's expectancy

Strengths: Multiple, extreme speed being the utmost asset

Weaknesses: Destruction of original human bodies used to create vampires. The original human body is the starter. If captured and destroyed, this creates a major weakness for this technology.

Maintenance: Disposable

Competition Availability: Yes

VAMPIRES

Origin: Metaphysical Forces

Known Engineers: The Seculars Scientists

Uses: Weapons, Extend life's expectancy, Trackers

Strengths: Multiple, extreme speed being the utmost asset

Weaknesses: Destruction of original human bodies used to create vampires

Maintenance: Blood transfusion or ingestion

Competition Availability: Yes

SHADOW HUNTER

Inventor and Engineer: Tim Undeapsided

Uses: Weapon, Human Location Finder, Object Tracker,

Clone and Vampire Detector

Strengths: Very accurate location finder

Weaknesses: Not user-friendly

Maintenance: Chargeable once a month

Competition Availability: Yes. They are less accurate and full

of glitches.

MECHANICAL HORSES

Inventor: Hanifa Ducktrinor

Engineer: Mustapha Kreedor

Uses: Sport, Weapons, Replace real horses

Strengths: Flight, Possession of strong metallic body armors

Weaknesses: Destructible

Maintenance: Regular oil change

Competition Availability: No

MECHANICAL CAMELS

Inventor: Hanifa Ducktrinor

Engineer: Mustapha Kreedor

Uses: Sport, Weapons, Replace real camels

Strengths: Flight. Possession of strong metallic body armors

Weaknesses: Destructible

Maintenance: Regular oil change

Competition Availability: No

NIQABAYA 1.0

Inventor: Hanifa Ducktrinor

Engineer: Mustapha Kreedor

Uses: Concealer, Safe mode of transportation, Spy

Strengths: Provides invisibility advantage

Weaknesses: Does not conceal body temperature

Maintenance: None

Competition Availability: Yes, many in the non-Seculars' circles

MUSTAPHA'S TELEPORTATION DEVICE

Inventor & **Engineer**: Mustapha Kreedor

Uses: Concealer, Instant Mode of transportation, Spy, Safety Weapon

Strengths: Provides invisibility advantage, Speedy mode of transportation

Weaknesses: Trackable at times

Maintenance: Regular calibration of GPS

Competition Availability: Yes

JABAL THAWR X.O

Inventor & **Engineer**: Mustapha Kreedor

Uses: Concealer, Instant Mode of transportation, Spy, Safety Weapon

Strengths: Provides invisibility advantage, Speedy mode of transportation

Weaknesses: Trackable at times

Maintenance: Regular calibration of GPS

Competition Availability: Yes. The same technology was

used for **Mihsser's** prison.

FOR FURTHER READING (2)

1001 Inventions & Awesome Facts from Muslim Civilization by National Geographic Kids

Alif the Unseen by G. Willow Wilson

Cure Your Waswas Forever by Hassan Khalid

Generation M by Shelina Janmohamed

Jannah Jewels by Umm Nura and contributing writers

Lost Islamic History by Firas Alkhateeb

Muslims in Brazil by Habeeb Akande

The Azurean Trilogy by F.A.Ibrahim

The Crimson League by Victoria Greffer

Harry Potter Series by J.K. Rolling

---

[2] The suggested list doesn't indicate that the author agrees with the opinions of the writers of these books.

GLOSSARY

Abaya: dress

Adhan: the first call to the prayer

Akhiret: the after-life

Al Fatiha: the opening chapter of the Quran

Al Goraba: the strangers of the future predicted by the Prophet of Islam

Al Muwaqqit: the Time Keeper

Aleihi Salam: Peace be upon him

Alhamdullilah: Praise be to God

Alim: scholar

Allah: God in Arabic

Ameen: I agree, so be it

Ashura: tenth day of the month of the first month in the Islamic calendar; Muharram

Assalamu aleikum: may peace be upon you

Awliya: a Muslim person with a strong faith, a saint

Awrat: intimate part of the human body

Bakhour: incense

Basmala: saying, "In the name of God, the Most Gracious, the Most Merciful"

Bi'ithnillah: with the permission of Allah (God)

Bismillah: in the name of God

Code fitnah: an alert mode that signifies that the Ducktrinor family is in danger and that escape is the next step; a state of emergency

Dawah: invitation to Islam

Deen: religion

Dhikr: remembrance of God made with a rosary, a counter, or bare fingers

Djamat: congregation

Djinn: a genie

Dua: supplication

Eid al-Adha: second religious holiday for Muslims

Fajr: dawn prayer

Fard: Obligatory

Feerasat: a miracle performed by a non-Believer

Fitnah: chaos

Genjutsu: a Japanese combat technique that uses illusionary and mystical methods

Habibti: my beloved friend

Halaqa: education semi-circle around a teacher where students are educated by and have exchanges with a teacher

Hanbal: clear, pristine

Hawqala: Laa Hawla wa laa Quwwata illaa Billaah—There is no might nor power except in Allah.

Hijri: Muslim calendar

Ibadat: act of worship

Ikhlas: purity

Ilm : knowledge

Imam: Muslim leader

Iman: faith

Injera: an Ethiopian dish made out sour dough; a beige pancake-looking porous flat bread

Insha'Allah: if Allah wills

Isha: last prayer of the night

Janazzah: Islamic funeral ritual, funeral service

Jihad: struggle

Jumah: Friday

Jutsu: a Japanese combat technique or a spell

Kabir: grandiose feeling

Keeramat: miracle performed by a believer

Keffiyeh: a trademark and traditional Middle Eastern square headdress made out of cotton

Khimar: a long head covering

Kôrôkô: old school person, nerd and most likely a believer

Kufi: a rimless hat for Muslim men

La Rayba: without any doubt

Madhab: a Muslim school of thought

Madhabib: Islamic schools of thought

Magrib: the fourth required and daily prayer for Muslims

MashaAllah: Allah has willed it

Mawlid: the Prophet of Islam's birthday

Merhaban: Hello

Mubarak: good

Muezzin: the person that performs the first call to prayer, usually on the minaret of a mosque.

Muhajaba: a female that wears the hijab thoroughly and with a lot of care

Muhajirun: the immigrants

Mujahid: warrior involved in a jihad

Mujiza: a miracle perfomed by a Prophet

Musalla: a prayer rug

Naam: Yes

Nasheed: a Muslim acapella song

Nikah: marriage contract

Ninjutsu: a Japanese warfare tecnhique that combines martial arts and mysticism

Qadr: the decree of Allah

Radihallahu anhu: may Allah be pleased with him

Rakat: one installment in a prayer

Ramadan: month of fasting for Muslims

Sahaba: companion

Salams: Peace greetings

Salat: prayer

Shahid: martyr

Shaytan: Satan

Sim: "Yes" in Portuguese

Subhanallah: Glory be to God

Sufi: a Muslim Mystic

Surah: chapter of the Quran

Tachahood: a prayer

Tafsir: exegesis

Taijutsu: a Japanese technique that uses body parts that seeks to optimize natural abilities and gifts

Takbir: a shouted declaration meaning "God is the Greatest."Also a word believers use to say "Allahu Akbar-God is Great!'" In all, it's a motivator and the formal start of a prayer.

Tamam: alright

Tayihat: a prayer

Wassalam: Goodbye. **Masalam** is also a variant to say "Peace out"

Waswas: satanic whispers

Wudu: ablution

Ya Latif: The Most Subtle, The Gracious, The Refined and Benevolent

Ya Mubeen: The Evident

Yalla: let's get going

www.ingramcontent.com/pod-product-compliance
Lightning Source LLC
Chambersburg PA
CBHW032255020726
47495CB00001B/121